GHOSTS IN SUNLIGHT

Book Two – Phil and Rena

~

Gretta Curran Browne

SPI
Seanelle Publications Inc.

PROLOGUE

'Hurt the mother, and you make an enemy of the son."

Old French Proverb

London
September 1980

_____/

By the time he was sixteen years old, Philippe Castineau Gaines had developed two real passions – the constant physical practice of oriental martial arts, and the creative beauty of true art.

Two weeks after his sixteenth birthday he sat down at the easel in his bedroom and began sketching the line work of his first painting of his father, working from a photograph – a photograph of a young American soldier who had died in Vietnam at the age of twenty-four – a photograph of Marc in green combat helmet, the chinstrap hanging down, his dark eyes grinning at the guy holding the camera, his hand raised towards the helmet in lazy salute.

He sat sketching for hours, unaware of time passing, the pencil in his hand moving in delicate feather-light touches.

1

He always wore headphones and listened to rock or soul music while he painted or sketched, yet this did not interfere with the intense concentration he always gave to his work. Nothing existed for him but the music and the developing sketch on the canvas.

Tonight he was listening to Queen's `*Bohemian Rhapsody*' pounding through his headphones, unaware of the constant ringing of the doorbell.

Only when a fist began to pound on the door did he stop and look round, then take off his headphones to listen.

He sighed, turned up his eyes, and then stood up muttering to himself, `Forgot her key again!'

He went into the hall and opened the apartment door blithely, about to make some joking remark to her ... until he saw the two police officers, male and female.

After the first few sentences, he stared at them in some confusion; then as they entered the flat and talked on, quietly and carefully, he slowly began to shake his head in disbelief. It was impossible.

What they were saying was not possible. He did not believe them, and he told them so.

`You have made some kind of mistake. The wrong name, wrong address.' He smiled faintly at the absurdity of it. `What you say can't be true ... it just can't.'

His attitude was positive and final.

The policewoman glanced apprehensively at her colleague. This was going to be even more difficult than she had anticipated.

At the hospital their footsteps were slow, but direct. The two police officers walked each side of him down a long corridor that looked very white and felt very cold, but all else was a blur.

Finally they stopped at a door on the left. The young policewoman caught his arm, holding him back while her male colleague went inside.

As they waited the policewoman spoke to him softly, but he did not reply, his stare fixed rigidly on the closed door. Still she regarded him with compassion. He wore blue jeans and a red sweatshirt and he was a very good-looking young lad, but his manner was as cold as ice.

He was frigid with terror.

The door opened.

The policeman, silently and gravely, beckoned them both to come inside.

The policewoman gestured for him to go in first.

He stepped through the door, unprepared for the chilliness of the room. He shivered, suddenly and violently, and it broke his trance. A man dressed like a doctor was speaking to him, but he was not listening.

He was staring at the woman lying on a trolley bed in the centre of the room, her slim body covered to the shoulders by a white sheet. He walked forward slowly and looked at her, and he felt his last faint hope drain away.

They had tried to clean her up, make her presentable, but the blood was so thickly matted in her hair it was impossible to remove.

He slowly stretched out a trembling hand and let his fingertips touch her face in a helpless caress, and continued his silent gazing.

Her face looked so pale, and she looked so young. Younger than thirty-five. Too young to be dead.

The policeman spoke gently to him, hesitantly, asking the vital question.

`Is it...?'

`My mother,' he whispered.

He was still shivering violently. The policewoman attempted to put a hand on his shoulder but he jerked away from her, taking a startled step back, staring at her as if she had struck him.

He did not want her comfort, did not want anyone's warm touch. The coldness inside him was like a protective shield, his only armour against the hatred building inside him, dense and dark and dangerous.

Her killer – nothing else stirred inside him now save thoughts of the man who had killed her.

The police had said his name – a name he had never heard before – a name he would never forget.

Find him, get him, destroy him.

He turned his head and looked at her face, her pale, lovely face; and in that moment he swore it.

Find him, get him, *annihilate* him. And he would – yes he would – somehow, some way, some day.

Throughout the return journey to the flat in Hampstead, he sat in the back of the police car in silent coldness.

From the driver's seat — a distance that seemed miles away — the policeman kept speaking to him with grim gentleness, but he gave no answer, his face turned toward the window, staring out blindly at the dark lamp-lit streets.

He was thinking of how she had scrimped and saved and worked so hard to give him everything he needed, paying for his private art classes with

Mr Hughes, his karate lessons in the church hall, even providing the fees when he wanted to move on at fifteen to a more sophisticated form of martial art.

'It's after midnight,' the policewoman said, but he was listening to the voice of his Wing Chun teacher, a master in the centuries-old system that prepared Chinese warriors for combat: *Others may seek only to grasp the bird's tail, or play with the monkey, but you must face the tiger ...*

The policeman was asking him about his father, but he didn't want to think about his father, not tonight.

He was thinking of how she cried a lot, not regularly or openly; but secretly, alone in her room, locked away with her photographs and love-letters, listening to her favourite songs on her old record-player, and only in summer. Always in summer. The rest of the year she never cried at all.

Sometimes, though, late at night, in the dark of winter, he would suddenly hear music coming from her room, and always the same slow song ... *'A candy-coloured clown they call the sandman. Tiptoes to my room every night. Just to sprinkle stardust and to whisper, Go to sleep, everything is alright ... In dreams I walk with you − '*

The car stopped. The singing voice of Roy Orbison stopped.

The private forecourt of the red-bricked block of apartments was brightly-lit, the green lawn in the centre neatly trimmed.

Inside the flat, the policewoman spoke to him in a sad, almost chiding tone. 'Listen, Phil, you can't stay here. Not all on your own. Is there anyone else you can stay with tonight?'

He thought of Chef and Sofia, but he shook his

head. 'No, I want to stay here,' he whispered, and gazed slowly around the living-room, so neat with her tidiness, 'I want to be ... with her.'

`Phil, can you give us the name and address of someone who knows you?' the policeman persisted. `Someone who can pop in and keep an eye on you. Someone in the other flats, perhaps?'

`No,' he said quietly, `I don't want to see anyone from the other flats. Not now, not yet ... not tonight.' But he knew from the glance they exchanged they were determined, and eventually he gave them Chef and Sofia's address.

The policeman nodded, putting his pen away, satisfied. `This Chef, is he a cook?'

His real name is Albert.'

"And he knows you, does he? Do you mind if we pop over there, on our way back to the station, just to let him know what's happened?'

Pop over there, on our way back to the station — it was a detour of at least six miles out of their way. But he didn't care where they went. He just wished with all his soul that they had never come into his life. And now all he wanted was for them to be gone.

A spring inside him was winding up, tighter and tighter, and if he didn't slow it down soon, his armour of coldness would shatter and break into a roaring agony, and he would start crying like a child at the horror of what he had seen — his beloved young mother, dead.

The policewoman touched his arm again, spoke to him in a hushed voice, words he didn't even try to hear.

They left the room, moving out to the hall, and he heard her voice again, more audibly this time.

'He's still in shock.'

'Not surprising. Only sixteen, poor lad.'

She suddenly turned back into the room. 'Phil, are you *sure* you're going to be all right?'

He nodded his head with a desperate insistence.

Slowly, hesitantly, she turned away, then abruptly brisked forward with a command to her colleague. 'Let's get over to this Albert and his wife. I don't feel right about this, leaving him here all on his own.'

The hall door closed.

The sudden silence was eerie. He stood alone in the empty desolateness of the flat, so strange now, without her.

He wanted her to come home ... in the way that she always came home, at the same time every night, after her evening shift at the restaurant.

For a long time he stood unmoving in the vacuity of the silence, a tearful haze swimming over his eyes, pictures of her floating in his mind — just this morning, how *happy* she had been, excited, triumphant, like a perverse schoolgirl who had boldly defied the rules and proved everyone wrong.

She had done it. The night before. She had finished her book.

And there it was, on the desk by the window, a proudly stacked manuscript waiting for a padded envelope and a professional opinion.

He moved towards it ... her book, her gift to Marc, her promise from a long-ago morning. The story of Marian, the story of Marc, the title: *Some Kind of Wonderful.*

Phil lifted the typed title page and turned it over, gazing at the poignant dedication she had written inside: *For Marc – still tender is the night.*

Outside the window the rain had started to pour, drowning the world in a filth of melancholy and blackness, its clattering uproar filling the silence.

He turned away from the window and slowly wandered around the sitting-room, emptied of her presence. But no matter where he looked, there was not a thing that did not remind him of her.

He paused by the left alcove; the shelves were lined with photographs of Marc, and of himself in various stages of childhood ... but amidst the array of family pictures stood a brass-framed photograph of Marian sitting up in a hospital bed holding a newborn baby in her arms. Her eyes shone and looked deeply blue, and her face was the face of a very young girl, exuberant, joyous, excited ... *I was a child and she was a child, in this kingdom by the sea* ... He shook his head, squeezed his eyes, not wanting his readings of Edgar Allan Poe to intrude into his memories.

Memories?

Is that all he had left now?

Bewildered, he stared around him. How could it be? How could his happy home and his loving mother disappear in a day? A night? An hour? A bloody minute of violent destruction.

Violent destruction?

The coldness returned ... it crept over his heart and his mind and into his black eyes until all warm emotions had numbed. Only sixteen, he looked as dangerous as a young French girl in Paris had once looked, when she too was sixteen. A foreign relation he had never met.

Again he was thinking of the man who had killed her. The police had said his name —

The doorbell rang.

He stood silent, waiting for whoever it was to go

away, but the bell rang and rang and he remembered it was the middle of the night, and the two police officers had gone to tell Chef and Sofia.

As soon as he opened the door Sofia pounced on him, wrapping him in her arms and hugging him so tight he could barely breath. `*Angelo mio! Oh Dio! Oh God! Oh my baby, my bayyybeee*!'

Part One

Phil

1984 — 1993

"The clear physical resemblance had not prepared me for the mesmerizing reality. The first time I saw him I thought a ghost had sauntered in out of the sunshine — and the sensation I felt was like a free fall down an elevator shaft. Here were the familiar eyes, in a familiar face, yet examining me with all the detachment of a stranger."

Truman Capote

'Ghosts in Sunlight.'

ONE

Massachusetts
September 1984

———————————————/

A bright and warm New England September. Massachusetts in a noon-day sunlight.

It was the taxi that drew Jacqueline's attention, made her pause curiously by the bedroom window. A white Harvard taxi turning off the country road into the private lane that led up to the house, slowly winding its way through the gaps in the green trees until it finally came to a halt at the end of the landscaped garden.

A young man stepped out.

Jacqueline stared at him curiously – and time stopped.

He was beautiful. The most strikingly beautiful young man she had ever seen. Tall and young and strong, with hair as black as jet.

Marc! Oh my darling, after all these years you've come back to me! You've come back, chéri!

Watching him undetected from the window of her bedroom, Jacqueline gazed down at him as he paused to speak to the taxi driver, the sunlight glancing off his leather jacket ... his favourite black leather jacket.

Oh Marc! Everything I did was for you. All my love was for you. And now you know that. And now you've come back to me.

She quickly turned away from the window, a hand to her cheek, her mind racing. She must look her best. After all this time – she must look her best!

She rushed into her dressing-room, flung open the doors of the closet and began searching through her dresses ... Chanel, Dior ... the very best money could buy ... She finally chose a Chanel dress in soft pearl-grey silk with matching grey stilettos. Her black hair was swept up into a neat chignon. She removed the small gold earrings and replaced them with a pair of Japanese pearls.

Above the pounding of her excitement she heard the doorbell ring. With one shoe on and one shoe off she rushed out onto the landing and called down to her housekeeper:

`Eddie! It's Marc! He's come back! He's at the door!'

Mrs Edwards appeared at the bottom of the stairs and gaped up at her. `Marc?'

The doorbell rang again.

`Quickly!' Jacqueline urged. *`Ne le faites pas attendre!* Don't keep him waiting! Let him in. Tell him I will not be long.' A beaming smile. `Oh, Eddie! *It's Marc!* He's come back! I saw him with my own eyes.'

Mrs Edwards gaped until Jacqueline disappeared back into her bedroom, then she turned towards the front door, shaking her head with a sigh of deep despair. When would Jacqueline accept that Marc would *never* come back to her.

So here it was ... *the house in Massachusetts* ... the forbidden house. Large and elegant, a stately multi-level house of the old Colonial style with a half acre of green slope leading up to the front door.

Phil stood outside the door waiting for his ring to be answered, waiting calmly, his manner cool and dispassionate. He did not intend to stay long. He had asked the taxi to wait.

A woman eventually opened the door – a sturdy grey-haired woman in her late sixties. From her dress and manner he knew she was some sort of housekeeper.

`May I see Mrs Gaines,' he asked politely.

The housekeeper stared at him oddly, her blue full-moon eyes blinking in strange puzzlement, like someone awakening from a deep sleep, wondering if they are still dreaming – or seeing a ghost.

She looked him up and down, taking in his blue jeans and black leather jacket. But then her eyes settled on his black hair and dark eyes, and her own eyes began to blink rapidly.

Now twenty years old, Phil was no longer a boy, but a young man. His years of dedication to the study of martial arts had made him lean, strong-limbed and fit. He was gentle-mannered, but had no fear of any adversary's muscular strength. He had studied a system of martial art that used speed and subtlety to overcome an opponent's natural advantages. By the time he was eighteen he could execute a flying kick at an angle of 180 degrees before a coin had dropped to the floor, followed by a swift strike to the face completed in 0.5 of a second. He had trained with a master, yet he rarely displayed any show of aggression to the world, always remaining respectful and polite – a natural trait he had inherited from his mother.

The housekeeper was still blinking at him dumbly.

`May I see Mrs Gaines,' he repeated. `Is she home?'

`Who *are* you?' she said at last. `What's your name?'

14

`Gaines,' he replied with slow deliberateness. `Phil Gaines.'

Truly startled now, she took a step back. `You're English.'

`Yes.'

`Holy Moses ...' Realisation of who he must be had dawned on her. Without saying another word she slowly opened the door wider, beckoning him to enter.

He followed her down the hall into a beautiful large drawing-room with cerise silk on the walls.

`Now,' she said shakily, as if short of breath, `I'm going to tell Mrs Gaines that she has a visitor, but that's all I'm going to tell her.'

He looked at her curiously. `Why?'

`Because you're English, and well, years ago, there was a whole lot of trouble in this house over an English girl ...' 'She glared at him moon-like again. `And if you are who I think you are, then I know there's going to be even more trouble — I can feel it in my bones.'

She didn't wait for his reply, turning and rushing out ... leaving him alone to gaze around the room.

The first thing that caught his eye was a photograph on a table by the window — a gold-framed photograph of Marc in full regimental uniform.

He walked over and lifted it; a sudden sadness sweeping over him as he gazed down at Marc's smiling face. A sudden yearning to be able to roll back time, bring back the past, and see that beloved face again – *in life* – not just in a photograph. He had lived too long with just photographs.

The curtain fluttered slightly in the breeze from the open window. A golden ray of sunlight shone directly onto his own face, making him turn his head slightly, to see he was not alone.

She was standing in the doorway, staring at him, her face a portrait of emotion.

He gazed at her silently. She was tall and slender and looked no more than forty-five, although he knew she was in her sixtieth year now, but she was still an incredibly beautiful woman. She wore a grey silk dress and grey stiletto shoes. She looked like a French aristocrat. He knew instantly that she was Jacqueline Castineau.

She finally spoke to him, but her words were mixed up in a moan, half words that trickled away as he stepped towards her, out of the sunlight, and her vision cleared.

`You are not Marc,' she whispered.

`I am Marc's son.'

She shrunk back in shock, her head shaking. `No, no,' she breathed, `how can that be?'

He knew her thoughts were swirling in disarray, but he continued to look at her with effortless detachment, a distance of twenty years and two deaths stood between them.

`Marc's son – how can that be?' she repeated.

He shrugged. `You were once a mother, so you must know the facts of life. And I'm one of them.'

She walked further into the room, smooth and graceful, but her black eyes were now burning with anger. `I knew there was a girl in England, yes. But I did *not* know there was a child. How could your mother be so cruel as to keep this fact from me?'

`Cruel? *My* mother?' He smiled derisively. `When it comes to cruel mothers, Madame, you should take a look in the mirror.'

Shocked, she stared at him. `How can you say ... you do not understand, you do not know −'

`I do know,' Phil interrupted. `I know she wrote two letters to this house, my mother, asking if she could have Marc's military identification tag and Vietnamese Cross, asking to know where Marc was buried, asking if she could visit his grave. His father, Alexander, he couldn't answer her letter, because Alexander was dead. But you ... you read those two letters, didn't you? And you didn't even have the decency to reply.'

She stood thoughtful, her mind churning back to the past, remembering the stupid English girl who didn't even know how to write an intelligent letter. She had thrown it away in disgust. Then a second letter that she did not bother to read but immediately tore up.

`I blamed her, you see. The English girl. I blamed *her* for Marc's death. Blamed her for causing such discord between us. But she may have treated Marc better than the American Army did. Oh yes, how wrong I was. I should never have trusted them. I gave them my son in full health and youth, and they gave me back a corpse. *Oh,* it was insupportable! The way they tried to console me with a bit of tin. A Vietnamese Cross – in exchange for my son.'

`In exchange for my father.'

Jacqueline stared at him, her face a study in pain, her hand touching her heart, still unable to believe that this young man was real and not the ghost of her son who had just strolled in out of the sunlight.

But then he spoke again, and she heard the unfamiliar English accent of his voice, yet the face ... the height ... the way he stood ...`Oh ...' she finally breathed, 'you are *so* like Marc.'

`I'm also like my mother.'

17

`But why...' Jacqueline asked, still bewildered. `Why did Marc not tell me about you? Did he know? No — ' she shook her head emphatically, `No, he could not have known! You must have been born *after* he went to Vietnam. How old are you?'

He removed a paper from his pocket and handed it to her. `Here, keep it as a gift, my birth certificate.'

Jacqueline took the certificate and stared at it. `Philippe Castineau Gaines ... Eighth of July 1964 ... A year before Marc's death ... yet no one told me about you ... why?'

`You tell me why? Your husband knew. Well, he was *told* about me, by Marc himself.'

Jacqueline was so shocked she had to sit down.

A voluptuous sofa covered in cerise velvet stood in front of the fireplace. She sat down on it thoughtfully, as if wondering if this could be true.

`Alexander *knew* Marc had a son?'

`Yes, Alexander knew.'

Her eyes went very dark and still. Then, suddenly, a strange and bitter smile moved on her face. `So, Alexander had his revenge on me after all ... He always vowed that he would.'

Slowly she lifted her head and looked at him, and the look on her face suddenly changed into a trembling, beautiful smile.

`May I call you Philippe?'

`I prefer Phil.'

`I prefer Philippe ... it was my father's name," she said softly. "He was a jeweller in Paris. Oh, many years ago. He was killed by the Gestapo...' While she spoke she turned a gold bracelet around on her wrist. `It must have been Marc who named you Philippe.

`Yes, it was.'

`My own name is Jacqueline.' She pronounced the J with `zha' sound. `Zhacqueline.'

He did not repeat it, did not give voice to her name.

`To think ...' she said reflectively, `all these years I thought Marc had left me nothing. Nothing but the sound of his voice in my dreams. But he *did* leave me something. All these years I have had a grandson, and did not know. Marc's son — ' Her eyes were beginning to sparkle.

`Marc's son —' she repeated, and suddenly she looked young and zestful, glowing with purpose and excitement.

`Have you come from England? Or do you now live in America?'

`From England.'

`To find me?' Her smile was radiant. `Yes, and I know why you did so. Because deep in your soul you know you are a *Castineau*. Just as Marc was. Just as I am. Just as your namesake and great-grandfather was. It was your *French* blood that brought you to Massachusetts. You could not stop yourself. You knew you *had* to come.'

She patted the sofa beside her. `Come, Philippe, sit beside me so we can talk. We have wasted many years, but now we must get to know each other.'

`Sit beside you?' He sighed, his voice cool and neutral. `Don't you know how sick I feel just being in the same *room* as you?'

His words hit her like bullets; all the blood seemed to drain from her face. She could only stare at him as he calmly fired again.

`Don't you realise how despicable I feel being in the same house as you. Especially *this* house – the one my mother was considered unfit to enter.'

`Then why ... why did you come here?'

`I came here four days ago. To New England. I've been to Fort Devens. I've been to St Teresa's cemetery in Harvard. I've even been to see Bill Simons over in Shirley. You remember him – Alexander's best friend – nice man, very hospitable, and very *talkative,* especially when he realised I was Alexander's grandson.'

He was looking directly at her eyes.

`I've also read Alexander's book. And I've read my mother's book. Marc always told her everything – did you know that? So, those are some of the reasons why I came here. You're looking at a pilgrim. A son searching for his father, searching for the truth. Now there's not much more I need to know. Now I can get on with my holiday in America, away from Massachusetts.'

`But before you were ready to leave Massachusetts,' Jacqueline realised, `you had to come and meet *me.*'

`You? No, no, I had no particular ambition to meet you, except as a means to an end. I've come here to get from you what is rightfully mine. I've come for Marc's military identification tag, the one he was wearing around his neck when he died.'

Jacqueline was stunned. `Rightfully yours?'

`You can keep the Vietnamese Cross. As you say, it's just a bit of tin. Marc never even saw it.'

`Rightfully yours?' Jacqueline repeated. `Why should you think anything of Marc's is rightfully *yours?*'

`Because what belongs to the father, passeth to the son. And I am Marc's son.'

`His *illegitimate* son!' Jacqueline flashed.

Phil smiled a little. `Yes, well, his illegitimate son. And that's why I'm not asking for much, nothing except this one small thing — Marc's military identification tag.'

`No!' Jacqueline refused. `No! I am his true next of kin. All that I had was taken from me, my father, my son, taken from me by war! But I will not give up that. I will not give up anything belonging to Marc. Not even his military identification tag. Not even to you.'

`Then you are the most selfish of women.'

Jacqueline's face hardened into viciousness. `You want it for *her*, don't you? That English girl. I remember now – she wrote in her letter that she wanted it. It was she who poisoned Marc against me, just as she has poisoned you against me. Why else should you feel sick to be in the same room as me — when you don't even know me?' Her eyes darkened murderously. `It was *she* who sent you here, wasn't it?'

`No.'

Without another word, without a backward glance, he turned and walked out of the room and out of the house.

Moments later Jacqueline heard the sound of the taxi's engine, and sat back. She was shaking, full of anger and agony – a raging agony she had not felt in years. And it was glorious – because for the first time in years she felt *alive*. Not half-dead, not half-living, but raging with passion for the challenge before her, the new *chance* that *Life* had now given to her.

She had seen the condescension and contempt in his eyes, seen a glimpse of the coldness and the cruelty he was capable of, but she did not mind, because all of those things were in her too.

`He's gone then?' Mrs Edwards entered nervously.

`He didn't stay long. Doesn't seem like he intended to either, seeing as how he kept the taxi-cab waiting outside.'

Jacqueline was slowly coming out of her shock, realising the enormity of what had just happened, a hand moving slowly up to her face.

`Oh, Eddie ... did you see him?'

`He's Marc's son all right. No doubt about that.'

`Oh Eddie, *Eddie* − did you see the blackness of his eyes? Did you see the way he walked, the way he stood, so dignified, just like my father, just like Marc. And the way his eyes looked at me, how *beautiful* he was! Oh, Eddie, my grandson, he's a true Castineau!'

Mrs Edwards was gaping moon-like again, because tears were spilling down Jacqueline's cheeks, big child-like tears.

`He hates me, Eddie. Oh, how he hates me. But I can't let him go. I can't just forget him. Not now that I've seen him. Not now that I know he exists!'

She was stammering almost piteously. `He behaved like a stranger to me. But he is *not* a stranger, he is *Marc's* son ... my darling Marc ... he would not want this; he would not want his son to hate me. He would want his son to love me as much as he always loved me. You know how much Marc adored me! That's why he named his son Philippe Castineau − in honour of me, in honour of my father.'

`But if he hates you, and he's gone − '

Jacqueline sprang to her feet in agitation. `I don't want any of your arguments, Eddie! Not about this. I will not allow it. People like you stare at life and see only the obvious, only defeat, that's why your lives are so tedious and your characters so simple. But me − I have fought the *Nazis* −I have never considered defeat.'

Her slender hands clenched into angry fists. She turned her dark eyes to Mrs Edwards.

`I can bring him back, Eddie.' She nodded emphatically. `He thinks he hates me now, but I can change that. He lied to me, I'm sure of it. His mother – that English girl – she *did* send him here. She *did* poison him against me. But I can change that. I can make her see how stupid she has been. How wrong she is about me. Oh *why* did I not keep her letters? All I know is her name.' She stopped suddenly. `But the bank will know ... the bank Marc used when sending money to her ... and if they still have the records, they will at least know where *she* banks in London – '

`But if she – '

`She will be no problem, Eddie, believe me. I know how to handle someone like her. A simple waitress, not very intelligent, what is someone like that compared to me? And he will see it too – Philippe – my grandson. He will see his mother and I together and he will realise that he is more like me than like her. He will see that he and I have the same blood, the same genes, the same ancestors, and the same name. Eventually, all that will count.'

Mrs Edwards was shaking her head worriedly. `Well, if you ask me – '

`Did you see way he was dressed, Eddie? Casual, yes, but utterly clean and perfectly groomed, with that certain *chic* so natural to the French. He reminded me so much of my father, so much of Marc – '

She stood up quickly, brisk and young again, full of excitement, snapping out orders like the young Resistance leader she had once been.

`We need a plan. But the first step is to find him, find out where he came from, and where he has now gone. For that we will need expert help. We have a fight on our hands, but we will win, we always do.'

Eddie sighed, filled with compassion and despair. She knew that Jacqueline was sick, knew she needed the help of a psychiatrist. But who would dare to suggest it? Even her lawyer was terrified of her. Jacqueline was still a powerful antagonist, as her lawyer once called her. Few dared to cross her.

Eddie shrugged. `Well,' she said, `do what you must, Mrs Gaines. All I can say is good luck.'

Jacqueline turned a beaming, beautiful smile on her housekeeper. `I don't need luck, Eddie. I never have. I have always relied on my own resources. And I will win my grandson over to my side in the end. I *will* win, you know. I always do.'

`Yes,' Eddie nodded, and suddenly she felt great pity for Marc's son. He hadn't a chance in hell of walking away from this.

The following morning Mrs Edwards found Jacqueline in the library sitting at her desk, speaking into the telephone.

` ... You are certain of that? He was on the seven o'clock flight from Logan to New York? Then you know what you must do ... Yes, of course I understand. I don't care if you have to search every hotel in New York to find him. I don't care if you have to search every address in England to find his mother. I'm paying you and your investigators good money, more than you have ever been paid. So I want no arguments. And I don't care what it costs. I just want you to *find him!*'

TWO

New York
September 1984

_____/

It took Phil only three days to find Jimmy, thanks to the help of the Vietnam Veterans' Association. The address, a seedy apartment house in the Bowery.

The paint-peeling front door was wide open, there was nothing to indicate who lived in which room, and the dank stairway had the sour and musty smell of a house rotting with decay.

Phil stood in the hall, unable to believe that Jimmy lived in a place like this. And which room?

He knocked on the first door.

`Yeah? Who is it?'

Phil didn't know what to say, so he knocked again. Seconds later the door was opened by a bullish bald-headed old man with an unlit cigarette in his mouth.

`Yeah?'

`I'm looking for Jimmy Overman.'

`Who?'

`Jimmy Overman.'

`What's he look like?'

Phil remembered Marian's description of Jimmy. `Tall, about six-one. Thin. Blond hair. Used to be a soldier.'

`Oh, the weirdo! Two flights up, then second door. But yuh betta bang loud. If he's out he won't hear yuh, but if he's in his TV'll be blasting.'

`Thank you,' Phil replied, but the door had

already slammed in his face.

Two flights up, then second door, Phil knocked. He could hear the sound of a television but it was not blasting, normal sound level. He knocked again.

The door opened, but the man who stood there was not Jimmy. Not the Jimmy of his mental image. This guy was mid-forties. He had more grey hair than blond, shaved close in a crew-cut. His blue eyes looked slightly vacant. A jagged scar puckered up one eyebrow into a quizzical expression. He was also missing an arm.

`Jimmy Overman?'

`Lord Almighty!'

He disappeared, and moments later Phil heard the clink of a bottle rattling against a glass.

Phil slowly pushed the door open wider and stepped into the room. Its cleanliness surprised him. The bed was neatly made, everything in its place. Army training, he supposed. Few soldiers lost the habit. The colour television was on, an armchair positioned in front of it. By the window were a small table and two chairs, and it was there Jimmy stood, gurgling down a shot of bourbon.

`I'm sorry to disturb you,' Phil apologised.

`Jesus Christ!' Jimmy put down the glass and wiped his mouth with the back of his hand. `For a minute there I thought you were an old buddy of mine.'

`No.'

`No, I can see that now,' Jimmy said slowly. `You ain't him. Not my buddy. But this country is full of ghosts, you know? Oh, sure! I see them all the time. Even in daylight. Turn a corner and there they are, all my old buddies, laughing and jostling each other, then I come up and *phit* – they're gone

- vanished into thin air!'

A wary, confused expression was forming on Jimmy's hard-lined face. The puckered eyebrow rose higher. `You ain't Marc. You ain't a ghost. So who the hell are you?'

`I'm Marc's son.'

`Lord Almighty!'

Trapped silent for a time, Jimmy stared, as motionless as a still life while his mind searched back down the avenue of a long yesterday.

Phil moved forward and held out his hand. `My name's Phil. I just wanted to meet you, Jimmy.'

Jimmy's one hand came out and grasped Phil's hand in a clasp as strong as a vice. `I remember now ... the little kid in London ... with Marian ... kept climbing onto my knee. Was that you?'

Phil smiled. `I can't remember, but Marian told me you came to see her once in London, after your first tour in Vietnam' ... "*He was so nice,*' Marian had said sadly. `*He had lost his boyish Elvis Presley leer and he looked a thousand years old, but he was so nice, so kind...*'

`Then in 1975,' Phil said, `when the war was over, you sent her a card from New York.'

`Yeah, so I did, on the tenth anniversary of his death ... I wanted to remember it somehow, let her know that I still remembered, still cared about what happened in 1965 — '

Jimmy stared through the window, but he was not seeing the street below, only shadows under an orange Saigon sun.

`1965,' he said softly, `when the world was young ... the year the Los Angeles Dodgers beat the Minnesota Twins in the World Series ... it seemed to matter then, baseball, our transistors constantly tuned to Armed Forces Vietnam who were beaming it live to us boys in Tigerland ... even out on patrol most GI's had their transistors plugged into their ear. Yeah, it seems funny now, but it still mattered then. We still cared who won at baseball....'

He turned suddenly. `Thanks for coming, Phil, searching me out. It was a nice thing to do. Just what I'd expect from Marc's son.' Tears were pushing, but Jimmy blinked them back. `But aiyyyy – listen, I'm not being very polite. Sit down, will you? Have a drink?'

Phil hesitated. `I was hoping I could take you out somewhere – to a restaurant or a bar. Wherever you like?'

`Nah!' Jimmy shook his head. `Thanks, but I don't care much for the outside world these days. Guess it's because it's so long since I played a part in it all. No, I'm happiest here in my room with my television. Do you like television?'

Phil nodded. `Sometimes.'

`Then stay awhile, will you?'

They sat talking until three o'clock the following morning. And during that time Jimmy told Phil things that brought tears to both men's eyes. A casualty of the Vietnam war, Jimmy's real disability was not his missing arm, but an illness which the Vietnam Veteran's Association had fought to get officially recognised – Post Traumatic Stress Disorder – guilt at being a survivor, a sense of alienation from the normal world, constant depression, and a high rate of suicide.

`So you see, I'm not doing so bad,' Jimmy smiled, easing himself into the armchair. `Some vets are so messed up after their experiences in Nam, they can't adapt to normal civilian life and have to live out in the wilds. They're the ones who are *really* paying the price – those poor guys alone with their ghosts. But me, well, as long as I'm left in peace here in my room, with the television on all the time ...'

`Why do you like the television so much?'

`Stops me thinking,' Jimmy admitted truthfully. `Helps me to forget.'

`Do you have a family?'

Jimmy's face changed. `Yeah ... I used to have a family, once. A father and a sister, as I recall. Nearly drove me nuts. Both of them. Always talking about how wrong the war was. How wrong America was. When I came back after my third tour in 1970, there was no homecoming welcome, not for any of us. We vets were an embarrassment to all decent people in the United States.'

He poured another drink.

`God! I *still* get mad when I think of the treatment handed out to soldiers returning from Nam, especially the draftees. To me, those guys weren't villains but victims – young men, some only kids, drafted out to fight a war they didn't understand in a sweating jungle that nearly drove them insane ... and after surviving the hell of it, after spending months in muddy bunkers living on tinned ham and lima beans, and after seeing their buddies maimed or blown to pieces by Charlie's trip wires and booby-traps – what happens then? They fly home to be greeted at the airport by crowds of unwashed hippies shouting, `*How's it going, baby killers? How many children did you kill at My Lai? How many villages and women did you bomb?'*

Jimmy clenched his one fist furiously. `No matter that most GIs were innocent. No matter that the North Vietnamese were also aggressors, backed to the hilt by the Chinese and Russians. No matter, no matter, no matter ... No wonder so many vets prefer to live alone in the wild.'

Phil was bewildered. `If it was such hell, why did you keep going back?'

Jimmy shrugged. `I honestly don't know ... but after Marc's death, after my first tour, things back home didn't seem the same anymore. I couldn't get excited about having enough money in my pocket to buy whatever I wanted, stupid things like that ... not while I knew there were guys getting their blood blown out through their ears in Nam.'

`How did you lose your arm?' Phil asked.

`Same way I lost my leg from the knee down.' Jimmy grinned and pulled up his trouser leg, knocking on what looked like a plastic leg. `I was on short time, only two weeks to go before my DEROS, and Charlie decided it was about time I had some punishment. It still hurts, you know, my lost leg. When it stops hurting, I'll know I'm dead.'

Jimmy sat back and sighed. `Couldn't manage the false arm, though. No matter how I tried, it just kept sticking out in front of me like I was continually pointing at something. Gave up in the end. Took the damn thing off. Use it now to bash cockroaches.' He chuckled. `Lord Almighty, between my lost leg and my lost arm and the near-miss of a bullet taking away a piece of my eyebrow, I don't know why I'm still alive!'

Despite his disabilities, Jimmy insisted on getting up from his chair and frying them some supper: fried eggs and bread and strong steaming coffee. And no, he wanted no help.

Jimmy suddenly frowned. `Know something, Marc, this is the first time we've talked so long in years.'

Phil looked at him steadily. `Jimmy ... I'm not Marc. I'm Phil.'

Jimmy frowned again, then smiled with bemused uncertainty. `Well, you know, you're a helluva lot like my buddy Marc. He was a good listener too.'

Phil grinned. `I can believe that. He once said you talked so much he had to beg you to let him share the air.'

Jimmy laughed. `Yeah, Marc said that all the time.' He shook his head, puzzled. `But how do *you* know that?'

`I'm his son, Jimmy. I've read all his letters.'

`No kidding!' Jimmy was struck with amazement. `You're Marc's kid? Well, whaddaya know!' He held out his hand to shake, beaming with delight at this discovery, and Phil realised that Jimmy's grip on reality was slipping.

Whether it was due to the weariness of long hours of talking, when he was normally used to spending his time sitting silent before the glare of the television screen, Phil didn't know why, but he decided to persuade Jimmy to go to bed.

*

Phil saw a lot of Jimmy in the following week. And by some change of heart, Jimmy even agreed to go outside with him.

They went to Manhattan, the Village, and other places Phil wanted to see around New York – anywhere outside the Bowery – a place that Phil could not feel relaxed in.

Twice he had been forced to step over a drunk lying comatose on the pavement; a third he was sure was a corpse, but all his efforts to get someone to phone for an ambulance had met with a waving hand of disinterest. `That drunk? Nah, he'll wake up soon enough – soon as his gut wants feeding from a bottle.'

`Why do you live in a place like the Bowery?' Phil asked Jimmy.

Jimmy paused, a rain-cloud passing over his eyes. `I didn't always live in the Bowery, you know. I lived in other places, nice places, but the people weren't nice. No, sir. Treated me like they thought I was crazy or something. Always sniggering at me.' He shrugged. `Can't think why.'

He looked around him in bewilderment, like a saddened stranger who no longer felt welcome anywhere in America.

`But the Bowery, well, it's not Boston or Washington, but it's a place where I can come and go and nobody gives me a second look. Nothing odd about a one-armed man amongst a load of no-hope zombies. But now, listen—' he asked curiously, `do you think it's because I've got only one arm and this here puckered-up eyebrow – do you think that's why those people kept sniggering at me?'

Phil looked at him. `The nice people who lived in the nice places?'

`Yeah.'

`No,' Phil shook his head. `They sniggered because they couldn't see past their own eyeballs, Jimmy. Because they were born with mean little souls.'

`A lot of nice people in nice places are like that,' agreed Jimmy, `mean as monkeys underneath.'

`What about money?' Phil asked. `Are you okay for money?'

`Yeah, I've got my army pension, you know, so I'm not too badly off,' Jimmy explained. `And I don't spend much. Don't go out much neither. I get all the entertainment I want from my television. Usually I only like coming out for my groceries and the occasional bottle of bourbon.'

Jimmy suddenly stopped. `What about you? Are you okay for money?'

Phil nodded, but did not explain that when the flat in Hampstead had been sold, all the money from the sale had come to him. A posthumous gift from Marc, from Marian; his immediate future was secure.

`I'm fine, Jimmy.'

`Are you sure now? Because if you need any money I could – '

`No, Jimmy, not a cent. I've got all I need.'

Jimmy held out his one hand, palm up. `Now give me your promise? Tell me no lie.'

Phil grinned and slapped Jimmy's hand with his own. `Swear to God.'

`Good.' Jimmy nodded with satisfaction, and walked on. `Nice to know we're both doing okay.'

`You'd never know you had a fake leg,' Phil observed. `You don't even limp.'

`Practice, boy, practice.'

They ate in cafes and small restaurants and sometimes stopped for a few drinks in a bar, and Phil tried not to look embarrassed when Jimmy would suddenly switch off from reality and stop to have a conversation with one of his ghosts – talking cheerfully to an empty space in the street, or to the empty barstool beside him.

He also kept confusing Phil with Marc, and Phil decided the kindest thing to do was play along.

In a bar – after one of Jimmy's conversations

with a ghost on the empty barstool beside him – Jimmy turned back to Phil and grinned, looking pleased as punch.

`You know who that was – McKenna! You remember him, don't you? The lippiest grunt in my platoon. From the Bronx. Used to make you laugh because of what he had painted in black on the front of his green helmet – *Izzat an order?* – You remember?'

Phil laughed. `Sure I remember.'

Others were laughing too, at Jimmy, behind his back. Sitting at tables and looking at the crazy guy at the bar as if he should be locked up. What else could he be but crazy – having a conversation with an empty barstool?

Like Phil, they had been unable to see the ghost of Michael McKenna, a young Irish lad from the Bronx who had died saving Jimmy's life.

`Out there in Nam,' Jimmy said, his voice croaky, `we weren't fighting for any great ideal. In the end, we weren't even fighting for America, we were fighting for each other – for our buddies – for the guys in our platoon. It was us or Charlie. All the way. Us or the Cong.'

Not ten feet away, a smart-faced bucko in a snazzy suit was sitting at a table with two blondes, continually looking at Jimmy then making snide comments which made the three of them howl with laughter.

Jimmy seemed unaware of them.

He suddenly turned to Phil, the lucidity back in his eyes, and more amazement. `I can't believe it, you know. Me sitting here with Marc's kid, all grown up now. What happened to the years in between?'

Another howl of laughter from the table behind.

`They just drift by, Jimmy, the years. That's why we've got to make the most of them while we can.'

`Drift by? Hell no — they speed past you while you're not looking. Least, that's how it seems to me. And the older you get, the faster they go.'

Jimmy smiled, a sad smile. `Not that I care much. Damned if I do. My only fear is that when my time comes, I'll die out here on the streets, flat on the sidewalk, like some tramp.' He shivered slightly. `That's one of the reasons why I don't like to go out much these days. Why I prefer to stay at home with my television.'

Another howl of laughter from the table behind.

Phil glanced towards it and saw the smart-mouthed bucko in the snazzy suit getting up and walking towards the men's room.

Phil stood up. `You stay right here, Jimmy, I'll be back in a minute.' He gestured to the bartender to give Jimmy another bourbon.

In the men's room, Bucko was standing by the sink looking at himself in the mirror when Phil walked in. He didn't even glance round, taking out a comb and raising it towards his hair.

`Hey,' Phil said to him quietly, `you know that tall thin guy sitting at the bar?'

Bucko turned, curious. `You mean, the one-armed guy? The loon?'

`Yeah, the one you've been making fun of all night, entertaining your two women, and none of you being too quiet about it either.'

Bucko's expression changed. `Say, what *is* this?'

`This?' The sudden strike to the face broke Bucko's nose, a guaranteed eye-closer, blood spurting like a tap onto his snazzy suit. Before he could even react, Phil grabbed him by the shoulders and bounced him hard against the wall.

`Next time you decide to entertain your women by making fun of a harmless, mixed-up, disabled man, make sure he's not the owner of a Purple Heart, Bronze Star, and Vietnamese Cross for gallantry.'

Phil left him slumped over the sink, and showed no sign of any disturbance when he sat down again beside Jimmy and smiled. `You okay?'

Jimmy nodded. `Yeah, I was just talking to the bartender there. Did you see *Kojak* on TV the other night?'

`No.'

Jimmy gritted his teeth. `Makes me mad. You can bet your last dollar that whenever there's a psychopath roaming the streets in cop shows or soap operas these days, he's always a Vietnam Veteran. A walking time bomb. A dope-head. Hell, these people who write these shows, they don't know shit. Never been near Vietnam.' He knocked back his bourbon. `Well, I'm not gonna watch *Kojak* no more.'

Phil grinned. `They're not all portrayed as bad guys. What about *The A-Team?*'

Jimmy's eyes brightened. `Sonofagun! I forgot *The A-Team*. Yeah, they're all supposed to have fought in Nam, aren't they? And then there's this new guy *Magnum*. He's a Vietnam Vet who's not so bad and almost sane – which is more than I can say for that *English* guy in the show – the one with the snooty voice and dinky little moustache. Now, if *he* ain't crazy, I'm Clint Eastwood!'

Phil was waiting for Bucko to come out of the men's room and show his bloody nose to his two women, give them another howl of laughter, but still no sign of him.

`Come on, Jimmy, let's go.'

36

Phil called on Jimmy the following afternoon. The television was on as always. Jimmy smiled his boyish smile, looking real pleased to see him.

`Coffee?'

`Thanks.'

Jimmy chuckled. `You know who was on TV today? Phil Silvers. You always loved that show. That rascal Bilko. Do you remember how we used to sit in front of the television at Devens and howl? Course, Bilko'd never get away with any of that stuff in a *real* army.'

There was a lump in Phil's throat, a terrible sadness in his heart as he watched and listened to this man who had been his father's best friend. `*Jimmy? – nicest guy in the world.*'

And look at him now, a broken man, a misfit, his mind trapped in a time warp from which he couldn't escape.

But Phil was going back to England the following morning, and he was worried. Very worried about Jimmy.

When the coffee was poured, he sat down at the table with Jimmy, and took a deep breath.

`Jimmy, I'm not going to be able to come around again. Not for a while. Tomorrow morning I fly back to England.'

Jimmy looked sad. `To Marian?'

`No, to Cambridge University. I start my first year there next week. But before I go, I want to know — ' He paused, and looked directly into Jimmy's eyes. `What are you going to do with the rest of your life, Jimmy?'

Jimmy seemed taken aback, his lips moved, but he didn't speak. He sat back in his chair, turned his face towards the window, and went into an endless stare, tears slowly trickling down his cheeks.

`Don't cry, Jimmy. I was just wondering, that's all.'

`No, grown men don't cry.' Jimmy's throat rumbled, then he croaked. `To tell you the truth, I suppose I'm just hanging around waiting to die.'

Phil brought back to mind all the symptoms he had looked up in the past few days about Post Traumatic Stress Disorder, suffered by forty percent of Vietnam veterans.

`Do you ever feel guilty about being a survivor?'

`Sometimes, yeah, sometimes.'

`Have you ever contemplated suicide?'

`Suicide? Hell, no! I've seen too many GIs wounded, in pain and covered in blood, maybe even a limb blown off, some with their chests hanging open, but *all* were desperate to survive, desperate to live ... young GIs, some no more than kids, crying out for life, even if it meant life as a cripple ... crying out for life.'

Tears were pushing again, but Jimmy blinked. `So those times when I *have* thought of ending it all ... I think of those boys crying out for life, and I know I couldn't do it. It would be like some kind of insult to their memory.'

A minute later Jimmy had switched back and was cheerful again. `My buddy Marc, you know, he loved Saigon when he first saw it. Know why? Because it looked so French, reminded him in ways of Paris. But then Vietnam was once part of the old colonial French empire, wasn't it?'

He chuckled. `I remember one day, just a few days after we'd arrived in Saigon...'

Phil had stopped listening. It was all just memories – the sum of Jimmy's life. A reject of society, a man suspended in time and trapped in the past. A lonely, lonely man, with no real purpose in life except surviving from one television show to the next.

Not exactly out of the blue – because Phil had already decided his own future career – he had an idea.

`Before you lost your arm, Jimmy, which hand did you write with?'

`The one I've got left – my right hand.'

`So would you do something for me, Jimmy? When I get back to England, would you write to me there, say, every few weeks or so?'

Jimmy smiled. `Sure I will. I always liked writing letters. These days, though, I got no one to write to.' He frowned. `Ain't got much to say either.'

`That's okay, because what I want you to write to me about, Jimmy, is Vietnam. All your memories, all your buddies, what happened to them, and what happened to you. All the little details you can remember, funny and sad. Just a few pages every week. Would you do that for me, Jimmy?'

Jimmy's face beamed, as if there was nothing he would enjoy doing more, not even watching television. '

Write about Vietnam? Sure I will, Marc. Anything for a buddy.'

THREE

New York
September 1984

——————————————/

`Gotcha!'

Phil had just returned to his hotel on the corner of West 63rd and Columbus, had just entered the foyer, when he heard the voice behind him. He turned to the young brown-haired man who had obviously mistaken him for someone else.

`Just kidding.' The young man grinned. `I've always wanted to say that to someone. Gotcha! Hope I didn't scare you?'

Phil assessed him quickly: he wore a three-piece tailored suit which must have cost a fortune, blue silk tie, and he looked like he had come straight from a business meeting in Wall Street. Either he was a resident of the hotel just trying to be friendly, or an off-the-street diner heading for the restaurant.

`My name is Tom Kennett,' he said. `I'm a detective for a firm of private investigators. Let me give you my firm's card.' Like a magician he produced a card through his fingers. `And you, I have been reliably informed, are Mr Phil Gaines.'

Phil frowned. `So?'

`Now I do understand this must be something of a surprise for you,' said Tom Kennett with solicitude. `And it's also very difficult for me. So can we just step aside here for a minute and talk.'

`About what?' Even as he asked, Phil knew

about what.

'The fact is, Mr Gaines, I have two of my colleagues waiting in a car outside, and the three of us are in a grim predicament. We really do need your help. We have a job to do for our firm, an important job, but we are running out of time. Only you can help us out of the jam we're in.'

Phil stared, amazed at this performance of charming audacity.

'You see, this is our problem – we were ordered by our firm to find out where you were staying in New York, which we did, yesterday afternoon. And now we have been ordered to escort you to the suite of Mrs Jacqueline Gaines at the Plaza Hotel before you leave for England, which, according to our investigations, is tomorrow morning on a British Airways flight at 8.15 from Kennedy.'

Tom Kennett sighed apologetically. 'So now you understand why we would be very grateful if you would come with us this evening. To the Plaza Hotel.'

'And if I refuse to go?'

Kennett screwed up his lips and looked thoughtful. 'Well, we can't strong-arm you out of the hotel. That wouldn't be very polite. And we have been ordered not to use violence. Not that we ever do. Violence is not our style.'

'I'm very relieved to hear that.'

'So, if you refuse to come with us tonight,' Kennett continued in an amiable, conversational tone, 'I suppose we could always arrest you in the morning before you board your plane at Kennedy. Show the airline staff a fake warrant for your arrest. Tell them we are FBI and you are responsible for two murders in two states and the cops have been looking for you everywhere –

haven't they been watching their televisions, for God's sake?' Kennett grinned. `Works every time. Especially when you mention the word television. Makes it more real.'

Despite everything, Phil couldn't help liking Kennett. The man was either extremely clever or an absolute clown.

`So you see, Mr Gaines, it would be much easier all round if you just came along with us now.'

Phil stared off towards the centre of the hotel lobby as if pondering the consequences of his decision. He finally made it, and looked at Kennett. `Okay, let's get it over with. Let's go to the Plaza.'

`Now you're talking! Look, son,' said Kennett, who was no more than thirty. `I know this is all very inconvenient for you, but where's the harm? She's just a little old lady after all, your grandmother. A poor old lady just wanting to find her grandson.'

`A little old lady?' Phil almost laughed. `Evidently, you have never met her.'

`No, but I believe in karma. And helping old ladies is good for my karma.'

Outside the hotel the two colleagues were standing by a silver-grey BMW, attempting to placate the doorman who was shouting furiously at them to move their car.

`It's *against the law* for any car to park inside these yellow lines! The space between these yellow lines is for taxicabs and limos delivering and collecting guests from the hotel! And it's *against the law* for any other vehicle to park here!'

Kennett flickered a glance at Phil. `I told you we were in a jam.'

As soon as the two investigators saw Phil and Kennett coming out together, they pointed. `And that's just what we're doing – collecting a guest. Look.'

The doorman turned, looked at Phil with recognition, then turned back to the car. `I see one guest, and I see three men to collect him. Know what that means to me? It means that this here vehicle is no taxicab and no hired limo. So it's *against the law* for it to be parked here!'

`Aw, shove it up your ass,' said Kennett, opening the back door of the car for Phil to get inside. `We can park where we damn well like. We pay our taxes to the City, which is more than any of your guests do. Know what you are – a *toady* to foreigners. A disgrace to your father!'

As the car moved off into the early-evening traffic, Phil looked wryly at Kennett sitting next to him. `Being civil to hotel doormen – not good for your karma?'

Kennett laughed. `Well, you know, there is one huge difference between your sweet grandmother and that blowhard doorman. Your grandmother is paying us a jumbo rate with a sizable bonus on top. And for that we don't take no interference from some ten-cent tip-technician.'

He sat back and relaxed. `Now let me introduce you to my two esteemed colleagues here in the front, Mr Tony Martinez and Mr Stephen Ward. The three of us always work as a team and we always get results.' He pointed to each of the two in turn. `He's the balls of the outfit, and he's the brains.'

`And what are you?' Phil asked Kennett.

`He's the biggest prick in the State of New York,' said the driver, grinning at the guy in the passenger seat. `That right, Stevie?'

`Yep.'

`I am the *negotiator*,' said Kennett with authority. `I know how to handle people without any unpleasantness. Right, Stevie?'

`Right, Tom.'

`Did you phone the Plaza?'

By the time they reached the Plaza Hotel, Phil decided he had been hoisted by the Marx Brothers, three well-dressed clowns. As he got out of the car the driver shook his hand firmly. `Adios, amigo.'

Stevie stretched and did likewise. `Hey, Phil,' he grinned, `don't let us down when you get inside. Don't strangle your grandmother. We'd feel responsible. So keep the peace now.'

Only Kennett escorted him into the hotel, after putting on a pair of dark glasses.

`Now this really *is* getting theatrical,' Phil murmured.

After stopping at the main desk, and while waiting for the elevator, Kennett took the dark glasses off.

`Maybe you're right,' he murmured. `They're not exactly a natural requirement for wandering around the Plaza. It was just a final little touch to impress your grandmother. Little old ladies always expect you to look the part. Get real disappointed if you don't. Comes from watching too much television. All of America watches too much television. It's the nation's God and all the presenters are hallowed apostles.' He nodded his head slightly, and Phil continued to look amused.

`But these shades are valuable tools of our trade, you know,' Kennett went on. `For instance, if we *had* been forced to arrest you at Kennedy, pretending we were FBI, all *three* of us would have been wearing shades. Know why? No one would believe we were FBI without them.'

`I still can't believe any of you are private detectives,' said Phil. `If you want the truth – not one of you look the part. Or is that the idea?'

`You got it – that's the idea.' Kennett grinned, pleased. `But tell me, just out of interest, why, in your opinion do we *not* look like private detectives?'

`Well, three young guys, all dressed like Wall Street yuppies – silk ties, Gucci shoes and Rolex watches – '

`You *noticed* all that?' Kennett looked impressed, then looked at his watch, and down at his shoes.

`Wouldn't wear anything else,' he said, and laughed. `So what did you expect? Tough guys with snap-brim hats like Philip Marlowe or Mike Hammer? Nah – that's *old* time! Old Fifties and Sixties Hollywood stuff. And this is the Eighties, friend, the *Eighties*.'

*

The sitting-room of the suite was yellow and white, and mirror bright. Jacqueline smiled her brilliant smile.

`So, Philippe, we meet again.'

Phil looked at her silently, certain that Kennett was still standing outside the door, stunned. The little old lady he had expected was tall and slender and black-haired, wearing a close-fitting beige jersey dress, designed to show her mature but still lovely figure to perfect advantage. Her style, her sophistication, her charm – the way her dark eyes had glowed as she had clasped Kennett's hand in both of hers with a delighted smile – all made her look a much younger woman than she actually was, and implied a sensuous energy and attractiveness that would never age.

Kennett had stood, open-mouthed, even as Jacqueline dismissed him by closing the door in his face.

`This is all a waste of time,' Phil said. `I don't know what you hope to achieve.'

A waiter had wheeled in a trolley of silvered-covered dishes. Jacqueline gestured for him to take it over to the dining table by the window. The table was dressed in a lace cloth, lighted candles and gold-rimmed white china, and already set for two. A second waiter carried in a bottle of champagne in an ice bucket.

Jacqueline said, `I thought it might be nice if we dined as we talked, Philippe. It's not yet seven, so I presume you have not dined?'

`I'm not hungry.'

`Nevertheless, you will at least have a glass of Roederer's Cristal with me, won't you? It was Marc's favourite, you know. I'm sure he would like you to try it, and would consider it very ungracious of you to refuse.'

`Nevertheless, no, thank you,' Phil said. `I see no point—' a waiter was holding out a chair for him, the other was pouring him a glass of the champagne – `in causing a scene,' he finished with a sigh.

As soon as he had sat down opposite her at the table, Jacqueline gave a slow easy smile. `Roederer's Cristal, as Marc used to say, is the champagne of champagnes. The late Tsars of Russia drank nothing else.'

She lifted her glass, letting the glow from the candlelight illuminate its sparkle. `All I want,

Philippe, is a little time for us to talk together without accusations or anger. And after all my trouble in finding you, surely you will allow me that?'

`I would find all this easier,' he said evenly, `if you would stop calling me Philippe. It's not a name I am used to, or feel comfortable with.'

`Then I shall call you Phil,' she said agreeably, and nodded for him to taste his champagne, smiling in triumph when he did so and she saw his instant appreciation of its cool and soothing seduction.

`I knew you would like it,' she said. `All the French have a natural appreciation for good wine and perfect champagne.'

`Yet I am English,' he said curiously, eyebrows raised. `So it seems we English know a good champagne when we taste it too.'

She smiled almost teasingly. `You are half-French. Your father was a Parisian, born in Paris.'

`My father,' he said quietly, `was an American soldier, the son of an American. So don't tell me he was French — not when he paid for his American citizenship with his blood.'

`And that is all you know of him,' Jacqueline said softly, `because that is all he left you — the American legacy of Vietnam. But there is so much more you need to know — things that only I can tell you. Things about Marc, about Alexander, about Paris, about my father, Philippe Castineau. Things about your paternal family. Things that your mother does not know. Will you not let me tell you some of those things, before you make a final judgement about me? Will you not at least hear my side of it? It would be a fair thing to do, I think. And I'm sure Marc would agree.'

`Very well,' he said, `I'll listen.' Then he looked up inquiringly at the two waiters who had finished serving food onto their plates.

Jacqueline read his expression and instantly dismissed the two waiters with a wave of her hand. She did this with a grace that was not offensive, simply expedient and not unexpected.

When the waiters had retired from the room, leaving them to continue their conversation in privacy, Jacqueline smiled, looking at ease and appreciative, and then spoke softly as if shyly venturing a confession.

`Not everything I have done has been right. But then, you must understand....'

He sat back and let her talk without interruption, and without touching a morsel of the food on his plate, finally turning his eyes away to gaze out of the window at the figure of Abundance atop the Pulitzer Fountain.

But throughout he continued listening as she told him of her life in Paris, her work for the Resistance, her father's murder by the Gestapo, her early years in America, her disastrous marriage, her complete devastation at Alexander's betrayal, writing down every word she had said to Alexander in confidence – using *her* words to win himself a Pulitzer prize ...

He glanced at her face and saw the faraway look in her eyes as she spoke – as absorbed as a small child lost in the telling of an enthralling story in which she was the heroine.

Then the tone and story changed.

`But, oh! ... how can I tell you my love for my son? How can I explain to you the love between a mother and her only son.'

He didn't need her to explain the love between a

mother and her only son. He had experienced sixteen years of it.

But she told him anyway, occasionally waving her hands as though trying to describe with her hands what she could not articulate, occasionally speaking in French and not realising it, an unstoppable monologue, explaining everything in the only way she knew how – from her own point of view.

When she had finally finished speaking, her eyes drifted from the window across the table to him. Her eyes, so dark, illuminated by the candlelight, were glistening with tears.

He sat there, saying nothing, looking at her intently.

She whispered, `Well, Philippe?'

`Well,' he said, pushing back his chair and standing up. `Thank you for dinner, Mrs Gaines. But now I must leave. I have an early start in the morning.'

`But you said – '

`I said nothing. You manoeuvred me into agreeing that you should be allowed to talk about yourself without suffering any accusations or anger from me, and I have complied.'

`But ... did nothing I say mean anything to you?'

`It might have meant more to me, if you had once – just once – mentioned my mother. Made even the smallest inquiry about her. But she was never of any interest to you, was she?'

He stared at her coldly, then suddenly changed his mind and sat down again. `Well, Madame, whether you like it not, I am going to tell you about that English girl named Marian Barnard.'

`Oh, *please,* please do!' Jacqueline gushed. `I want to know *everything* about her. Marc told me so little. And now I so much want to meet her. I so much want to talk with her about Marc. I want to make her understand how wrong she is about me. I was hoping you *would* – tonight, tell me about her.'

A long silence.

`She was not like you,' Phil said finally. `She would not have considered herself brave or daring or reckless. She didn't know about such things. She hated hurting others, and often feared for her own courage. But she was the sun and rain and earth to me. She was kind and loving and as ordinary in her ways as ... as a childhood morning full of bowls of cornflakes and fresh milk. An ordinary mother, watching over my boyhood, helping me to put the pieces of a jigsaw into place, her fingers leaving a timeless imprint on my life, never to be erased, no matter how long I live. Do you understand?'

`Oh, yes,' she agreed. `I understand so well. That is how I think of my father.'

`But to Marc ... Marian was someone else,' Phil went on. `Someone quite different to the person I knew. To Marc she was a beautiful girl, the love of his life, constantly crossing sky and ocean – just to be with her. He wanted to give her the world, marry her, and bring her to America. He wanted you, as his mother, to welcome her.'

`Yes,' Jacqueline agreed, moving restlessly. `But you see – '

`To you, though, she was someone else again. To you she was not good enough. An unintelligent waitress. An immoral slut. My mother.'

`I was wrong, so *wrong*,' Jacqueline said penitently.

`And you do regret it now, don't you? The way you insulted her. The way you hurt both of them.

Marian and Marc. My parents.'

`Yes,' Jacqueline nodded. `So much I regret it now.'

`Now that you know they had a son?'

Her hand reached out to him. `Will you forgive me?'

`No.'

Jacqueline fought off her panic – an unprepared moment of terrible alarm – which quickly gave way to a feeling of exasperated anger.

Oh, how *foolish* young men were. How stubborn. How *naïve*. Did he really believe she would take `No' for an answer? She would not take `No' for an answer, and she was a good fighter when it came to getting what she wanted. She had learned early in the Resistance, and instructed others with the same duty: *Whatever the obstacle, the mission must be accomplished.*

Marc had also said `No' to her, at first, but she had quickly found a way to persuade him. And as bitterly as she now regretted forcing that promise from Marc – she was ready to use the same tactics again with his son. Except this time she would not use a Bible. This time she was better prepared.

`Wait, please!' she begged as Phil stood to leave. `I have something for you!'

`Marc's military identification tag?'

`No, something much better.'

He had called her the most selfish of women, but she would prove him wrong. She rushed over to the escritoire and took a slip of paper from a drawer. He was almost at the door when she rushed over and handed it to him.

`For you.'

He stared at it, and thought at first it was some

kind of joke.

He shook his head to clear it, and stared again, but there it was, filled out in black ink – a cheque from the Chase Manhattan Bank payable to Philippe Gaines, and signed by Jacqueline Gaines – $1,000,000. One million dollars.

He looked at her and smiled. `Very funny,' he said, and handed the cheque back to her. But she pushed it back into his hand, deadly serious.

`You must allow me to make amends,' she insisted. `You must understand how important this is to me. I lost my son, but now I have found my grandson. You must allow me to give you a fatted calf.'

`A million bucks is one hell of a fatted calf.'

`So?' She made a careless gesture with her hand; diamonds flashed before his eyes. `You are my grandson. My brother died out in the Congo, and now you are my only living relative. So who else should I give it to?'

She smiled at him, almost flirtatiously, knowing that money was the greatest persuader in the world.

`Do you not know how wealthy I am, Philippe? When I married my husband I did not marry a rich man. He married a wealthy woman. Did I not tell you that my father was a Parisian gentleman, a jeweller, a man who dealt in gold and diamonds? The Gestapo got his life but not his wealth. No-n-no, we Castineaus were far too clever for that.'

Phil looked at her smiling face, and thought of his mother, penny-pinching all her life – selling the only diamond she had been lucky enough to possess. Her engagement ring.

Jacqueline sighed, `You should have had this years ago. Your mother should have had some too.

But I shall make amends to her. I shall see she has every luxury. Really, it's too bad, my grandson growing up without the Castineau wealth to support him.'

`My mother wants nothing from you,' he said softly. `And neither do I.'

He tore up the cheque.

Jacqueline stared at him, incredulous. It was impossible! No young man would tear up a cheque for a million dollars.

`Nothing,' he reiterated, letting the torn pieces fall before her eyes. `Not a cent. Not from you.'

She stepped back, stung, as if it was salt being thrown in her eyes. She quickly turned away, her hands gripping the back of the sofa, her voice beginning to shake.

`Why ... *why?*' she moaned. `Why do you hate me so? Has it always been?'

`No, not always. Until a week ago you were just a stranger who lived in a house in Massachusetts. All I ever wanted from you was my father's military identification tag. But when I went to see Bill Simons and was told – what Jimmy forgot to tell Marian all those years ago when he visited her in London – that Marc's father had died upon news of Marc's death, I realised then that the vindictive tyrant of the family was not Alexander, but you. Because it was *you*, wasn't it, who after Marc's death ordered his bank to stop the monthly payments to Marian Barnard?'

`Yes, but you see, I did not know there was a child! If I had – '

`Oh, so it was only *her* you wanted to punish – the waitress. The girl you knew Marc was deeply in love with. And so despite his instructions that she be supported from his *own* money – from his *own* trust fund – even in the event of his death, you brought in your clever lawyers and had Marc's instructions rescinded.'

`But please, you *must* understand – after Marc's death I was so tortured with grief ... I was deranged.'

`No!' Phil snapped savagely. `You were deranged *before* Marc's death. Long before. And don't give me all that sob stuff about how you suffered in the war. How you were *forced* to kill Nazis. You loved the violence. It was the only time you felt passion! When you were killing, destroying, getting your revenge. You revelled in it! The war, to you, was nothing to do with good and evil – it was all about *power*. The power you felt every time you killed, every time you gave an order, every time someone knuckled under to you.'

She was staring at him, eyes wide, without voice, only words in her ears, words scourging her with remorseless intent.

`Especially Marc. You revelled in emasculating Marc even more than you delighted in humiliating Alexander. So don't try and use the war, or Marc's death, or anything else as an excuse for your badness.'

`B-Badness?'

`All I know is that you treated my mother with as much contempt and malevolence as any Nazi treated a Jew – so it doesn't wash with me, Saint Joan. You're a selfish, malicious, evil bitch. And it's about time somebody told you so.'

Jacqueline sprang out of her shock, lunging forward, grabbing him fiercely, her hands holding onto the lapels of his jacket, her eyes manic with rage. `It was *her*, wasn't it? The English girl! Your mother! It was *she* who sent you here to torment me!'

He caught her hands in his own, removed them from his jacket, and pushed her away.

`My mother is dead! If you had been listening when I spoke about her, you would have realised that immediately. Everything I said about her was in the *past* tense. Strange you didn't notice that – a woman who claims to have been the true literary voice behind her husband's prize-winning book.'

He gave her one last disgusted look. `But that was just one more of your lies, wasn't it? A damned disgraceful lie to cover up all your other lies ... taking away Alexander's victory and talent and claiming it all for yourself. Poor Alexander.'

Jacqueline was unable to utter a sound. Not even when the door clicked shut behind him.

The suite had two bedrooms.

Mrs Edwards, standing in her own bedroom with her ear pressed to the door, had heard it all. She opened the door slowly but did not enter the sitting-room, just stood and stared in disbelief at Jacqueline's motionless figure. On the carpet, near her feet, were the scattered pieces of the torn-up check.

Eddie shook her head. After all these years living with Jacqueline, she would not have believed it possible. Poor Alexander had not been able to stand up to her, nor Marc, nor any single person that Jacqueline had ever come in contact with. She was possessed by a ruthless conviction in her own power, and in any battle of will, she always won.

But yes, tonight it had actually happened. Jacqueline had finally met her match, and lost.

Eddie closed the door quietly and turned back into the bedroom. But would she give up? Eddie wondered. Even now, would Jacqueline give up?

Returning to his hotel room, Phil immediately opened the small refrigerated mini-bar and poured himself a shot of bourbon. Since his mother's death he had a particular detestation of strong drink, and rarely drank anything stronger than wine – but it was not every day he was given a chance to tear up a cheque for a million dollars.

Was he crazy?

He knocked back a slug of bourbon. Shuddered. Threw the rest down the sink.

A million dollars.

Maybe he was as crazy as her?

No, only a sleaze would forgive for money.

Slowly, the terrible tenseness that had gripped and held him, began to leave him. His muscles relaxing, his mind clearing. He thought over all Jacqueline had told him about her reckless and violent teenage life, and wondered what kind of woman she might have become, if the Nazis had never invaded her beloved Paris.

Would she still have become a psychopath? Or would she have put her intelligence and talents to better use?

Strangely, he found himself, at last, feeling some compassion for her.

Not much, but some.

In her suite at the Plaza, Jacqueline sat listlessly on the sofa, staring into nothingness. Eddie tried to comfort her.

`Aw, he'll come round! Now he's had his vengeance, he'll start thinking about that million dollars and wonder if it was worth it.'

`No,' Jacqueline said quietly. `There will be no forgiveness. Not from him. I know that now. I thought he was like my son. My beautiful son who died in Vietnam. I thought he was like my father. My wonderful father who died for France. But he is not like either of them – he is like *me*.'

Eddie didn't know whether to agree or disagree.

`I knew it that first day I met him,' Jacqueline continued. `When I saw the way he looked at me. Dear God, my heart – in that moment I saw a memory of myself as I had been when I was young. So proud, so aloof, so heartless! Like me, as I was then, he is beautiful, but cold and immovable. Like me, he will never allow anyone to stand in his way. And like me – he will *never* forgive an enemy.'

`An enemy? Aw, you're no *enemy*. And what's there to forgive? Okay, so you stopped Marc from marrying his mother. But that's all in the past. And anyway – his mother is dead now.'

Jacqueline winced, and bit her lip. Such lack of subtlety still appalled her.

`If only his mother was *not* dead,' she said a few moments later. `If only his mother was still alive – then there would be some hope, some chance of a reconciliation, some way to win him back. But now it is too late.'

`Oh, come on, it's never too late.'

`You do not understand him, as I do,' Jacqueline said softly. `In France there is a saying ... "Hurt the mother, and you make an enemy of the son".'

She closed her eyes. `And I hurt them both. His mother *and* his father. And now both are dead. No, no, he will never forgive me, I see that now.'

FOUR

New York,
September 1984

_____/

The following morning, three hours after Phil had caught his flight and left New York behind him, Jacqueline visited her lawyer.

`I have come about my grandson.'

Lewis Belfort's eyes widened. `Your grandson? I didn't know – '

`Yes. He gave me his birth certificate as a gift.' She threw it across the desk.

Belfort picked it up, read it carefully, noted the legal stamps and signatures, and then looked at her in amazement. `So ... Marc had a son?'

`As you can see, he is now twenty years old.'

Belfort nodded, and thought he understood her problem. `And now he has come to you looking for money, has he?' Belfort smiled confidently. `Well let me put your mind at rest, Jacqueline. The child was born out of wedlock. He is illegitimate – '

`He is magnificent!' Jacqueline cut him short. `I gave him a cheque for a million dollars and he tore it up in my presence.'

Belfort swallowed. `A ... million dollars?'

Jacqueline smiled. `Oh, Lewis, he would have been *superb* in the Resistance. He would not have been bribed. My father would have been so proud of him.'

Lewis Belfort was losing track, flummoxed by Jacqueline's reaction, and unsure what she wanted from him now.

`I want him legitimised. As Marc's son. And my

grandson. You have his birth certificate there before you. And as you can see, it bears Marc's signature.'

Belfort looked again at the certificate. `Yes, Marc must have been present when the birth was registered.'

`Yes,' Jacqueline echoed, her dark eyes transparent with pain. `My darling Marc was present when the birth of his son was registered. But he never told me....'

And as Jacqueline sat staring back into the past, all the mistakes of her own making came back to haunt her, taunt her − blades of bitter sorrow shooting through her for the lives that had been wasted ... her own life, and her son's life. The baby grandson she could have loved.

Oh, regret was bitterly sharp when she looked back on what she had not known, yet could have known, if only ... if only...

`Jacqueline?' Lewis Belfort touched her shoulder. She looked at him and he saw her suffering, her despair.

`How was I to know Marc would be sent to Vietnam?' she groaned. `How was I to know Lyndon Johnson was going to betray us. How was I to *know?*'

She sat down and finally told Lewis Belfort the full story of Marc and the English girl, and the action she had taken to prevent their marriage.

`But I didn't *know*, Lewis, I didn't know they had a child ... I didn't know ... the girl ... I didn't know she would remain faithful to Marc, remain unmarried ...'

Lewis Belfort looked into the black desolation of Jacqueline's eyes and pitied her, as he had never done before. He had never seen her so vulnerable, and wanted to comfort her.

`And now their son – ' she whispered. `Oh, how he hates me, Lewis.'

`I'm sure,' Lewis said, `that in time, some sort of understanding will be reached between the two of you. Perhaps if you were to – '

`No, no,' Jacqueline shook her head hopelessly, and repeated to Lewis Belfort the same words she had said to Eddie. `Hurt the mother, and you make a steadfast enemy of the son ... No, he will never forgive me, it is too late for me to hope for anything from him."

*

The plane was somewhere above the mid-Atlantic, Phil reckoned, but he was too wide-awake to sleep, and too restless to read. He thought of all the places he had been, and all the people he had seen, during his time in America.

The only person he did not think of was Jacqueline. Nor would he allow himself to think of her ever again. She belonged to the past, and now he was concerned only with the future.

He knew exactly what his goals were, and he knew nothing would stop him, no matter how long he was forced to wait. He would personally publish his mother's book, and he would personally destroy the man who had killed her.

FIVE

Cambridge
1984-1987

_____/

It was a thirty-page letter written on lined foolscap in close neat words, so neat in fact, Phil suspected Jimmy had written it at his own disjointed pace, then had painstakingly copied it all out again, neatly, to make it more readable.

An act of true decency and true nice-guy consideration, from a man with only one hand.

Yet every word was powerful with authenticity: the nuts and bolts of everyday life of soldiers in Vietnam; the long scorching days out on patrol in tiger-striped camouflage; the jungle with its blood-sucking leeches; the dark nights of silver stars watched by young men in green helmets who smoked Cambodian Red and dreamed bamboo dreams, all wishing and wondering and counting the days until they could go home again – back to the place they called `The World.'

The sheer guts and truth of Jimmy's storytelling surprised Phil, although he had known that Jimmy would be incapable of writing anything other than the truth about Vietnam. No ballyhoo or baloney, no fake sentimentality – all of it was as real as the skin on your face. But much of it was mixed up, out of order, and out of shape.

After reading it carefully three times, Phil took out his own foolscap pad of paper and began rewriting Jimmy's pages, not taking away or adding anything, but giving it form, chronology, removing a paragraph from page twenty-two and using it as the opening paragraph:

In the beginning, every American soldier in Vietnam was sure of only one thing – "Ho Chi Minh ain't gonna win". That was in the beginning...

Phil worked for hours, oblivious of time passing, committed to the task before him, lost in the images and words, some of it written in Namspeak, the regular language of the US soldiers out in the field – `Give 'em some rock 'n' roll!' (automatic fire). `An Angel hovering above.' (A helicopter coming in to pick up the wounded) `Men, I want you to welcome our latest FNG.' (Fucking New Guy). `On short-time.' (Less than 30 days left in Vietnam).

The door of his room suddenly flew open –Phil looked up in vague disorientation, snapping back to the conscious present, to his surroundings – his room at Cambridge – and saw that his visitor looked even more disorientated.

`I'm sorry,' David Gallagher muttered. `Oh God, I'm sorry, I've walked into the wrong room.'

He appeared to be almost weeping with rage. Phil looked at him curiously.

`Something wrong, David?'

`Oh God, yes ... It's Coles. Bloody Mr Coles! This time he's really upset me, that's why I walked into your room instead of my own.'

`That's okay.'

Now that he *was* in Phil's room, David Gallagher seemed reluctant to leave it, hovering indecisively in the silence.

Phil sighed patiently. `Do you want to talk about it?'

`Yes, oh God, yes. I can't tell you how much I hate Coles. From the first day I got here he's been making snide comments about my looks...' Tears glistening in his eyes, David sat down in the armchair and blurted it all out.

David Gallagher was the same age as Phil, both were reading English at King's, and both had rooms on the same staircase. But there the similarity ended. Whereas Phil was dark and undoubtedly masculine, David had the golden hair and fresh-faced looks of a choirboy. Sensitive and poetic and intellectual, he was unable to cope with the constant jibing of Stephen Coles, a man of extreme arrogance and intimidating wit, who seemed to have chosen David Gallagher as an easy prey for his predatory humour.

`All my life I've been called a pretty boy, and I've *always* hated it,' David Blurted. `Sometimes I wish I could have a real bad car accident and get my face all smashed up, then maybe creeps like Coles will leave me alone.'

Then David felt like a blubbering fool, and said so. `I'm sorry, I've no right to come in here burdening you with my problem.'

Phil shrugged. `I can't see the problem myself. You don't look that pretty to me. But then people usually only see what they want to see.'

`What do you mean?'

`Coles – I think *he's* the one with the problem.'

`You do?' David looked at him earnestly. `In what way?'

`Well, you know, some of these overtly macho guys ... it's all a front. A cover-up for their own weaknesses.'

David looked down at his clenched hands for a long moment. When he spoke again, his voice was very quiet. `I understand what you're saying. But I don't know what I can do about it. All I know for certain ... is that I have suffered this kind of thing before, and I can't go through it again. Not with a man like Coles, and *definitely* not for the next three years.'

Phil sat looking at David in that dark thoughtful way of his. `Why don't you just tell Coles to bugger off and go screw himself?'

David blinked. `Charming, of course. But I didn't come all the way to Cambridge to start using language like that. Don't you know that men such as Tennyson, Wordsworth and Byron all studied here? So did Prince Charles.'

Phil shrugged. `Well I can't speak for Charlie, but I doubt that a man like Byron would have taken any personal crap from a lecturer.'

`No—' David said thoughtfully, `No ... not Byron. And come to think of it ... judging by his portraits ... Byron's face was somewhat on the pretty side too – don't you think so?'

`I know his tongue was as smooth as a razor – cut an opponent dead with just one sentence, perfectly phrased.'

`Yes, yes, every time.' David nodded. His eyes suddenly filled with a quickened, reverent light. `No man ever succeeded when trying to intimidate Byron.'

Phil smiled. `So, go act like your hero, David. Tell Coles what he needs to be told, and put a stop to this thing now. Fight back and make it clear you're taking no more crap. Coles is out of order here, and it's up to you to tell him so. And tell him straight.'

`Right, that's just what I will do, and right away.' David jumped to his feet determinedly and headed for the door.

Phil turned his eyes and attention back to the pages of Jimmy's letter. Back to the world of soldiers in Vietnam.

The following day David Gallagher was still feeling exhilarated and immensely relieved as he walked beside Phil across the grounds. `I still can't believe I stood up to Coles, strong on every point. And afterwards, God, I felt bloody marvellous!'

Phil laughed. `So there's hope for you yet, David. You may even make it all the way through the next three years to your degree.'

David felt so good, he accompanied Phil all the way into town and into an art shop. The young girl behind the counter had a perfect heart-shaped face, long chestnut hair, and very attractive.

`Now *that* is what I call a pretty face,' Phil whispered to David with a grin.

He bought an easel and a number of canvases. David helped him to carry them, still looking somewhat surprised.

`Do you paint?' David asked curiously. `I mean, *seriously* paint?'

Phil turned his head with a wry smile. `No, David, I'm buying this easel to hang my ties on. And these canvases, well, I thought they might be useful for blocking out the beautiful view from my window. Of course I bloody paint!'

`And my God – you have talent!' David said a few days later, coming up behind Phil unexpectedly and staring at the canvas on the easel. `You really do have *talent!'*

Phil glanced round at David, then at the open door of his room. `Don't you ever knock, Gallagher?'

`I'm sorry,' David apologised, `I did knock, but you obviously didn't hear me. Must be the headphones.'

Phil, as usual, was wearing headphones and listening to soul music while he painted. `And looking at this—' David exclaimed, staring at the painting of a young dark-haired girl with soulful sapphire-blue eyes – `makes me wonder why on earth you chose to study literature instead of art?'

Phil ignored the question and delicately dipped his brush into black paint. `So what do you want?' he asked.

David racked his brains to remember what, then smiled vaguely. `Do you know, I've completely forgotten.'

Phil sighed, and continued to paint.

David sat silently for a long time, just watching, while Phil continued to ignored him.

David didn't mind being ignored. As long as Phil did not object, David would have been happy to sit there all day long. This room was the only place in the world he wanted to be. It had an attraction for him that was hard to describe. Even more than his own room, sitting here in a high-back chair, legs stretched out, he felt safe and content.

And in the weeks and months and years that followed, David Gallagher ventured towards Phil's room as often as possible, on any pretext, although he did not understand why he did so.

Friendship, David finally concluded – that was the reason he was constantly lured like a magnet towards Phil's company. Happy, invigorating, genuine friendship. Something David had known very little of in his boyhood years.

Phil, in contrast, seemed to have no need of anything or anyone. And so he had lots of friends.

Sitting in his usual chair, looking over at him, David realised how impossible it was to summarise Phil Gaines, to rubber-stamp him into any category. An enigma in many ways, Phil did not reveal himself to others, refusing to be drawn into any personal revelations about himself, often with a smile of gentle mockery in his eyes.

It was true that Phil did not reveal himself to others, not because he was in any way sepulchral about his privacy, but simply because he felt no need to do so, and saw no reason why he should.

Not even when he received the life-changing telephone call from New York did he trouble himself telling others.

The call came in May, 1987, at eleven o'clock at night, but still early evening in New York.

Phil's first thought, when Lewis Belfort introduced himself over the telephone, was to wonder how Jacqueline's lawyer knew where to contact him.

`Don't ask me how, Mr Gaines, but your grandmother seems to have been kept well informed of all your activities since she last saw you ... or perhaps I should say, since she last *spoke* to you.'

Was there a difference? Phil instantly knew there was. It made him shudder to think he might have been unaware of hidden eyes watching him.

`Spoke and saw? Where's the difference? I know when I last spoke to her – three years ago. So when was it that she last saw me?'

`The last time? Oh, that was a few months ago. When you came to New York to see Jimmy Overman. She always came to New York whenever she knew you were over from England on a visit.

But as I say, I can't tell you how she knew.'

Again Phil shuddered. So for the past three years, Jacqueline had been keeping tabs on him.

`Has she been to Cambridge?'

`Yes, I believe she has. Three or four times, as I recall. It was her greatest hope, I must tell you, to go to Cambridge for your graduation ceremony. She had no doubts about you securing your degree. She even predicted honours.'

Was, had, did – all words belonging to the *past* tense.

`Your grandmother is dead, I regret to say, Mr Gaines. Less than a month ago she was informed she was suffering from cancer. Her death following so quickly was quite unexpected.'

It didn't take many seconds of thought for Phil to work it out. A woman like Jacqueline Castineau would never allow herself to descend into fragility or a sick dependence upon others. So, an efficient sorting out of her affairs, then a self-administered drug to end it all with dignity.

`She killed herself, didn't she?'

Lewis Belfort's voice sounded appalled at such a suggestion. `Most certainly not! As I have told you, Mr Gaines, your grandmother died of cancer.'

Phil was not convinced.

`It was for the best – and end to her suffering,' Belfort murmured.

`When did she die?'

`Three days ago. Her funeral was held this morning at Saint Teresa's Catholic Church in Harvard, Massachusetts. I have just flown back from there. There was quite a crowd, I can tell you. Friends from all over America. Even a wreath from Ted Kennedy. He's the State Senator of Massachusetts, you know. Your grandmother was always a great supporter of the Democrats – '

`Well, thank you for letting me know,' Phil cut him short, not caring to hear all the details of the funeral.

`If you will just give me a few minutes longer, Mr Gaines, I promise to be brief.'

`About what?'

`About your grandmother's will. She has left her estate in its entirety to you.'

`I don't want it,' Phil replied immediately. `I told her when she was alive, and I'm telling you now – I don't want anything from her. She was Marc's mother but she was nothing to my own mother or me.'

Lewis Belfort sighed. `She expected this to be your reaction. She warned me that you would be difficult. That's why she instructed me not to inform you of her death until after she was buried. She knew you would probably refuse to attend her funeral. But, Mr Gaines, I must stress ... your grandmother spent the last three years of her life living in bitter regret. And she really *did* want to make amends. Not only to you, but also to Marc. Especially to Marc.'

`Marc?'

`In her will, your grandmother wishes it to be made clear to you, that the legacy of the Gaines estate in its entirety comes to you, posthumously, from her son Marc, your father. What should have been Marc's shall now be yours. She pleads with you to accept it on Marc's behalf, and with her apologies.'

After a long pause, Phil said, `The Gaines estate in its entirety? What exactly are we talking about?'

`Oh ... the country house in Harvard, the townhouse in Boston, the apartment in Paris;

stocks and shares, bank accounts, various other assets ... Your grandmother was a very astute business woman, Mr Gaines, so apart from the two houses and apartment in Paris, in actual money in GBP currency we are talking about a total of approximately fifty-three million pounds. And all of it now belongs to you.'

`And Marc's military identification tag? Do I get that too?'

`Oh yes, that too. Absolutely everything.'

An hour later Phil was sitting on the window seat in his room looking down on the garden below, still thinking about everything Lewis Belfort had said to him.

Jacqueline ... here in Cambridge ... hidden and unseen ... watching him, keeping tabs on him, knew his every move. She even knew when he was over in New York visiting Jimmy – `*Don't ask me how, Mr Gaines, but your grandmother seems to have been kept informed of all your activities since...*'

Kept informed?

Under normal circumstances this realisation would have made him sick to the pit of his stomach, but now it was over and so it didn't matter. Now he was considering Jacqueline's actions from a detached perspective, analytically ... Only one thing could have bought that kind of surveillance. Big money. Lots of BIG MONEY.

He thought of Tom Kennett in New York. Even then Jacqueline had used private investigators, no expense spared.

He thought of the millions he had just inherited. Enough BIG MONEY to hire his own investigators.

He thought of the man who had killed his mother – and all at once, as if scenes from a film were running across his eyes, he was sixteen again, sitting at the back of a courtroom ...

Close-up: The defendant, James Duncan, a businessman in his forties, described as a `successful publisher'.

Close-up: The witness-box, a police officer reading from his notes, then stepping down – his place taken by an old man, a witness – `Yes, sir, he just stood there, watching her bleed to death on the road, just stood there, smoking a cigar.'

Close-up: The defence lawyer, pleading mitigating circumstances on behalf of his client. A skilled and eloquent lawyer – a bastard liar.

Scene: Same courtroom, afternoon of same day, the verdict: the sentence statute, a fine of £150 plus a three-year driving ban.

Close-up: James Duncan, laughing with relief and shaking his lawyer's hand in gratitude and congratulation.

He had got away with it. He had killed a thirty-five year old woman and he had not been made to pay for it. No more than £150.

And amidst all the joyous handshaking, Phil saw not a hint of remorse as James Duncan, with a blonde bimbo on his arm, sailed past him full of smiles, unaware of the presence in court of his victim's son.

Scene: The street outside the court, James Duncan, exuberant, lighting a cigar, laughing, hugging the blonde, waving down a taxi.

Close-up: The Blonde, fluttering on her stilettos toward the taxi with excited gaspings `*Champagne, darling, champagne, what else?*'

FADE-OUT.

A film without an end, a long tunnel without an exit, a hatred without respite, a vendetta without retribution, the good die young and the iniquitous go unpunished ... until now.

Phil stood up suddenly and went in search of his old wallet, found it in a drawer, flicked through all the bits and pieces and found Tom Kennett's card – why had he kept it? It didn't matter why. What mattered was now and how.

Jacqueline, God bless her sick soul, had not only given him the idea, she had also given him the money to pay for it.

Again he looked at Tom Kennett's card, but he forced his mind to shift down a gear and thought, No, not yet, time enough. First, he had to get his graduation over.

Then he would move on and meet his opponent on the same pitch, beat him at his own game, and find some perfect but truly risk-free way of destroying him.

Again he heard a voice in his head from the past: Bill Simons in Shirley, Massachusetts – Alexander's best friend from boyhood: `... *Alexander was convinced of it, he kept saying it, every time he got drunk he would say it – she won't use a gun or a knife, nothing so obvious, but she'll find a way...*'

Phil smiled a little.

And he too would find a way. But first, his

graduation. Then the pitch and the game. If an unconscionable swine named James Duncan could become a successful publisher, then a multi-millionaire named Phil Gaines could also, and easier.

SIX

Cambridge
June 1987

_____/

It was a day to remember, that Friday in June 1987.

With three thousand graduates about to collect their degrees, and twenty thousand guests present to see them do so, Cambridge was alive with excitement as tourists lined the streets to see the procession.

At nine-fifteen the undergraduates of King's College were the first to proceed through the streets in a long procession of fours, en-route to the Senate House, followed by undergraduates from Trinity and St. Johns, until the graduates of all thirty-one colleges had been awarded their degrees in a ceremony that would last two days.

Phil Gaines and David Gallagher had both achieved their B.A. with Honours. And as both had a surname beginning with `G' they walked side by side, both dressed in white tie and white neckbands and black graduate gowns.

Chef and Sofia, who had taken Phil into their home and had been his surrogate parents from the age of sixteen, watched Phil with pride. He was a man now. Tall and dark and handsome. A graduate of Cambridge.

`Marian would be so proud,' Chef whispered.

Sofia was too emotional to speak.

Miss Courtney was fidgeting anxiously with her

broad-brimmed cream hat, convinced it was far too flamboyant for a lady of her age. She should never have allowed an Italian to choose her outfit for such a special occasion.

`Are you *sure* my hat is not just a bit too flashy?' she whispered to Sofia.

`*Bellissimo*,' Sofia sighed, but her eyes were on Phil, not the hat. `*Angelo mio*.'

After the presentation ceremony, the graduates from King's returned to the grounds of King's with their families where refreshments of strawberries and cream and white wine were served.

`My dear boy,' Chef said, smiling. `I am proud of you. You know that.'

`Yes, Chef, I know that.'

`And now?' Chef asked. `What are you going to do now?'

Phil was going to do what he had always intended to do. Only now he would be able to achieve his ultimate goal five years earlier than planned.

`I'm going to work in a publishing house in London to gain some ground experience, before I open my own house in a few years' time.'

Chef was startled for a second. `Your own publishing house? Your own business?' He gave Phil a cautionary look.

`It takes a lot of money to open your own business, Phil. And huge loans from the banks. Not a good idea. Not with borrowing being so expensive these days. Look at me – still struggling in my restaurant. Still worrying about costs and receipts and bills. And no pension for the self-employed. Only the small State handout of a pension, and who can live on that? So I must work on.'

`But, you see – '

Chef shook his head negatively. `Too many people are deciding they want to be employers instead of employed. Taking too many risks. Even Peter is planning to open his own restaurant now. Huge loans from the bank, his house put up as security, and now his wife and children's future is dependent upon market forces.'

`I won't need to borrow money from any bank,' Phil said quietly, and finally told Chef about the call from Lewis Belfort a month earlier.

Chef almost fainted. `I knew Marc was not poor. He always had enough money to fly over from America, and he bought Marian the flat ... but I never realised ... fifty-three million!' He reached for another glass of wine and downed it in two gulps.

Phil grinned `I think it's time for you to retire from slaving in that restaurant of yours, Chef. Time to start thinking about *la dolce vita*.'

`Me?' Chef stared at him. `Me, retire? You mean '

`*Alberto!*'

Sofia and Miss Courtney returned from wherever they had disappeared to. Sofia was smiling happily at everyone she passed, loving every minute of the occasion, but Phil noticed that Miss Courtney was still looking anxious.

`What's wrong, Missy?' Phil asked her.

`This hat – it's far too ostentatious,' she muttered self-consciously. `And matching cream coat and shoes! I feel like the Queen Mother.'

`You look *wonnnnnderful!*' Sofia assured her. `Sophia Loren wore a hat just like that when she married Carlo Ponti. Or was it Gina Lollobrigida when she married – who?'

She turned to Chef. `Alberto, who did Gina marry? Was it Roberto Rossellini? No, now I remember, it was Ingrid Bergman who fell in love with Roberto Rossellini —'

`But Sofia,' protested Miss Courtney, `all those women may have got married in this hat, but I am *not* getting married, am I?'

Sofia sucked a strawberry and eyed Miss Courtney speculatively. `Do you *want* to get married?'

Miss Courtney sighed and reached for another strawberry; she had always been childish about strawberries, just the taste of them made her feel young again.

`Sofia,' she said, `you are the kindest person in the whole world and we all love you dearly, but at times you would try the patience of a saint.' Miss Courtney chuckled. `Married! Me? My dear, I know you are an incurable romantic, but don't you know that I am seventy-four years old.'

`So? Marry a man seventy-four years old,' Sofia said simply. `Hold hands and smell the flowers together. Days of wine and roses – who says when they should begin? Who says when they should end? Now look at me, I'm fifty-eight,' Sofia said, subtracting five years from her age, `and I still hold hands with Alberto.'

Chef impatiently caught Phil's arm and turned him aside from the women, speaking in a low voice. `Let's get back to you, Phil – why publishing?'

`Does it really surprise you?'

`No,' said Chef after a moment. `No, nothing you do surprises me anymore. You're too much like Marc. He once flew all the way from America just to take Marian for a walk in the park. Did you know that?'

Phil nodded. `I know everything, Chef. It's all in my mother's manuscript.'

`My dear boy – ' Chef was smiling in amazement. `So that's why you locked her script away and refused to let anyone see it. I often wondered why. And also why you chose English instead of Art ... you know you *should* have studied Art, Phil, it's what you do best, you know that ... but Marian's book means that much to you?'

`It's more than a book, Chef. It's everything she worked towards. All the days studying for her A-levels in English. All the nights writing her book, struggling over sentences, determined to get it right. It was, in effect, her life's work. I can't let it all go to waste.'

`*You* were her life's work,' said Chef. `But yes, you're right. Once Marian saw that you were growing up, out every night learning your Kung Fu or studying art with Mr Hughes, that book of hers became her dream. Did it never occur to you, though, to just send it to a publisher?'

`It occurred to me, yes. It's what I thought I would do one day, later on, when I felt more reasonable about her death. But then one day – '

Phil sighed. `Chef, publishers bring out hundreds of books every year, mainly to fill their catalogues. Only a few get special attention. Promotion and Advertising. The rest have their fifteen minutes of success and then disappear into oblivion. So the only way I can ensure that Marian's book gets the attention it deserves, is to publish it myself.'

`And now you have the money to do it. *Fifty-three million!* Is that in pounds or American dollars?'

"Pounds. Pure Sterling. She had personally detailed all the final arrangements herself."

'Pounds - so even more in dollars.' Chef shook his head again and reached out to a passing tray for more wine. `You know, I think Sofia is right about you. The gods may have been cruel in the past, but now you seem to have all the angels on your side.'

Phil smiled as he looked beyond Chef's shoulder. `And here comes a guy who loves books almost as much as my mother did.'

`Phil, may I introduce you to my father?'

David Gallagher was deliberately full of false bravado to cover his nervousness as he introduced Phil to his father, a stern, broad-shouldered man from the green belt of Surrey.

`I was beginning to despair of ever meeting you in the flesh,' Simon Gallagher said, eyeing Phil genially. `Apparently we keep missing each other. But here we are at last, face to face. My son tells me you are his best friend.'

`A friend,' David put in quickly, clearly embarrassed by his father's use of such an adolescent term. `Phil has many friends.'

`We both do,' Phil rejoined. `Cambridge is a very friendly place.' He then introduced David's father to Albert and Sofia and Miss Courtney.

`Ah! This is the lady!' said David's father, clasping Miss Courtney's hand. `Do you know, my dear, in that outfit you look exactly like the Queen Mother.'

'Oh gracious ...' Miss Courtney's face turned a dull red colour.

SEVEN

London
September 1987

_____/

Phil's new home was a spacious three-bedroomed flat in a new block on Prince Albert Road in St John's Wood, directly overlooking Regent's Park. It had a large south-facing terrace, video-entry phone, twenty-four-hour porterage, and furnished for his every need. He had looked at other properties, but had finally chosen this flat because it provided him with all the advantages of Central London living.

As well as the tranquil green view of the park.

One night, as September came to a close, he glanced at his watch and saw it was eight-thirty – so only three-thirty in New York ... Time to take the next step.

A minute later, with Tom Kennett's card beside the telephone, he was dialling the area code for New York.

`I'm so sorry, but Mr Kennett no longer works for this firm,' chirped the telephonist. `He has his own firm now. I can give you the number.'

Two telephone calls later, Phil was still trying to contact Tom Kennett, but now, at last, Tony Martinez had given him the number of Tom's cell phone.

As the number started to ring, Phil suddenly heard a voice in his head from the past, the voice of his Wing Chun master ... *Others may seek only to grasp the bird's tail, or play with the monkey, but you must face the tiger —.'*

'Yeah, hello? ...' Tom Kennett sounded like he was chewing a burger. The connection was loud and clear.

Three minutes later Kennett gave a chuckle, which expanded into laughter. 'Yeah, I remember you. Mr Phil Gaines. The guy with the grandmother.' He laughed again. 'Some grandmother! Did I feel a schmuck! Even my *sister* didn't look that good.'

'But seriously,' said Phil, and went on to explain very carefully what he wanted from Kennett.

'What d'you mean?' Kennett sounded hurt. '*We* are the best!'

'In New York.'

'You bet! Listen, you don't get into my tax bracket unless you keep getting results. And we always do. Because we are the best. We've even got our own firm now, but you won't find us in the *Yellow Pages*. No, sir. It's all word-of-mouth recommendations.'

'And that's why I'm ringing you, for a word-of-mouth recommendation, to give me a start ...'

Five minutes later Kennett was chuckling again. 'Boy, you must be just like your grandmother.'

'Was it you she hired to tail me whenever I was in New York during the past three years?'

'Ah, now, listen —' Kennett sounded disappointed, 'why did you have to go and spoil things by asking me a question like that?'

'Because I'd like to know the answer.'

'Which is *confidential*. Everything we do is confidential. So I'm not saying we did, and I'm not saying we didn't. Anyway, it was the old firm your grandmother employed – we left there nearly a year ago.'

`Do you know she died?'

`Yeah, I heard. I also heard she left you a huge heap of dough. So we did you a favour picking you up that night, didn't we? Though none of us could ever figure out why you kept turning your back on her. I mean – ' he chuckled again, `if *my* grandmother was that loaded, I wouldn't care if she – '

`But seriously,' Phil interrupted again.

`Okay, let's get serious. Let's see if we can give you what you want. Well ... okay, now listen....'

Kennett mumbled something. Then he mumbled something else.

When Phil asked him to speak more clearly, he said, `The number ... I'm just looking here for the number of a particular firm over there in London that we've used a few times ... a real high-class team. And like us, you won't find them in the *Yellow Pages*. No, sir. Word-of-mouth recommendations only.'

`Is it the same firm that was employed to keep an eye on me in Cambridge?'

`I couldn't say, couldn't tell you, not even now. I told you – everything in this business is confidential. Or it *should* be. How else is a client gonna trust us? Who wants to pay good money to a team of private investigators who gossip like actors ... okay, here we go, I've found the number...'

Phil wrote down the number. `Are you sure they're good?'

`In England – they're the best! Real neat and very elite. Like I said, top-class.'

Phil grinned. `That's what I want.'

`And listen,' Kennett added, `if you *really* want the best, then go straight to the top man there. He's ex-CID, an ex-cop who retired at fifty and started up his own firm. If you say I recommended you, he'll see you get the best. Hang on, I'll give you his name ...'

*

From the second-floor window of his office near Baker Street, Joseph Irving watched the driver of a black Mercedes as he stood pressing coins into the parking meter on the opposite side of the road.

A tall young man with black hair and a charming look of *savoire faire* about him. He wore a perfectly tailored dark blue suit, pale blue shirt, and dark blue tie. The meter fed, he walked across the road toward the building and Irving noticed his black shoes were perfectly polished.

Irving sighed appreciatively. Sloppiness of dress was something he had always despised, especially in plain-clothes police officers.

Joseph Julius Irving was fifty-nine years old and looked a personification of the perfect English gentleman. Always impeccably dressed in Savile Row suits and Jermyn Street shirts, he was as British in every way as the Houses of Parliament. English dignity oozed from his every pore. So it was no surprise that few people ever successfully guessed his true occupation.

Phil stood outside the front door of the black-railinged Victorian terraced house, and smiled a little. If Joseph Irving himself had not given him instructions, he would wonder if he was at the right address, There was no outward indication of the business that went on here. The brass plate on the front wall bore the names of a firm of chartered accountants: *Jones, Lipzburgh, Trippett &*

Associates.

He pressed the bell. A female voice spoke through the Entry phone. As soon as he gave his name and the time of his appointment, the door was buzzed open.

He passed through a glass vestibule and was met in the hall by a grey-haired woman who looked as prim as a civil servant. But she greeted him graciously, and invited him to follow her upstairs.

As they moved down the hall and up the staircase to the second floor, Phil noticed that all the doors of the other rooms were closed, but he was given no time to think about it, because his escort chatted to him all the way up from the bottom step.

She was Mr Irving's PA, she informed him, but she did not provide her surname. `Oh, just call me Anna,' she said brightly. `Everyone else does. Even my mother.' Her laugh made him smile, because her personality was obviously nothing as prim as her looks.

`Here we are,' she said, knocking on a door and opening it.

Joseph Irving was still standing by the window when Phil entered the large office which appeared ideal for a senior accountant – right down to the dark green walls, white marble fireplace, genuine Regency desk and armchairs, and a number of eighteenth-century oils on the walls. All of it elegant and old money.

`Mr Gaines, how very nice to meet you.' Joseph Irving smiled genially, shook hands firmly, then moved to his desk and invited Phil to sit opposite him.

Anna asked if either gentleman would care for some refreshment. `Some tea or coffee?'

Phil shook his head. `Thank you, nothing.'

When she had left the room, Joseph Irving clasped his hands together on the desk and looked paternal. `Now, how may I help you?'

`I need information, as much of it as possible,' Phil withdrew a folded white paper from his pocket, opened it and placed it on the desk, `on this man, James Duncan.'

Irving picked up a pair of spectacles from his desk and put them on, showing no reaction as he read while Phil said, `As you can see, in 1980 he lived at that address in Berkshire, and he's still living there.'

`You've telephoned occasionally to make sure,' Irving guessed.

`Yes, and apologised for dialling a wrong number. He lives there with his wife, a blonde woman named Joanne Duncan. I don't know if they have any children. I don't think they do.'

`You've been there,' Irving guessed again. `You've looked at the house and the people who live inside it?'

`Yes, in 1980, but not since then. Neither of them are people I enjoy looking at.'

`His occupation?' Irving's eyes moved down the page.

`As you can see, in 1980 he worked for a publishing house, Garland Press. Yesterday afternoon he was still working there, which is not surprising as Garland's is a family-run firm owned by his father. From what I have been able to ascertain, Garland's has a somewhat distinguished name for publishing good literature. But beyond that—' Phil shrugged, `that's all I know.'

Joseph Irving gave him a long thoughtful gaze, observing again how totally relaxed he appeared to be, despite the reason for his being here. Unlike other clients he did not twitch or cough or finger his tie repeatedly. Neither did he look guilty about his desire to seek unusual methods in obtaining what he desired. Nor did he betray the slightest hint of being riskily emotional or overtly vengeful. He was, it appeared, a most suitable client to do business with.

`So,' Irving asked, `what exactly do you want us to do?'

`Why not tell me exactly what you *can* do?'

Irving's expression did not flicker. `I thought Mr Kennett had already informed you of the services our firm provides. There is little we cannot do. All our staff are highly skilled professionals. All ex-police operatives. We can provide twenty-four undercover surveillance, electronic surveillance, executive and diplomatic protection, personal investigation ... just about everything. However, we are *very* expensive.'

Joseph Irving smiled apologetically at the young millionaire. `But then you *did* say you wanted only the best.'

`Yes, and I don't care what it costs.'

`Nevertheless, we will not cheat you nor overcharge you. On that you can rely.'

Irving placed Phil's written information about James Duncan to one side. He picked up a pen in readiness to make notes. `Now, I would like to know a little more about you,' he murmured. `Just a few relevant details.'

Phil smiled. `Oh, I think you know quite a lot about me already, Mr Irving. I suspect you could even supply the name of every girl I slept with in Cambridge.'

Joseph Irving lifted his head slowly and gave

him a wonderfully innocent stare. `Cambridge? Mr Gaines, I have never set eyes on you before today.'

`Not you personally, no. Just as you, personally, will not set eyes on James Duncan. It will be left to your operatives. But you knew who I was as soon I contacted you. As soon as I mentioned my name. As soon as I mentioned Tom Kennett. And *I* knew – as soon as you said, "Ahhh yesss."'

Irving continued to look splendidly baffled ... His operatives – skilled men of experience – treated him like a king. Yet instinctively he knew that this young man regarded him with no awe at all ... and he was astute and straight to the point ... just like his grandmother.

He sighed, removed his glasses, rubbed an eye, and allowed himself a second to remember that particular French lady, and not without some delight. The dinner they had shared together at the Grosvenor had lasted four hours, and her charm had not only inspired him, but utterly captivated him.

And now, here before him, was her grandson and heir. However pragmatists may deplore it, it seemed to him like another of those little touches of ironic melodrama that often occur in life. Or as the French say, *C'est la vie.*

He replaced his glasses and said sternly, `You seem very sure, but you are quite mistaken. However, let us move on. Let us deal with the facts of the matter before us ... Now, may I ask you the situation behind all this? The reason why you want to obtain as much information as possible on this man?'

Irving looked at Phil questioningly, and when Phil made no immediate reply, Irving explained, `I always find it helps me to assess the needs of a client more clearly if I know the situation. I cannot give orders empirically. I cannot operate on theory. I need to have valid information in order to know if the client's motives are within our boundaries. And we *do* have boundaries. We are not interested in helping petty criminals, for instance.' He looked a little apologetic. `Not, I hasten to add, that you in any way appear to be of that type.'

Phil considered, his eyes dark and thoughtful. `Very well,' he said at last. `I'll tell you my reason.' Then, unflinching, he took his time as he told Joseph Irving in a quiet voice the precise details of the situation.

When he had concluded, Joseph Irving did not speak for some seconds, but there was condolence and understanding in his eyes.

Condolence for a young boy having to identify his dead mother, then having to watch the perpetrator and his wife laughing gleefully as they headed off for a champagne celebration.

And understanding of the son's determination to execute some sort of revenge. The practice of *vendetta* was as prevalent in Corsica and parts of France as it was in Sicily, the unspoken law that allows the family of a murdered person to seek vengeance on the killer.

But not in England. The English had always been far more subtle and less violent in their methods of retribution, but just as effective, nevertheless.

`I would like to help you,' he said sincerely. `But you must understand, we do not operate outside the law. Nor would we want to help *you* to break the law as a result of our investigations on your behalf. I must have your assurance on that. You intend to do nothing illegal?'

`No, nothing like that, nothing illegal.' Phil looked at Irving with the clearest honesty. `I simply want to see James Duncan get what he deserves. I want to see him ruined. Utterly destroyed. No hope for him, no help, nothing. He's fifty-two years old so his father must be over seventy and ready to completely retire. After which, if James Duncan takes over, I want to see his business decimated, and rapidly so. I want to see him bankrupt and paupered, unable to afford champagne. I want to wipe the smirk off his face for ever. I want to make him pay a lot more than a fine of £150 for the crime of killing my mother.'

Joseph Irving sat back in his chair, and looked grave. `So what you really want,' he said quietly, `is to kill the man.'

Phil's dark eyes moved to the wall above Irving's head, as if pondering. `Yes,' he admitted, and his voice was very calm. `In 1980 the law denied me justice. In 1980 I would have settled for a jail sentence for James Duncan, but when I saw him walk away from the court laughing, then I wanted his life .. And it would have been easy to kill him. Very easy. One winter night in 1980, when I was sixteen, I stood in his garden in Berkshire, I watched his car pull into the drive, watched him step out, watched him bend over to get his briefcase. One swift move and I could have had a knife in his back. One of Chef's carving knives. I knew the exact spot to make the thrust. But just as I was about to make my move, that's when I saw my mistake – Chef's carving knife.'

Joseph Irving was studying him intently. `Why?'

`Marian ... all the years she had worked in Chef's restaurant. From before I was born, and then after I started school. All the years she had struggled to bring me up well ... to be decent and respectable and as well behaved as anyone else's son. That had always meant a lot to her. In a way, her whole life was one long prayer that I should turn out well. That I should be a credit to Marc, and prove that, if nothing else, she was a good mother ... and then James Duncan was gone, walking into his house ... and I knew I had missed my chance ... I had let it go.'

A silence had fallen on the room. Joseph Irving sighed, `I'm glad you held back. But I do know how you feel.'

`No, you don't. Only I know how I feel.'

Phil shrugged. `But that's all in the past, The mad demented dreams of boyhood. Now I have grown up, more mature, more reasonable. Now I merely want to ruin him. And I will.'

Joseph Irving sat silent and watching, and the eyes of the two men met, and for a long time neither spoke

Then Joseph Irving smiled, a small enigmatic smile, and at last Phil knew that Irving understood and agreed and was on his side.

`So, to begin,' Phil said, his tone calm and practical, `I need to find out his weaknesses and his strengths. How successful he really is, or is not. How financially stable his father's firm is, or is not. The names of the most *financially* successful authors on their list – which are not, by the way, necessarily the most prestigious or famous. I would also be interested to know....' Irving made notes of everything he said.

An hour later, when the meeting concluded, the two men rose and Joseph Irving inquired, `How soon do you want this information?'

Phil considered. `I've been very patient, I've

waited a long time, and I'm prepared to wait a while longer. Just as long as it takes.'

`Good.' Joseph Irving smiled as he escorted him to the door. `One does hate to be rushed.'

As they shook hands, Irving suddenly patted Phil's arm paternally. `Now remember, we do nothing illegal. And neither must you.'

Five nights later, the offices of Garland Press were broken into without the alarm going off. Two of Irving's operatives went about their business calmly and efficiently and without turning on a light. Both wore a small torch strapped to their foreheads and both wore light surgical gloves. Everything was done without haste or mistake. Although it all would have been done a lot swifter if Garland's accounts had been on computer. Everything about the place was old-fashioned, even the old manual typewriters. The only machine that was activated was the photocopier.

Four hours later, after all the files and documents had been copied and carefully replaced in cabinets and drawers, the counter on the photocopier was returned to its original setting, the paper tray refilled. Even a used coffee mug, which someone had left on top of the machine, was placed back in the exact spot it had been found.

When the staff arrived for work the following morning, there was nothing to indicate that a break-in had taken place, or that anything had been disturbed. The two operatives were, as Tom Kennett had promised, top-class professionals.

A third operative, who had been detailed to take care of the house in Berkshire, cruised behind Joanne Duncan's Alpha Romeo as she drove to her hairdressers in the High Street.

He watched her go inside, then followed her in and looked around the salon, looking for his wife. He smiled a sheepish apology to the receptionist. `Sorry, wrong hairdressers. It's the one further up.'

Although only a few seconds, it had been long enough to see Mrs Duncan being led to one of the sinks, confirming she would be away from the house for at least an hour.

When she returned two hours later, tripping into the hall on ridiculously high stilettos, her blonde hair wildly glamorous and lacquered as hard as cement – there was nothing to make her pause and wonder, nothing to indicate that anything in the house had been disturbed.

Even the drawers of the desk in the study, where James Duncan kept all his private papers, remained securely locked and apparently untouched.

Yet the following morning Joseph Irving was handed a report containing specific figures from James Duncan's credit card and private bank statements.

EIGHT

London
October 1987

_____/

Phil stood in Joseph Irving's office and could not help smiling as he stared at the thick file of photocopied documents containing all the inside information he needed on Garland Press and James Duncan.

He looked across the desk at Joseph Irving with approval, wondering if it would be imprudent to ask questions. He said, `Thank you.'

Irving smiled. `My pleasure.'

`I thought you did nothing illegal.'

Irving's expression did not flicker as he affected deafness. `I'm sorry, I didn't hear that.'

Phil was unable to hide his amusement. `Mr Irving,' he said sincerely, `you are not only a perfect gentleman, you are also the most serene crook I have ever met, and I admire you enormously.'

`And I like you too,' Irving replied smoothly. `Because despite your present activity I don't believe you are really a scoundrel. You are simply a young man living in a Heaven-or-Hell world where the good must be applauded and the wicked must pay. In time you will find the middle ground, as most people eventually do.'

`I'm sure I will,' said Phil, and smiled again. `I'm not too old and not too young, so anything is possible.'

But this time Irving did not smile, his eyes were

fixed on the thick file of papers and he looked a
little grave.

`In this case, I'm afraid we were forced to
circumvent the law slightly. But then in this case
we were prepared to do that, because the law can
be rather ambiguous at times, can't it? Sometimes
it just doesn't even up.'

`No,' Phil said, and knew that Joseph Irving was
referring to a particular law which, in 1980, had
allowed a man to walk away laughing, even though
he had killed a thirty-five year old woman.

`Ask any police officer,' Irving sighed. `They do
their job, often at great risk to their own lives, and
succeed in getting the criminals to court. Then they
have to listen to two lawyers disagreeing about the
law. Arguing endlessly about what is strictly legal,
and what is not. In the end it's left to a judge or
jury to decide, and they don't always get it right.'

Phil said nothing.

`Much of our work, believe it or not, is for the
police,' Irving continued. `Only in special cases, of
course. And only when a certain line has to be
crossed. But then most private investigators have
to work close to the edge, or how else could they be
investigators. How else are they to flush out the
real criminals? No drug baron is going to open up
his books and show the police a list of the firms he
is currently using to launder money from narcotic
sales.'

They talked for a further fifteen minutes, then
Phil stood up and lifted the thick file of papers.
`Well, I am very grateful to you, Mr Irving. And as
for these — ' he tapped the file, `whatever I do in
the future, I won't do anything downright criminal,
I promise you.'

`Good.' Irving smiled in a paternal way, and

spoke as if to a beloved young relative. `I would be very disappointed if you did.'

*

From the window Joseph Irving watched Phil as he left the building and walked over to his car.

Anna knocked and entered carrying a tray of freshly percolated coffee. `Oh, has he gone? I've just made him the coffee he requested!'

Joseph Irving did not answer or glance round. She laid down the tray and joined him at the window, and she too watched Phil unlock the boot of his car and place the thick file of papers inside.

Irving sighed. `Down there, Anna, is a young man who will not be content until just one other man in this world knows how dangerous he is. Yet that other man doesn't even know of his existence.'

`Hmm ... now that *is* interesting.' Anna narrowed her eyes. `And will he be back?'

`Oh yes, he'll be back. In his own good time. This is just the beginning for him. He has a long way to go, and other things to do. But meanwhile, as he is willing to pay whatever it costs, we shall continue to work on his behalf.'

`Meanwhile?' Anna was surprised. `In what way?'

`Garland Press,' Irving said. `From their personnel records it seems they are presently seeking a new secretary. The pay is so bad they are not having much luck. Now which of our female operatives would enjoy a nice, cushy job for a change?'

`Quite a few, I'm sure.'

`Will you see to it?'

`Certainly.'

Irving looked at her and smiled. `I knew you would.'

NINE

London
1988 –1990

_____/

Phil and some of his closest friends from Cambridge had now entered the world of publishing. All worked in different firms and different departments – sales and marketing, editorial, production and design, foreign rights – and all learned as much as they could, because they knew their present positions were temporary.

In the year that followed their first meeting, Phil and Joseph Irving kept in regular contact. Even though Irving's fees were high, they made hardly a dent in the huge income that Phil was earning from his grandmother's legacy.

Phil had been stunned to discover the extent of Jacqueline's investments. She owned shares in three lavish hotels in New York, a newspaper in Paris, properties in Boston and Washington. Endless investments, enormous sums of money in various banks. All of which now belonged to him. Without lifting a finger or doing a day's work, his personal income, after tax, was in excess of £4,000,000 a year from interest payments alone.

In August 1988, James Duncan's father died, but James Duncan did not – as he had hoped – inherit the company.

`He was so distraught about his father's will, he made everyone's life a misery for weeks,' Joseph Irving reported to Phil. `But he has calmed down somewhat, and seems to have reluctantly resigned himself to the situation. Garland Press is now owned in three equal parts by James Duncan and his two sisters, Helen and Felicity. It's common knowledge within Garland's that Duncan utterly despises his two sisters – neither of whom are involved in any way with the business. Nevertheless, Garland Press is now a limited company and they own two-thirds of the shares, so James Duncan has been denied the sole autonomy he desired.'

Phil considered. `The two sisters?'

`Both were devoted to their father, unlike the son. The eldest sister, Helen, visited her brother's office a week ago and loudly accused him of —' Irving looked down at his report – `being an avaricious bastard who had spent the past ten years wishing their father dead so he could move into his office and chair.'

`Ah, so there's a degree of animosity there.'

Joseph Irving was highly amused by the understatement. `Possibly, Phil, quite possibly.'

`Good,' said Phil.

*

In December 1989 Joseph Irving said to Phil, `I think this will interest you. It seems our man at Garland Press does not possess the talents of his father. He has made severe cuts to all advertising budgets and is in danger of losing his two most lucrative authors.'

`Howard and McAllister?'

`Yes. He insists he won't lose them, of course, and seems quite confident of their loyalty.'

`Then he's a fool,' Phil said contemptuously, `because he *will* lose them, and soon.'

Joseph Irving folded his hands on his desk, his eyes bright with mirth and curiosity. `How soon?'

Phil smiled. `Everything is more or less set up, offices found, equipment bought. So, all being well, we should be able to open in about three months.'

TEN

London
1990 –1993

_____/

In April 1990, it all started with the poster.

A poster of a beautiful painting – a head-and-shoulders portrait of a dark-haired young girl with sapphire-blue eyes gazing soulfully at the viewer; the background surrounding her was a cloudy mixture of various shades of blue and silver. And the book the poster advertised – *Some Kind of Wonderful* – by Marian Barnard.

David Gallagher, the Editorial Director of the newly opened Gaines Publishing Ltd, could not believe there was still a month to go to the official publication date: orders were rolling in. But then, with such a massive advertising campaign backing it, most bookshops wanted to have at least a few copies of the book in stock when it was eventually published.

In their offices on Shaftesbury Avenue, Phil grinned at David. `As Sidney Sheldon once said – "If you want to win, you have to know how to play the game."'

`Not exactly,' David corrected, a stickler for accuracy when it came to quotes, `"If you want to win, you have to learn to be a *master* of the game."'

`Well, one eventually leads to the other,' Phil replied. `And anyway—' his secretary interrupted him: a telephone call from the distributors.

He returned to his own office and left David Gallagher wondering if he could keep up with

Phil's inexhaustible energy. No other book in the world was as important as this launch book for Gaines Publishing – not in Phil's view. In the months leading up to its publication, he had left no call unanswered, no contact unmade, and no minute left spare in his determination to see it succeed.

By May the poster for the book was displayed at airports, underground stations, bookshops – almost everywhere. Every national paper and women's magazines carried a full-page advert to coincide with publication.

And so, naturally, curious book-readers were interested, and seeing the book there in front of them, they picked it up, looked at the cover, read the blurb on the back, liked the quotes from the favourable pre-publication reviews, and bought it.

`A customer cannot buy something the shop doesn't stock,' Phil had said when instructing his reps. `So I want to see this book in as many shops as possible.'

Some Kind of Wonderful entered *The Times* bestseller list at number nine. A week later it was number three.

All the staff at Gaines Publishing – which consisted of eight in Editorial and twelve in Sales and Marketing – were buzzing with excitement. Then a telephone call from *Bookwatch* informed them it had moved up to Number two.

Miranda Alvin, the Sales Manager, was discussing the proofs of a jacket for a cookery book with the art manager, Ben Anderson, when David Gallagher popped his head around the door of her office and grinned, `*Wonderful* – it's number two!'

`What!'

Miranda stared at David, and then at Ben – then

threw down the proofs and did an excited little victory dance on the spot. `Oh, bloody bloody bloody *brilliant!'*

The art manager stared at her in wide-eyed amazement, and scratched his dyed-blond short hair. Miranda Alvin was a woman of mystery to Ben, and usually she terrified him. She was a Cambridge Honours graduate who had read English at King's with Phil and David. She had long wavy Titian red hair, dairy-fresh skin, red glossy lips, dressed in St Laurent, and had a reputation for being cool, composed, and insanely intelligent.

But look at her now!

She stopped jigging and grinned at David. `What is Phil's reaction?'

David shrugged. 'Oh, you know Phil – '

Phil was showing no outward reaction, covering his excitement with breathtaking skill as he followed the progression of Marian Barnard's book up the bestseller list. It consumed him, obsessed him, but no one in Gaines Publishing knew why. No one – not even David Gallagher – knew that the author, Marian Barnard, was Phil's mother.

Just publishing the book was not enough – not enough! From the time of publication he had been tense and restless and barely able to sleep at night as he realised how close he was to fulfilling the greatest dream of his life. His gift to his mother, her gift to Marc ... From Day One he had been on the phone to *Bookwatch* tracking its progress ... tracking it ... tracking it ... every move up.

Until, finally, three weeks after publication, the great day came, the one he had been so desperately waiting and praying for. As soon as Phil heard, he slammed down the phone and sprinted down the corridor into David Gallagher's office. Miranda

Alvin was already in there.

`We've done it! – *numero uno*!'

David Gallagher let out a whoop and within minutes all hell broke loose as the news was spread by Phil's secretary. Phones were put down, conversations halted, computers deserted.

`*Wonderful*—' David Gallagher told them. `It's reached the top! Number one.' Everyone cheered. Number One! Jackpot first time! It was all heady stuff.

`Wow, look at that!' Ben said in amazement – Miranda was so excited Phil had lifted her up and swung her around. He was so happy there were tears in his eyes.

`Come on, everyone,' Phil announced. `Time to celebrate! Time to close up and have a party.'

`What – another one?' David Gallagher had only just recovered from the launch party, but he went along with the mood and asked, `Where? Here? Shall I send out for champagne?'

`You have to be joking!' Phil laughed. `No — ' he had already decided where, had already chosen the place where he wanted to celebrate the success of Marian and Marc's love story – `The American Bar, at the Savoy.'

*

Three months after Marian's book, Gaines Publishing brought out a second major book that had every male reviewer raving about it – *Tigerland: A Cry for Life,* by Jimmy Overman.

'Not since Oliver Stone wrote his script for Platoon *has a story about Vietnam been told with such power and authenticity by a Vietnam Veteran,'* said *The Times 'The book is perfectly*

*structured, the writing superb, and Jimmy
Overman tells his spirited and occasionally tear-
blurring story as if it all happened only yesterday.
Once I started reading Tigerland I could not put it
down...'*

All the reviews were excellent, which made
David Gallagher push even harder to get Phil to
change his mind about bringing the author over to
England for interviews, and even television. But
Phil would not be persuaded.

`No, no, he's a private man, very closed in on
himself. I don't think he'd be able to cope with
interviews.'

`Why? Because he's disabled? Because he's
missing an arm and walking around on a plastic
leg? Don't you see? That would only increase his
interest value. Everyone loves a wounded soldier.'

But a wounded soldier who suddenly stopped in
the middle of an interview to have a conversation
with an empty space? Talking cheerfully to a ghost
only he could see? No.' Phil shook his head, he
would not take the risk of anyone laughing at
Jimmy.

Jimmy was crying as he read the reviews. `Lord
Almighty ... if I'd've known way back when you
asked me to write ... that you were going to turn
my letters into a book! ... I still can't believe it, you
know?'

He wiped his hand over his eyes. `See here now
... this guy in the *Daily Mail*, he says ... "*Read this
book and you'll never sit through another
preposterous* Rambo *film again without howling
in derision.*" Jimmy's puckered eyebrow rose
higher. `Who's Rambo?'

Phil shrugged. `It's a film, Jimmy, about an ex-Green Beret who went back to Nam and destroyed most of the Viet Cong single-handed.'

Jimmy laughed. `Nah, that was John Wayne who did that. In 1968. Did you see that film, *The Green Berets*? Wayne in a toupee, defying all the odds. Biggest error in that film was a shot of the sun going down in the East – in all my life I've never seen the sun setting in the East, not even in a mixed-up place like Vietnam. And you know, when *The Green Berets* was shown to the troops in Nam, they laughed for days.'

Phil opened his black leather briefcase again, surprised by his own excitement, now the moment had come. Although Jimmy had seen a copy-edited manuscript six months earlier, and had sat answering all Phil's technical queries with patience, Jimmy had seemed bemused and unimpressed by the pile of typed pages, as if he could not comprehend the reality of them ever being turned into a *real* book.

So Phil had not sent him a proof copy nor an advance copy, but had waited until he could present Jimmy with copies of the published book.

`Here's the book, Jimmy.'

Jimmy stared at the glossy hardcover book that Phil took out of his briefcase and laid on the table. He just stared and stared, then his eyes moved down the cover to the name of the author, *Jimmy Overman*. His eyes were like two pools of iced water.

Jimmy blinked, and at last his eyes finally saw the image that had been faintly superimposed over the jungle green background of the cover.

`It's the photo!' Jimmy exclaimed. `The one I took of Marc in his green helmet and cammies, the one I sent to Marian all those years ago.'

`You agreed I could use it, Jimmy. The designer gave it the hazed-over look to get the effect we wanted. A misted photograph of a young American soldier in combat helmet and jungle fatigues.'

`Yeah, I know I said you could use it. It's just ... you know, *seeing* it again, after all these years, it takes me back...' The tears were spilling fast, Jimmy searched his pocket, drew out a hankie and mopped his eyes.

Then in a snap, his expression changed and he was grinning like a delighted boy. `But aiyyyy – lookit that! The photo I took of Marc on the cover of a book by Jimmy Overman. Didn't I tell him we would always be buddies? Didn't I?'

Phil smiled. `You did, Jimmy.'

`But you know what I wish sometimes,' Jimmy said wistfully, `I wish that Marc had lived to see the Bob Hope show. Ah, it was great! Every Christmas, from 1966 to 1970, Bob Hope came over and did a show for us guys in Nam. We all loved it. Did I put that in my letters? About Bob Hope?'

`Yep,' Phil replied, tapping the book that was four hundred pages long. `He's in there, large as life. Bob Hope. Some of his jokes too. And Ann-Margaret in her mini-skirt.'

`Ann-Margaret!' Jimmy sat for a moment in ecstatic stillness. `Boy, was she something. None of us were listening to her sing. Couldn't take our eyes off her legs – long and golden as a summer's day in Oklahoma.'

Phil turned over the book so Jimmy could see the back cover – a full page black-and-white photograph of Jimmy which Phil had taken six months earlier.

`Hey, is that me!' Jimmy sat smiling at the photograph of himself in a kind of childish awe. `Good-looking guy, ain't I?'

After a silence, he raised his eyes. `Say, listen. Any chance my book could get published here in America?'

Phil nodded. `We've got eight New York publishers bidding for it right now. That's one of the reasons I'm over here.'

Jimmy's face restyled into shocked disbelief. `Eight publishers? You're kidding me!'

`No.' Phil took a deep breath, and attempted once again to succeed in his ambition to get Jimmy out of the Bowery.

`The thing is, Jimmy, this book is going to make you a hell of a lot of money.'

`More money? You've already paid me a bundle!'

`That was an advance, Jimmy, an advance against royalties. But I know for a fact that one New York publisher has already made a top offer for the American rights to your book, and it could be a lot more by the time the auction is finished.'

`Lord Almighty!'

`So you see, Jimmy, it wouldn't be charity. You wouldn't have to take any money from me. You could pay your own way ... if you went to that place in Connecticut.'

Jimmy eyed him suspiciously. `You sure it's not a loony bin? I don't want you to start acting like my doctor now, wanting to put me away. Because let me tell you something – I am *saner* than most people walking the streets of New York.'

`I know that, Jimmy, I know that,' Phil assured him, hand raised. `You're the sanest guy I know. That's why I visit you so regularly. Because you're such good company, and because you were Marc's best friend.'

`Yeah, that's what I thought ... I thought you and me were buddies.'

More tears were burning in Jimmy's eyes, and it truly worried Phil. More and more, lately, Jimmy seemed to be on the edge of tears; the least little thing could trigger him off. Except when he had spent his days writing about Vietnam. Then he had been as perky and full of life as a twenty-five year old.

`I got a job to do!' Jimmy would say in those days, sometimes abruptly leaving Phil in the middle of a meal in a restaurant to rush home and write a letter to him.

But now Jimmy had written as much as he could remember, the book was completed, and as his only friend, Phil felt he had to do something to ensure Jimmy didn't end up dead in the Bowery.

`You see, this book of yours, Jimmy, it's going to grab America by the heart – '

`You think so?'

`And once it's published over here, and it hits the bestsellers, with your name on the front and your picture on the back, all these druggies and drunks around here are going to know you've got money. A lot more than your disability pension. It's not going to be a safe place to be.'

Jimmy turned his face toward the window and went into one of his endless stares, a common trait amongst long-timers in Vietnam – a look in the eyes known to Vets as `the thousand-yard-stare.'

After a lengthy silence, Phil said, `Well?'

Jimmy shrugged. `I dunno.'

`Will you at least think about it?'

`If I'm gonna be rich,' Jimmy said petulantly,

`why can't I just move to Park Avenue?'

`Wherever you move to, Jimmy, you're still going to be alone. Unless of course you meet a woman and decide to get married. Your only forty-nine, so any chance of that?'

Jimmy chuckled. `Are you kidding? With only one arm and one leg, what woman would have me? Anyway, I'm too tired for women these days ... There was a woman there a while back, name was Ruth, kept coming up here saying she wanted to keep me company, wanted to cook me a nice meal. Not a bad cook either. But hell, it wasn't worth it. The damn woman kept talking non-stop through my television programmes.'

Jimmy sat back and frowned.

`And when she wasn't flapping her yap through my television programmes, she was sitting there shelling pistachio nuts, cracking them with her teeth – all the way through a re-run of *Columbo* – cracking pistachio nuts with her teeth. I felt like strangling her. Couldn't do it, though. Not with only one hand. So in the end I picked up my old plastic arm there, the one I use to bash cockroaches, and then I told her I had a leg just like it. Asked her if she wanted to see the way I took my leg off every night before going to bed.' He chuckled. `Never saw her again. And boy, was I glad!'

`But you still feel very lonely at times,' Phil persisted. `You said you did. But this place in Connecticut ... you'd have the privacy of your own room when you wanted it – even room service for your meals when you didn't feel like mixing. But plenty of company nearby if you did.'

Jimmy sighed. `Okay. This place. Tell me some more about it. What kind of people live there?'

`All are ex-soldiers of one rank or another. Vietnam Vets suffering from PTSD in varying degrees. Most, like you, are in their late forties or early fifties. Men who just can't take the noise and confusion of civilian life anymore. All they want is a haven of peace. Green lawns and green trees and comfortable rooms where they can watch their televisions in peace or, alternatively, mix with the other guys for a game of pool, a beer, a few hours conversation.'

`All Vietnam Vets?'

`Every one.'

Jimmy's growing interest was evident. `Well, I suppose, being Vets, it would give us something – ' he sighed, almost plaintively, `something interesting to talk about.'

`And if you moved there, and then decided you didn't like it, you can leave whenever you choose. It's just like a hotel.'

`I could do that? Leave whenever I choose?'

`Sure.'

`And no cockroaches?'

`No cockroaches.'

`No stinking smells?'

`Shoes shined every day. Laundry done twice a week. Good food.'

`Sounds good.'

`Why don't you let me drive you out there tomorrow, just to take a look at the place. See what you think of it.'

Jimmy smiled. `Reckon I might.'

Phil would always remember that drive in his hired BMW along the wide freeway and then through the countryside of Connecticut. For a while he and Jimmy talked about everything and anything –

good, sane, intelligent and entertaining conversation with quite a few laughs. Then with startling suddenness, Jimmy turned and commenced a conversation with an invisible guy in the back seat.

Phil listened, hands firm and steady on the wheel, eyes noting the passing scenery as if there was nothing unusual going on, nothing strange about Jimmy giving a lecture to a young black GI named Brig, who was obviously an FNG.

`... so you'd better listen to me, Brig?' Jimmy said sternly. `I don't care how much you felt the draft back there in Motown. Out here in Nam there is no Mason-Dixon line. No black or white. No rednecks or blue-collars. Just American soldiers. This is an army that sees only two colours – mean green and olive drab. You got that?'

Phil turned off the main road and within minutes they were driving through woodland. Jimmy came out of his own inner cosmos and looked around him. `Say, this place has got a nice mosey feel to it. Wouldn't mind taking a walk around here. Nice and peaceful. Can we stop awhile?'

`We're almost there.'

Jimmy's expression became sharp as Phil turned the car into a leafy driveway, then along a long gravel path flanked by sweeping green lawns and tall pine trees in the near distance. The house was a mansion of grey stone and many wide windows; lazy green ivy clung leisurely to one of the walls.

`What's this place called again?' Jimmy asked.

`Silver Waters.'

`Silver Waters – why's that?'

`There's a beautiful lake only a short stroll away.'

Phil stopped the car in front of the main entrance. He turned and looked at Jimmy. `Do you like the look of it?'

`Looks the sort of place a millionaire might own.'

`But do you like it?'

`Yes."

`Okay.' Phil opened his car door. `Let's take a closer look.'

As they started up the stone steps, the front door opened and a broad-shouldered man came out to greet them, standing on the top step and grinning.

`So it *is* you!'

Jimmy paused, looked up, and locked a startled gaze on the man. `Sonofagun! Lewis! What the hell are you doing here?'

`Came out to meet our new FNG.' Captain Lewis pointed his thumb at Phil. `You know, when Phil here told me he was bringing out Jimmy Overman, I didn't believe it could be the same Jimmy Overman I knew. Thought you were dead. We all did.'

`Dead? Me? Are you crazy? I'm about to be famous!' Then Jimmy's mind clicked. `You mean, there's other guys here I know?'

`Two or three. Come on, we're all out the back having a game of baseball. Wait a minute – where's your other arm?'

Jimmy shrugged. `Left it in Nam.'

Phil was completely forgotten. He spent most of the afternoon wandering around, talking to the staff, watching Jimmy sitting on the back patio in the sunshine with a group of men, drinking beer and talking with his old animation, as well as listening and revelling in the conversation of some of the others.

`Christ, remember ol' Kingpin? That guy was such a sadist, such a vicious sonofabitch, no wonder his men fragged him ... No, I'm not kidding! I tell you – he was fragged by his own men. The skirmish with Charlie was all to the front, yet when the chopper brought Kingpin back to base, he had more holes in his back than anywhere else. His own men did it, had enough of him, so they wasted him out in the field and blamed it on Charlie...'

An hour later Jimmy was in the pool room, cursing Charlie for depriving him of his arm. `I'd give anything for a game, but it can't be done. Even the dumbest sucker knows you've gotta have *two* hands to play pool.'

`You could still mark the board,' one of the players suggested.

`Yeah, I could, couldn't I?' Jimmy agreed cheerfully, and then became as engrossed in the game as a referee, walking over after each player's miss to score the board.

Phil had never seen Jimmy looking so happy, but he finally dragged him away to take a look at one of the rooms.

`Lord Almighty!' Jimmy exclaimed, his eyes on the large television in the corner, `This place is as swish as the Waldorf.' He looked at Phil. `Is a stay here very expensive?'

`It's not cheap, Jimmy, but you can afford it now. The money you make from the book will keep you living comfortably for the rest of your life. Because, believe me, we intend to exploit all the rights.'

`All the rights? What does that mean?'

`Well, after America, there'll be foreign rights, translations. We hope to sell the book to at least twenty-two countries before we're done. Maybe even a film deal. So, believe me, you can *well* afford to live in a place like this.'

`And you'd be amongst friends,' Captain Lewis said. `Guys who know what you're talking about when you tune into Namspeak.'

Jimmy looked thoughtful, went into one of his endless stares. Then he turned his head and looked at his old buddy. `Lewis,' he said `what exactly do the men do around here? You know, when they're not playing pool or baseball or whatever. What else do they do?'

Captain Lewis shrugged. `Oh, you know, just lazin' and gazin'. Eating ice cream and watching television. Most of the time it's pretty quiet around here, very easy. The men have had enough conflict to last a lifetime. So here, well, it's all downtime, rest and recreation.'

`Sounds good,' Jimmy said quietly. `Sounds real good.'

`So? Phil asked him. `Do you think you might like to leave your room in the Bowery and come and live here, Jimmy?

Jimmy smiled. `Reckon I might.'

Two days later Jimmy was back at Silver Waters, to take up residence. Having seen the car approach, Captain Lewis and two others came down the steps to greet Jimmy voicing expressions of welcome and smiles of genuine pleasure.

While the two others helped carry Jimmy's suitcases up the steps, Phil drew Captain Lewis aside and spoke to him quietly, almost apologetically.

`You know I told you that Jimmy sometimes has mind blocks, flicks off from reality, forgets where he is. Well, he's not crazy. I want you to know that. His mind just goes off-centre now and again. He's — '

`One of us,' Captain Lewis said gently. `He's a Vietnam Veteran. A maimed survivor. That's all that matters here. And if Jimmy wants to talk a little crazy now and again, well, as far as we're concerned, he's got a Purple Heart, Bronze Star, and Vietnamese Cross that says he's entitled to do that.'

Phil smiled, reassured. `That's okay, then.'

`Hot damn!' Jimmy said emotionally, when the time came for Phil to leave. `What did I ever do to deserve you, son? You've turned my whole life around.'

`I'll keep in touch,' Phil assured him, and seconds later he pressed down on the accelerator as the car swished round on the gravel path and headed back to New York.

The following day Phil caught his flight back to London, with a final and accepted offer of $750,000 for the American rights to Jimmy's book safe in his briefcase. Fifteen per-cent of that would go back into Gaines Publishing, the rest would go to Jimmy.

From the moment the plane took off, Phil sat reading a script which David Gallagher had taken from the firm's unsolicited pile a week before: a thriller, by an unpublished Irish writer named John Houlihan.

David had said the script was better than good, and so it proved to be, keeping Phil engrossed and page-turning while ignoring the stewardess who hovered round him more than was necessary, offering him drinks and pillows and `anything at all' he might need.

Finally, he looked up at her.

`I'd like a cup of coffee.'

She looked sassily into his dark eyes. `How would you like it?'

`In peace,' Phil said.

*

Ten months later John Houlihan found his script converted into a book, and Phil Gaines was earning a reputation as a very shrewd publisher. In fact, although Lewis Belfort was the only mortal who knew it, Phil possessed the same natural astuteness for business as his late French grandmother.

And also, just like Jacqueline, he was not afraid to take risks, and never wilted in the face of potential danger.

Within two years the firm's staff had increased from twenty to thirty-five, excluding the reps on the road. It was a young firm and a happy one, even if the boss did work twice as hard as anyone else.

`I think you really like this business,' David Gallagher said to Phil one day. `All the deal making and so on. What is it the Americans call it? Being a player?'

`Russian roulette, publishing style,' Phil grinned. `Hit or miss. Waiting to see which book is going blow up in your face and leave you badly burned.'

`Not me,' said David with a sniff, `I prefer to do my job expertly and methodically and take as few risks as possible.'

`And that is why you are so indispensable, David.'

`Indispensable?' David thought about that for a moment, and then nodded. `You're right. A little praise does go a long way. The conundrum is — do you ever mean it?'

The phone on Phil's desk rang. He gave David an amused glance. `Saved by the bell.'

ELEVEN

London,
1992

_____/

The flat in Mayfair belonged to one of London's leading literary agents. From the entrance hall a gilded lift carried all visitors up three floors to a mirrored and carpeted private landing, vibrant with lights, and noisy with the buzz of cheerful voices coming from an open doorway. There was a party going on.

Although why the party was being held, Phil could not remember. All he knew was that it was a party for publishers and authors and anyone else who might be useful in the buying and selling world of London's literati, and his own presence here tonight was all in the line of business.

He was greeted by the literary agent himself, Martin Pellmann, a tough straight-talking American who had made London his own, as well as making a fortune for both himself and his authors.

`Phil!' Martin greeted him with a big smile and a hand thrust forward. `Glad you could make it.'

Phil grinned as they shook hands. `My pleasure.'

`There's a few people here tonight I want you to meet,' Martin said, putting a hand on Phil's shoulder and leading him into the buzz of the crowded living-room. `But first, how about a long cool drink?'

The flat was huge, high-ceilinged and mainly white in carpet and upholstery, with a splash of rich deep colours here and there.

Only ten minutes or so after his own arrival at the party, Phil saw them ... two people walking into the room ... a man and a woman ... For a moment he thought he must be imagining it, but there they were, the two of them, in the flesh, but it was the *man* his eyes were fixed upon.

A tall, silver-haired man in his fifties, built as square and as solid as a brick outhouse. His head looked as solid as the rest of him, firmly planted on a thick bull neck. He stood tall and self-assured and peacock-proud.

Phil stared at him, and felt a deep and murderous hatred flaming back to life, still hardly able to believe that there – just a few yards away – was the man who had killed his mother.

*

David Gallagher had always known that he would never become Phil's confidante in any aspect other than business. But he also knew that Phil's reservations did not apply only to him. Phil never let *anyone* get too close – never discussed his own feelings, and never explained his reasons for doing anything.

So David could only wonder what had happened to Phil at Martin Pellmann's party. In the two weeks that had passed since then, Phil had upset everybody by attacking life and work as if making up for lost time.

He had upset David by ignoring all his protests and immediately entering into long lunch negotiations with the agents of John Howard and Ken McAllister, offering advances that he knew Garland Press could not match, let alone top. It was blatant bribery and worse – it made no sense to David.

`Apart from anything else,' he said to Phil, `it was bad business, because neither author is worth a third of what you paid.'

Phil glanced up at him, then slightly smiled. `They *are* worth it, David. Every penny.'

`You should have left them picking up peanuts at Garland's,' David fumed on. `Because both are over the hill, out of time and out of touch, and they are certainly not right for us.'

`Then we'll *make* them right for us!' Phil snapped. `Both are good writers, and hardly over the hill in their fifties. They've just been neglected, let slide. When was the last time either of them got any promotion from Garland's? And without promotion even the *best* writers can fade from the public interest. Look at Agatha Christie – her sales had tailed away to library level until Collins put new and exciting covers on all her books and pushed her back into the public eye. Within a year her sales had risen by 40% and now most of them have been bought for television.'

`And you think we can do the same for Howard and McAllister?'

Phil gave David a slow, enigmatic smile. `I think it's a challenge we might enjoy.'

David was not convinced.

`And James Duncan is going to be absolutely furious when he finds out,' David added. `Both those authors have been with his house for years.'

`And James Duncan has profited a lot more from the association than they ever did. They owe him nothing. Not even loyalty.'

`He's still going to be very upset at the loss. Especially as you bought up all their backlists. I know they were out of print, but Garland's have their own contracts, their own clauses, have never signed the MTA, and he still may call in his lawyers.'

`Oh, his *lawyers* again!' Phil said in a voice of contempt. `Life is no legal bargain, as James Duncan will one day find out.'

Part Two

Rena

1993

TWELVE

Stockholm
June 1993

_____/

A warm late-June day in 1993. Opening his eyes onto a strange and unfamiliar place. His eyelids felt heavy but he forced them open and looked around the room. Scandinavianly white and gleaming. A hospital room. He wondered how he came to be here and tried to remember, but against his will his eyes closed again and he drifted back to sleep.

Seconds, minutes, maybe even hours later, he felt soft wisps of air passing over him; a soft unhurried sound very near. Then a touch: a soft hand gently placed on his brow, his wrist being lifted, his pulse being counted; still his eyes did not open. In the far distance somewhere, someone or something was playing music ... a radio?

Another touch, warm fingers smoothing up his left arm, as tender as the fingers of a lover ...

Something cold and rubbery was being wrapped around his upper arm.

His eyes slowly opened, and he saw her, bending over him – a girl, very blonde, very beautiful, dressed crisply in white – a nurse.

She spoke to him gently, in beautifully accented English. `You are awake now? You can understand when I speak to you?'

She had the bluest eyes he had ever seen. Scandinavian blue.

`Where am I?' he whispered.

`In hospital. You have had an appendectomy.'

`A what?'

`The surgical removal of your appendix.'

`Oh.'

Slowly, it came back to him: he had come to Stockholm on a flying visit to Bonniers for the Swedish publication of Jimmy Overman's book, because everything to do with Jimmy's book, even foreign rights, was handled personally by him.

He had not stayed long, preferring to retire to a nearby restaurant with the Rights Director to discuss other titles Bonnier might be interested in. The restaurant was cool and relaxing and the food looked excellent, but he was unable to do more than occasionally taste it. A pain in the lower right side of his body that had been nagging him on and off for weeks, suddenly became acute. No matter how much he tried to pretend there was nothing wrong, the charming man seated opposite him looked more and more worried.

It was only when they stood up to leave, and the agonising pain suddenly doubled him over, Kris Schneider immediately took charge of the situation, ordering the staff to phone for an ambulance.

`I am going now to take your blood pressure,' the nurse told him, and her voice was soft and unhurried and soothing on his awakening mind.

He watched her as she pumped the sphyg and studied the rising mercury, his eyes taking in every detail of her face: the Scandinavian blue eyes, the smooth line of her jaw, full pink lips, the long Swedish-blonde hair tied back for work, but which he could imagine all floating in the evening. Her freshness, the light gold of her skin, her sheer cleanliness, as if she had just bathed in a fountain of sparkling Perrier water. Everything about her was ultra feminine, exquisitely beautiful.

`The *doktor* will come to see you very soon,' she said, unwrapping the band from his arm. `But I can now bring you a drink, something light to eat – would you like that?'

She was smiling down at him, bending towards him slightly, and the scent of her reached his senses.

He tried to sit up and ask her a question. She immediately pressed his shoulders back down on to the pillows.

`Rest,' she said gently.

*

Her name was Rena Olsson, she was twenty-three, but that was all she seemed prepared to let him know about her. An ambiguous angel, she was beauty and perfection, his dream girl, and whenever she came into his room and lifted his wrist to take his pulse or put a hand on his brow while he dozed, he pretended to dream while losing himself in the closeness of her.

In the days that followed when she was absent, or off-duty, he spoke to the other nurses, finding out small things about her.

He wondered if his incredible attraction to her was due simply to her being a nurse, all those tender little touches. But when other nurses came in and performed the same duties for him, he felt nothing at all. Only when she appeared did his heart begin thumping in the way it always did when he saw her.

She was on duty and in his room when Kris Schneider walked in. Kris looked at her and lost his step, almost tripping over a chair. She turned and left the room.

Phil grinned at the expression on Kris's face and suggested, `To borrow a phrase from Jack Kerouac – "the only word is wow."'

Kris nodded, his lips silently forming the word as he sat down. Phil handed him a bowl of fruit. `Here, have a grape.'

Later that evening, while Rena was placing an Interflora bouquet of flowers from England into a vase, Phil asked her if she would kind enough to give him her home telephone number.

`In case, you know, I feel ill in the night.'

`So you ring for one of the nurses on duty.'

`Ah yes, but they don't speak English as well as you, Rena. That's why I thought your home telephone number would be very useful, in case of some verbal emergency.'

`No, I cannot give you my home telephone number.'

`Why not?'

She glanced at him over her shoulder. `Perhaps I am married.'

`Are you?'

`No.'

`Neither am I.'

She looked at him with her ice-blue eyes and gave him a shadow of a smile as she lifted the card attached to the flowers. It read: *Missing you darling, hurry home. Love Katie.*

`So who is Katie?' she asked.

`A friend, just a friend.'

Rena looked disbelieving. `Do all your friends call you darling?'

He shrugged. `It's an English thing, Rena. It means nothing.'

She gave him a small cynical smile, and walked

out of the room.

For the rest of the day, all her responses to him were ice-calm and uninterested.

*

Lying in bed that night, Rena found that sleep would not come, her mind continually going off on a spin, thinking about the Englishman.

The last few days seemed to have moved with a faster pulse, more funny and more exciting. Yet all this was new and strange to her, and she did not like it. It interfered with her efficiency, causing her moods to swing from excited and happy to pensive and confused.

It was not possible that she was attracted to him, was it? No – she was incapable of becoming romantically attracted to any man. For four years, since her nineteenth birthday she had been suffering from a sickness which she kept a close secret from everyone in her life. She could not bear any man to touch her.

But the Englishman – she had been unprepared for him. Unprepared for the lightning flash of spontaneous attraction she had felt in those first few moments of speaking to him ... But that was all, just a lightning flash, before she retreated back into her own isolation and refused to succumb to his flirtation.

Yet when she arrived for work the following day and discovered he had left the hospital earlier that morning, her predominant emotion as she stood at the open door of his empty room, was crushing disappointment.

She was barely back outside the door when she was told there was a telephone call for her.

She was hesitant as she put the receiver to her

ear, hoping yes, hoping no.

`Hej?'

`Rena?'

`Yes, Phil?'

`Ah, you recognised my voice.' He sounded amused. `So you noticed then – that I'd checked out?'

`Yes, I noticed.'

`Oh well, that's something for me to remember.'

`You are at the airport?' she asked. `You have ringed to say goodbye?'

`No, I am at my hotel, and I have ringed to ask you out to dinner tonight.'

`Do you not have to go back to England?'

`Not if you say yes.'

Rena's first sight of Phil outside the hospital environment caught her completely by surprise. He looked vital and full of energy and he was dressed in a black suit, as black as his hair, and his handsomeness almost took her breath away.

She looked around the lobby of the Grand hotel. `Are we going to dine here?'

`No.'

He took her to Mälardrottningen, a hotel of 59 cabins on what had formerly been the yacht of the American heiress, Barbara Hutton – a beautiful yacht now permanently berthed in its own lovely setting at Riddarholmen. They dined in the restaurant on the bridge.

`Why did you choose here?' she asked him.

`I rang a friend at Bonniers; he recommended it. Do you like it?'

`I like it very much,' she smiled, and gazed around the restaurant. `It's the first time I have dined on a yacht.'

The wine steward arrived. She had no particular preference, so Phil ordered a white burgundy. Chassagne-Montrachet.

She was the most exquisite girl Phil had ever dated. Gone was the cool crisp cotton whiteness of the nurse in the hospital. Tonight his dream girl was wearing a black dress that hugged her slender figure like a second skin. Her blonde hair was loosened from its regular plait and seemed even longer and glossier than he had imagined, like waves of cream silk.

`You're very beautiful,' he said.

She looked away.

Something was wrong.

He could see she was very tense and nervous, even when she smiled, but he knew it was not because of the unfamiliarity of her surroundings; she was a worldly woman in every sense, perfectly capable, assured and intelligent, with no pretence of simpering naivety or gaucheness. So why did she seem so nervous?

He said softly, `Rena, what are you afraid of?'

She turned her eyes to him, ice-blue and surprised. `Afraid? Why should I be afraid?'

He smiled. `No reason at all.'

`It was a strange thing for you to ask.'

`Forget it, please.'

After two glasses of wine she began to relax, her smile genuine, her conversation more free and natural. He watched her face as she spoke, fascinated by the changing expression in her eyes.

`Did you always want to be a nurse?'

`Oh no,' she replied seriously. `For a long time I wanted to be a mermaid.'

Rena was enjoying herself.

128

Much more than she had anticipated, and most especially because as the night wore on she found she could talk to Phil, very easily. He knew when to listen, when to offer his own point of view, and even when they disagreed, she enjoyed the disagreement.

Usually she found men not worth quarrelling with.

She thought back to the last man she had dined with – a year ago – a disaster. Lars had done nothing but talk about his work, his ambitions – himself.

Phil was different: his theme did not keep returning to the main subject of himself. In fact, that seemed to be his only taboo subject – himself. He shrugged her questions aside as if all the details of his life were no more interesting than slight trivialities, deftly bringing the subject back to her.

She liked him, and suddenly wished she didn't, not only because he was going back to England, but also because she knew he would not understand.

When the evening was over, she looked at him uncertainly. `Phil, would you mind if I returned home in a taxi, alone?'

Phil, who had been beckoning to the waiter, gave her a quick glance, quizzical. `Why?'

`I prefer it so.'

`Isn't this all rather strange, Rena?' He handed the plate containing bill and card to the waiter, then turned back to her.

`First, you had to go home to change out of uniform, you said, but refused to allow me to collect you there in a taxi, insisting we meet in the lobby of my hotel. And now you want me to allow you to travel home alone late at night. It's not a very gentlemanly thing for me to do, is it?'

`Sweden is not like England or America. We do not have such high crime rates.'

`You're not married,' he continued. `So what is it? Are you living with a man? Some guy who doesn't know you're out with someone else tonight?'

`No, Phil,' she said, lowering her eyes wearily. `I live only with my parents.'

`Your parents?'

`But even if I was married, or living with a man,' Rena added softly, `what would it matter? Today on the telephone you agreed that we would meet tonight as friends – just friends.'

`Okay, just friends, so why can't I escort you home?'

`Because there is no need for you to come all the way out to my home. A taxi will take me there just as safely.'

Phil studied her for a moment, then decided to let her play this out in her own time, her own way, at her own pace. `Okay,' he acceded, `if that's what you want, I'll ask them to call you a taxi.'

When the taxi arrived, he walked with her down the brightly lit steps of the yacht and opened the taxi door for her.

`I wish you wouldn't be so afraid,' he said quietly, `because there's nothing to be afraid about.'

`I am afraid,' she admitted. `The way you see me ... `I'm not like you think I am.'

`I think you're gorgeous.' He smiled. `Are you going to allow me to kiss you goodnight?'

He saw the stark stricken look on her face as she drew back in sudden panic. `No, please, you agreed, we would be friends – just friends.'

He barely caught her whispered farewell as she disappeared inside the taxi, slamming the door shut behind her. Seconds later she was gone.

He stared after the receding taxi like a man who had been struck. Her hesitations he could understand, her stark horror he could not.

He was still baffled when he got back to his hotel.

What now? sang Plato's ghost. What now?

At this doubtful hour, Phil hadn't a clue. He looked at his watch: 12:16.am, after midnight. Already she belonged to yesterday.

THIRTEEN

London
July 1993

_____/

It was almost two weeks since Phil had returned from Stockholm. He had tried unsuccessfully to forget Rena Olsson, put her out of his mind, but every now and then something reminded him of her: a question from David Gallagher about Bonniers, or a girl in a restaurant with blonde hair.

The anodyne was work. Throughout the past eleven days he had worked as if making up for lost time, immersing himself in it totally until he had no time to think. The phone on his desk rang: he picked it up and felt his heart sink when he heard John Houlihan's cheerful Irish voice.

`Phil, I've been trying to get you all morning.'

`Sorry, John, I was in a meeting.'

`Did you read my new script?'

`No,' Phil lied. `Not yet.'

`Oh...' Houlihan managed to convey a huge tidal wave of disappointment into that one small word. `Oh...' he said again. `So when – when did you think you'll get round to reading it?'

`Today. I'll start reading it today.'

`*Today?*' Houlihan chuckled and was instantly joyful. `You'll love it, Phil. It's fabulous. It's the book I was born to write. Even Nancy says so. It's my *magnum opus*. And d'you know what?'

Five minutes later Phil replaced the telephone in its sleek cradle. After a pause, he leaned forward and pressed down an intercom button.

132

`David...'

When David Gallagher walked into Phil's office, he looked baffled. `John Houlihan? Why did he phone you?'

`To know if I'd read his new script.'

David's face stiffened. `I didn't know he had sent in a new script.'

Phil pointed to a cabinet on which there was a large box. `It's over there. Came last week. Sent as always direct to me at my flat – marked *Personal*. I should never have given him my home address.'

David moved over to the cabinet and lifted the lid of the box, then closed it again without touching the contents, his anger consuming him.

`The spiteful sod ... sending it direct to you ... *I* was the one who discovered him and worked my back off to make him a success.'

Phil sat back in his chair. `I know that David.'

David tried to push away his anger, but he couldn't. After all, he had discovered John Houlihan. Lifted his script from the slush-pile and taken it home to glance through over the weekend, expecting nothing much, then finding himself awake half the night, unable to put down one of the best thrillers he had ever read. *Foreign Relations,* a fast-moving story about the IRA and Loyalists in Ulster.

That had been the beginning for John Houlihan. Success had come fast and Houlihan had loved it. It charged up his batteries and oiled his ego until he was writing at a furious pace, turning out two books a year. *The Final Demand*, quickly followed by *The Death of Napoleon Smith*. By the time he had started his fourth, his books were sitting on bookshop shelves alongside John Grisham and Stephen King.

And all thanks to David Gallagher, who had discovered him, edited him, and worked his back off for him.

`I put his books on shelves in every bookshop from here to Japan,' David said. `But even now, even *now*, Houlihan is still sending his scripts direct to you.'

`So why don't you ask him why?'

`I did ask him once.'

David would never forget the night he had asked John Houlihan why. The night of the launch party for Houlihan's third book.

`Why? You're asking me why I send my scripts to Phil?' Houlihan had looked at David for the longest time, slightly boozy-eyed, a man now in his late forties, physically going to seed, but still showing signs of the fairly handsome young man he must once have been.

Then a slow smile had finally come on Houlihan's face. `Well now,' he said, `I'll tell you just why. I'm a man's writer. I write books mainly for men. And I send my scripts to Phil there — ' he pointed, `because, like myself, Phil is ... well, a *real* man.'

Shocked, and deeply hurt – David had never forgiven Houlihan for that. In fact, from that night on he had despised him. But he was too intelligent to allow personal feelings to interfere with business. The discovery of John Houlihan had helped to establish David's name in the publishing world, and that had meant a lot to him, because – unlike Phil, who now seemed to care only about the business side of publishing – David loved books, and loved reading good writers.

And Houlihan had been a cracking good writer, until he had started his really serious affair with the bottle.

`So what did Houlihan say?' Phil asked. `When you asked him why?'

David shrugged. `He just answered with a load of rubbish. A pile of nonsense. He was drunk. It was just before he disappeared to write his fourth.'

`And now he's back, stone-cold sober, with a script that stinks like a dead dog.'

`Stinks?' David stared at him, mystified. `You're not serious? Listen, I may hate the man, but Houlihan is a cracking writer.'

`Houlihan *was* a cracking writer,' Phil corrected. `When he drank nothing but the best and not too much of it. But now he's cold sober— ' He shook his head ruefully. `I mean, who wants to read a thriller that takes twelve pages of gloomy introspection to reach every point? Not Joe Public. He has enough gloomy introspection of his own to cope with.'

David's gaze was a study in disbelief. `Is it that bad?'

Phil nodded. `It's awful, I promise you. Most pretentious load of garbage I've ever read. No story that I could find. And the writing itself is as soggy as a swamp. Chapter after chapter of overladen prose. Houlihan sets out to write a short racy thriller about the IRA, but ends up – well, at times it was so dense, so congested with obscure words and jabberwocky, so devoid of any clear narrative, I thought I was reading *Finnegan's Wake.'*

David looked wounded, as if Houlihan had not only failed him, but also betrayed him in a very grievous way.

`It will sell, of course,' Phil continued, `if we publish it. But it will ruin Houlihan's reputation irrevocably. And damage ours into the bargain. At

135

best it's the work of a mocking bird. Houlihan trying to imitate James Joyce. But Houlihan is a man looking at himself through a cracked mirror. He may be an excellent writer in the thriller genre, but another James Joyce he ain't.'

David removed the lid of the large box and stared agog when he saw the box was filled to the brim with typed pages.

Phil grinned. `Twelve hundred and eighty-eight pages, to be exact. Some short, racy thriller, eh?'

David immediately returned the lid. `Well, there's only one thing to be done with it,' he said determinedly, lifting the box and walking towards the door.

`Hey!' Phil exclaimed. `What are you going to do with it?'

David paused. `I'm going to do what I always do with Houlihan's scripts. I'm going to *read* it.'

`Okay,' Phil held up both hands, `don't take my word for it. Read it yourself and make your own judgement.'

Later that afternoon, David appeared in the doorway of Phil's office, bleary-eyed. `Well, I've read the first two hundred pages.'

Phil smiled. `Of Houlihan's *magnum opus?* That's what he called it. Said it was going to launch him among the greats.'

`An egotist *par excellence.*'

`So?' Phil asked. `What did you think?'

`Immensely interesting, it is not. A Promethean feat of the intellect, it is not. But it does contain a certain—'

`Cut the crap, David. Give it straight.'

David blinked his bleary eyes. `I was so impressed I had to keep stopping myself from nodding off.'

The following day, Friday, Miranda Alvin arrived at Phil's office to collect him for their lunch meeting. They always went out together for a working lunch on Fridays. The office was empty. Miranda looked at her watch – she was on time. So where was he?

Liz Walters, Phil's secretary, rushed down the corridor a few seconds later and informed her, `Sorry, Miranda, I forgot – Phil said to give you his apologies and tell you he can't make it for lunch today. He's had to dash off to a meeting.'

`A meeting.' Miranda frowned. `Who with?'

Liz hesitated. `I don't know. He just said he'll be back on Monday.'

`*Monday?*' Miranda smiled, astonished. `So where the bloody hell is this meeting – New York?'

`No,' Liz replied, as curious as Miranda. `In Stockholm.'

FOURTEEN

Stockholm
July 1993

———————————————————/

Swedish clocks were one hour ahead of England, but Phil made it to the hospital just in time.

He entered the lobby only a few seconds before the elevator door opened and the most beautiful girl in the world stepped out.

She was out of uniform but dressed very simply in flat white nursing shoes, a sleeveless vest that looked whiter than white against her golden arms, a red summer skirt, and a bag hanging from her shoulder.

His pulse was already beating fast from the fear of missing her, but now as he looked at her, she made his heart beat even faster, because despite the simplicity of her clothes, she looked startlingly, physically, sexually, stunning.

She didn't see him until he walked over to her and touched her arm. `Hello,' he said politely. `Remember me?'

She stared at him, her ice-blue eyes full of shock. `Phil!'

`Rena, I must talk to you,' he said, and was surprised when instantly she nodded.

`I want to tell you something else too,' she replied.

Puzzled, he smiled, and put it down to a mix-up in her English. `Can we go somewhere for a drink?'

`No, I have only a few minutes, then I must go.' She took his arm and drew him over to a quiet corner of the lobby. `Have you been in Stockholm again for business?' she asked.

He ignored her question and asked, `Why are you in such a rush? Have you got a date tonight?'

Choosing her words carefully, she said, `I want to tell you something else. After our dinner at Riddarholmen, I telephoned your hotel the next day to tell you, but you had gone back to England.'

`Tell me what?'

She was embarrassed, her face flushed. `After our dinner at Riddarholmen ...' she began again, `when the taxi came, and I rushed away, I did not mean to hurt you. I know I did, and I'm sorry.'

`You didn't hurt me.'

`It's true, I did.'

He was smiling. `So you've been thinking about me then? These past two weeks. You've missed me?'

She sighed impatiently. `No, I have not missed you. I only wanted to apologise to you. I wanted you to know that I so much enjoyed my evening with you, and I did not mean to be so rude at the end and spoil it for you.'

`Nothing is spoiled, Rena, not for me. Not if you'll allow me to take you out again. That's why I've come to Stockholm.'

She was puzzled. `You are not here on business? You are not going away from Sweden now? Back to England?'

`No.' He grinned. `I've only just arrived! I managed to throw my things into the hotel before getting back into the taxi and coming straight here. I remembered you didn't work at weekends. But I don't know where you live.'

It was her turn to be flustered. `So you have come only ... to see me?'

`Yes.'

After a long pause, she said, quietly, `Phil, I like you very much. I would be happy to spend time with you. But I can only be friends with you – platonic friends.'

`Platonic?' Phil could not help smiling – she had to be crazy. His eyes moved down to the lush ripeness of her breasts under the close-fitting white vest – her sexual attraction was ravishing. Few men would be capable of having a platonic relationship with her.

She had seen the look in his eyes, and immediately her own eyes were bright with anger.

`I was foolish to think it possible, even with you. You English men, I know you – you think all Swedish girls are promiscuous.' She pushed past him angrily, and then she was gone.

He immediately chased after her, catching up with her just a few yards away from the hospital. `All right, all right,' he exclaimed, `platonic friends, whatever you say, anything you say.'

`No, you don't mean it.' She tried to move past him but he prevented her. Her eyes looked up at him, but now there was a film of tears over their blueness.

`Rena,' he said quietly, `all I'm asking for is a chance.'

`A chance for what?'

`A chance ... to be platonic friends.' He could lie as well as any man. `Just tell me one thing,' he said. `Just tell me you're not a lesbian. I could cope with anything but that, a battle no man could win.'

`No, I am not a lesbian!' she cried, and her voice was choked with tears as she said, `But I hate men, all men, even you.'

It was the 'even you' which made Phil realise

that she did feel something for him. `Look,' he said, `let's go somewhere and sit down and calm down. Do you have a date tonight?'

`No.'

`Then why the rush?'

`I want to go home. I'm very tired. The hospital has been very busy all day, and I have been working without a break since eight o'clock this morning.'

`Well, then,' he suggested, `we could go somewhere relaxing and have something to eat, a few drinks, just talk for a while, a short while, and then we could go to bed early.'

The last evoked a look from her that made him add quickly, `Separately, of course. You to your home, and me to my hotel.'

She turned up her eyes like a persecuted schoolgirl. `You will not give up, will you?'

`No,' said Phil, and smiled.

She hesitated, looking quickly at her at her plain T-shirt and skirt. `We could not go anywhere special, I'm too tired to go home and change.'

`We'll go anywhere you want.'

And since restaurants were such an important part of Stockholm's social life, they had an extensive choice.

They met again on Saturday morning. Rena stared in amused amazement when she saw that Phil had hired a motorbike. He was wearing a leather jacket and jeans and he was gazing over the Harley Davidson with sighs of admiration.

`Now I know why you told me to wear jeans,' Rena said.

`More comfortable.' Phil agreed.

`But why a motorbike?' she asked him. `Can you

not drive a car?'

`Rena, I drive a car every day. This is more fun.' He smiled. `Come on, climb aboard. They gave me two helmets.'

It was years since she had ridden pillion on a motorbike, not since she was sixteen, and she felt both thrilled and frightened at the prospect.

`This is crazy,' she said, climbing behind him. `Drive carefully.'

`I always drive carefully.'

Then his foot went down and as the engine roared Rena's arms gripped his body tighter. Phil grinned to himself as they zoomed away: always more than one way to skin a cat, make a deal, or get the girl's arms around you.

The city and the suburbs were left far behind. Thick lines of green pine trees occasionally obscured the beautiful Swedish landscape.

Now, Rena thought suspiciously, now he will take me to some secluded place and try to seduce me. She had experienced it all before, all the tricks men played, though never on a motorbike.

They stopped for lunch; they later stopped by the cool blue waters of a beautiful lake; but in the early evening he brought her back to the city, untouched.

Rena was smiling as she climbed off the bike. `That was very enjoyable.' She removed her helmet and let her hair tumble around her. `I felt young again.'

`You *are* young,' Phil reminded her. `Only twenty-three.'

`Yes,' Rena nodded, as if it was something she had forgotten. `What now?'

`Well, let's see ... how about we get something to

eat and then go on to a movie?' he suggested.

`I'd like that,' she agreed. Throughout the day they had agreed and disagreed on a number of things, but they both loved the cinema – they had agreed on that. And as American and British films dominated in Sweden, again they had plenty of choice.

Phil disappeared inside the garage to return the keys of the bike. Later, as they walked through the city, he stopped to buy an English newspaper which Rena insisted on glancing at in the restaurant. Her puzzled confusion over certain words kept him busy explaining their meaning.

`I can speak English better than I can read it,' she confessed.

`You're better than me, I can't understand a word of Swedish, let alone read it.'

`Would you like me to teach you?'

`That sounds promising.'

`What?'

`You offering to teach me hurdi-gurdi. Does that mean you want me to come back to Stockholm again?'

She responded with her uncertain smile. `Do you like Stockholm?'

`Me? Oh, I just like Rena Olsson. But then you know that, don't you?'

She gave him a cool Scandinavian look. `Let's go to the cinema now.'

`Which reminds me,' he said as they walked along. `Bonniers have just published a book by Vibeke Olsson. Is she any relation to you?'

`No, no relation. Olsson is a very common name in Sweden. Even some of my friends are called Olsson.'

`Your friends?' He smiled at her. `Are they all

platonic friends? Like me?'

`Oh, shut up!'

In the cinema, in the darkness, she worried if this might be where he would try to touch her, get too friendly. Many men brought girls to cinemas simply for the darkness. But apart from the normal whispered exchange of comments at the beginning, she sat through the film warm and comfortable and completely engrossed, and left the cinema untouched.

`Tomorrow?' he asked, as they waited for her taxi. `Can we meet again tomorrow?'

`Yes,' she smiled. `Tomorrow. What time is your flight?'

`Not till the evening. Seven o'clock.'

`Then we will have most of the day. Would you like to see more of Stockholm? We could go under the bridges.'

`And what would we see under there?'

She laughed at his puzzled expression. `It's a boat trip, a two-hour cruise called "Under the Bridges of Stockholm". It takes you out to where Lake Mälaren reaches the Baltic.'

`Okay,' he agreed as her taxi drew up to the kerb. `What time?'

`Very early. I'll meet you on the waterfront. Outside the Grand Hotel at seven-thirty.'

`*Seven* – oh for God's sake, Rena, this cruise of yours better be worth it.'

`*Ja*,' she nodded, `it will be.' She looked at him and smiled. `And I will buy the tickets this time. I will show you Stockholm from the water, and prove to you that it is the most beautiful city in the world.'

And she did.

As the boat reached Lake Mälaren under the

morning sun, they leaned on the rail and looked down at the shimmering blue fresh water under a cloudless sky.

`Now you understand why I wanted to be a mermaid,' she murmured, gazing longingly at the water's blue depths. `I can swim like a fish, you know? I won medals in school.'

Their arms on the rail were only inches apart. He watched her face, and knew he had never wanted anyone so much in his life. She was so close, he wanted to reach out and take her in his arms and hold her tightly, but he didn't dare. He suspected there was something deeply traumatic behind her sexual frigidity, and knew it would be a mistake to even touch her.

As the boat veered back toward the salt water of the Baltic, he was confirmed in his decision. He had to let her play this out in her own way and in her own time, until they finally reached the end or the beginning. And amongst all his flaws he knew he possessed one definite virtue – extreme patience.

By Sunday evening, all Rena's fears were swept away. At last she had found a man who would make no physical demands upon her.

FIFTEEN

London
August 1993

_____/

David Gallagher was in Phil's office discussing a typescript when one of the phones on Phil's desk rang.

Phil picked it up. `Yes? ... No wait – no, don't put him through yet...' He looked at David. `It's John Houlihan.'

`Houlihan!' David's perseverance had reached its limit. `*The sod!* I've already spoken to him three times today! I've already told him the script hasn't a hope. And now here he is, taking not a blind bit of notice and going over my head to you!'

Phil spoke into the receiver. `Put him through.'

David listened with fury as Phil was patience itself with John Houlihan.

`Yes, John? ... Oh, pretty good. And you?'

A long silence from Phil followed ... the only sound in the room being Houlihan's voice crackling louder and louder through the receiver that Phil held a few inches away from his ear.

Finally, Phil spoke. `Sure I can hear you, John. I'm not deaf.'

David nodded wearily. Houlihan always shouted down a phone.

`You're speaking to the wrong man, John. The man you should be speaking to is David Gallagher. You know everything to do with your scripts is down to him, and always has been. If he says the book is good enough, we publish. If he gives it the thumbs down, we don't. Simple as that ... Why? Because he's the Editorial Director here! I don't have time to read scripts. I run a business.'

Houlihan's voice raged on through the receiver.

Phil sighed. `I'm sorry, John, but as far as your scripts are concerned, I rely implicitly on David Gallagher's impeccable judgement. Your previous books have all done well because they have always been under David's *super* supervision ... Yes I *have* read this latest script, but only as a courtesy to David Gallagher who wanted a second opinion.'

David grinned – now here was a man making a point. A point that even Houlihan might grasp.

David's secretary appeared at the door, beckoning him to come to his own phone.

For an instant David debated whether he should ask her to tell whoever it was to call back; but then, reluctantly, he stood up and left the room – before he had the satisfaction of hearing Phil giving Houlihan his own verdict on the script – the one Houlihan intended to launch him amongst the greats of literature.

Silence reigned for a few moments in Phil's office as he listened to John Houlihan, then — suddenly — the expression on Phil's face changed, as if he could not believe what he had just heard.

`No,' he said to Houlihan. `No, I don't know what you're talking about.'

In his own study, John Houlihan sat back in his chair and did a slow swivel, speaking with aggrieved slowness.

`Phil, you know what I'm saying, ... I don't care what David Gallagher says about my book, because what does he know? He may understand all the managerial moves in a book's process. He may even understand all the creative components that make a good story. But what the hell does he know about what goes on between a man and a woman? And *this* book – *Rage Of The Soul* – is, as you know, a painfully *intimate* story of a man and a woman. So how can someone like Gallagher possibly evaluate its worth?'

When Phil did not reply, Houlihan continued, more cajolingly. `How can you allow yourself to accept his decision? Feck's sake, Phil, you *know* what I'm saying. I *know* you do. You see, David Gallagher ... well, what you have there is a very nicely spoken pretty boy who looks as pure as a monk. True, he's intelligent, very bookish, very serious, and personally I think he should have become a professor at some university instead of a businessman. But at the end of the day, we both know what he is. So come on, Phil, let's talk about this, man to man.'

`Man to man? If you were here in this office, Houlihan, you know what I'd do man to man – I'd bounce you off the frigging wall!'

Houlihan reared up in his chair. `*What* was that you said?'

`You heard me, Houlihan! What makes you think you can get off with that kind of personal talk about one of my staff?'

`Hey, wait a minute! Now hold on, hold on there, Phil! All I was saying is that Gallagher ... well, he's shy ... doesn't talk, you know, like a man. Doesn't seem to know much about the sex thing —'

`The *sex* thing? So who are you? Some modern-day Casanova? Well you'd never guess it from your latest script. For three pages I thought I was reading about the Rain Forest in Brazil – turns out you're not describing the Rain Forest at all, but some woman's pubic hair! But you're right, Houlihan, you're *dead* right. Amongst all the jabberwocky, David Gallagher might not have realised the difference.'

`Now, hold on there, Phil, just hold on a minute. Now look, let me explain something to you. I understand about people like David Gallagher. I understand why you're annoyed. You're his pal, so I understand. Deep down I feel the same myself. I feel very sorry for those people. They can't help it. Those people — '

`*What* people? I'm talking to you about David Gallagher. I'm telling you to mind your own damned business. I'm telling you that the private life of anyone employed here is nothing to do with you. Listen, Houlihan – No! Just shut the fuck up and listen! This is a *business*. A business concerned solely with *books*. Nothing to do with anyone's private life. Not even yours! The truth is, Houlihan, we wouldn't care if you spent your nights shacked up with a kangaroo, just so long as you turned in a good script.'

At the other end of the line, Houlihan suddenly grinned, a stupid grin for a stupid reason. `Well, you've got plenty of spunk in you anyway, bejasus!'

He slapped his hand down on the desk. `You're all right, Phil. You're all right. Straight as a die! But now ... you said that you've read the script – so let's talk about it. If you think it needs some rewriting, then I'll do some rewriting ... but let's not get sidetracked anymore by all this David Gallagher business.'

`You're the one who sidetracked, Houlihan. You're the one who was bloody impertinent about my Editorial Director.'

`Yeah, sorry ... sorry about that, Phil. Only I'm

just a bit, you know, upset ...' Houlihan passed and hand over his eyes. `Phil, I'm *suicidal* here ... can we *please* talk about the script?'

After a very long pause, Phil said in a quiet voice. `Okay, let's talk about the script.'

When David Gallagher returned to the room, Phil was putting the phone down.

`Well?' David asked. `What did you say to him? Did you tell him the script was no good?'

`I told him he had made a mistake. Taken a wrong turning down a dead end,' Phil replied quietly. `I also told him that if he ever wanted to reverse back down the road to where he had started — back with an explosive script about Mafioso entrepreneurs or an IRA hit-man with eyes like steel gun barrels – we'll still be here for him.'

`But you rejected his script?'

`Yes.'

`Did he give you any trouble?'

`No.' Phil picked up the phone and began tapping out numbers. `No trouble at all.'

`Typical,' David muttered sullenly.

In his study in Islington, John Houlihan was sitting in his chair in a daze.

His wife, Nancy, a comforting and homely woman, also in her late forties, came into the room and looked at him anxiously. Houlihan turned his head and stared at her.

`Did you hear what he said, Nancy? That Phil Gaines. Did you hear?'

`No, pet, he was speaking to you on the telephone.'

`He said – that Phil Gaines – he said, "Why all

this mania to be a ghost of James Joyce when you have enough real live talent of your own?"'

`There now. Wasn't that a nice thing for him to say?'

Houlihan pressed his shoulders back against the chair and sat for a second squinting resentfully into the distance.

`Then he said to me – that Phil Gaines – he said, "Why don't you accept that you're a truly skilled *thriller* writer, who just took a wrong turning here."'

`Wrong turning? Well maybe he's right, Johnny.'

`"And when a new John Houlihan hits the shelves," he said, "that's what your readers expect – a thriller. Not a dark Irish lament as long as *War and Peace*."'

Nancy sighed. `He doesn't know our history or our heroes, Johnny. He's an Englishman.'

`He's a bloody basket case! That's what he is! Rejected my script. Said it was no good. Not even a rewrite would save it. Said it was ridiculous from start to end. Not only was it too long, it had no plot, no action, no excitement, *no balls!*'

`No what?'

`No kidding, Nancy, that's what he said. Came straight out and said it was no good. Anyway, what the hell does he know? He's only a publisher. If he knows so much about how to write a book, why doesn't he sit down and write one. But no. Can't do it. Got to rely on people like me to do it for him.'

`But he must know *something* about books,' Nancy ventured thoughtfully. `Because what he said to you, you know, about you being a good writer in the thriller style, but not so good in the *literary* style ... Well, isn't that what Mr Brennan, the schoolteacher who lived next door to us in Dublin, isn't that just what he told you? He did now, Johnny. I heard him myself. You must be fair.'

`Ah, fair my arse. What did Mr Brennan know about anything other than Greek and Latin? It might have served him better to have learned better English.'

`Merciful God, isn't that a terrible way to talk about a dear man who set you on the road to making a name for yourself. If it wasn't for Mr Brennan, God rest his soul, we'd still be living in a four-roomed corporation house in Dublin now. Not in this grand big house in Islington.'

`Yeah but ... Yeah but ... Yeah, you're right, Nancy. I shouldn't say anything bad about Mr Brennan. He was always very kind to me. But you see, Nancy—' He looked at her in a supplicating plea for understanding.

`I honestly don't think Mr Brennan was right in his evaluation of my work. You must remember, Nancy, it was over twenty years ago when he said that, and my writing then wasn't fully developed. I was a young man out working all day and coming home at night to a house of noisy kids.'

He angrily swished his arm through the air, taking a few imaginary swipes at those noisy kids of the past gathered round his chair, then he sat back and stared like a martyr at the ceiling.

`Dear God,' he said woefully, 'it was a hard life for a budding genius to suffer! The only place I could get some peace to do my writing was sitting in the bath with a blanket under me and wearing my overcoat. So of course my writing wasn't *literary*. I was too damned cold to feel literary. So I made my stories fast and hot. Exciting stuff that got my adrenalin pumping and warmed me up. And why not? What the hell? A few quid is all I was after in those days. Enough to treat myself to the odd glass of whiskey now and again.'

The mention of whiskey made Nancy nervous. Johnny had been teetotal for almost a year now, during which time he had not seemed to have given even a thought to whiskey, so busy was he writing his literary masterpiece. But look at him now – his poor martyred face!

`I'm still madly in love with you, Johnny.'

Houlihan slowly lowered his head and stared at her. `Did you *have* to tell me that? Just at this minute?'

`The thing is, Johnny, I don't think Phil Gaines meant anything personal by it ... you know ... turning down your book.'

`Phil Gaines? That basket case!' Houlihan was furious again. `And what's more – he's a bloody *rude* basket case too! Did you *hear* the way he spoke to me, Nancy? Threatened to bounce me off the wall! Just because I spoke the truth about his pal Gallagher – that blondey Angel Gabriel.'

`Ah, sure you know Phil probably didn't mean it,' Nancy comforted. `He's always been very nice to you in the past. And he's always been very nice to me as well.'

`Well that just goes to show you what a bloody hypocrite he is, Nancy. Because d'you know what he said about you? He said you were a kangaroo!'

SIXTEEN

Stockholm
August – September 1993

_____/

Phil seemed to have fallen in love with Stockholm, surprising Rena by coming back to it again and again – telephoning her as soon as he arrived at his hotel, then whisking her off to dine, followed by an early meeting the following day.

Every weekend, though, he found it hard to adjust to the climate in Sweden. He loved the long summer days, which were sunny and dry, but the summer nights – hardly any darkness at all. Sometimes the sun was still red in the sky at one o'clock in the morning.

`This is the land of the Midnight Sun and the Northern Lights,' Rena reminded him. 'We have bright warm summers and dark cold winters.'

Rena had to admit to herself that she enjoyed every minute in his company, yet whenever he tried to get close to her, even to just hold her hand, a chilly reserve came over her – as cold as snow-clad Stockholm in winter.

During the weeks, when they were apart, he phoned every night from London. She would always answer the phone coolly, pretending astonishment that he had called again, giving not a hint that she had been waiting restlessly for his call.

They would sometimes talk for more than an hour, late into the night, about everything and anything; the content did not matter. He had phoned just to hear her voice, and she had waited to hear his.

Was she falling in love with him? At times it felt so. His general compliance to her request for a non-sexual friendship bewildered her. With other men, there had been no middle ground. They gave her only two choices: lover or implacable adversary.

The latter was usually the result.

With Phil it was different, and she was helpless to understand it. Often, when he was not looking, she would sit with her eyes upon him, trying to puzzle him out, trying to understand the mystery behind his relaxed attitude. He had taught her to laugh again and she had not known that so much laughter was left in her. He always gave her a wonderful time, but she gave him nothing in return, except her company.

Even so, he spoiled her shamelessly. He sent her flowers and chocolates several times a week, delivered to the hospital. She would leave some behind and take the rest home; but before long her bedroom was filled with flowers, the entire *house* was filled with them.

`Who sends them?' her mother asked one night when she arrived home with more flowers and more Swiss chocolates. `The Englishman on the telephone?'

`Yes,' Rena replied quietly, `the Englishman.'

`What is wrong with him? Has he more money than sense? And why does he always send them to the hospital and not here?'

`I have not yet given him my address.'

`Why not?'

Rena didn't reply, just looked at her mother silently.

`What is wrong with him, Rena? That he does not wonder why you do not give him the address of your home?'

Rena sighed. `Yes, he wonders. But he has English good manners and he does not push the question.'

When they entered the sitting-room, her mother continued. `Why has he come to Stockholm seven, eight times now? And when he comes, why do you need to stay out with him all day, every weekend?'

`At least she does not stay out with him all night,' her father said, but not on her behalf, only in satisfaction.

Even during dinner, her mother would not let the subject drop. `Who is this Englishman, Rena? Why do you not bring him home for us to meet with him? Is he married?'

`No, Mamma, he is not married. He is a publisher. He comes to Stockholm to see business people.'

`At weekends?' Her father looked disbelieving. `No businessman in Sweden works at weekends. Only shopkeepers.'

Her mother persisted. `This Englishman – '

`At least he is not American,' her father interrupted. `There is too much of America here in Sweden. All the young, dressing always like Americans, buying their clothes from Marc O'Polo and Gul & Bla on Hamngatan – shops that seem to be more rich and American than America itself'.

Her mother nodded in agreement with him. To them, the Swedish youth appeared to be obsessed with all things American, but they were devoted only to Sweden. Both were history teachers in the same school, and both knew every detail of the preserved chronicles of the Vikings. There was not a thing they did not know and love about Sweden, from the arrival of King Gustav Vasa who had fought to free the Swedish people from the rule of Denmark, to King Gustavus Adolphus who had made Stockholm the capital and heart of the Swedish nation.

`This Englishman, Rena....'

When the questions continued, Rena was unable to take any more, `I feel unwell ... I think I must lie down.'

In her room she threw herself down on the bed and wished that Minna had not got married.

Six months earlier she had finally escaped from home, to share an apartment in the city with her friend Minna. But only weeks later, after a whirlwind romance, Minna had married and her new husband, an actor, had moved into the apartment with them.

So Rena had moved out, back home. Back to catching the train to and from work. Her parents had looked satisfied.

She had left once before, and once again after that, but always her parents found a way of bringing her back.

When the phone rang later that night, her father did not call her. She knew it was Phil. She leapt off the bed and ran downstairs to see her father putting the phone down.

`I thought you were asleep,' he said, but she knew he was lying. `It was the Englishman. I told him you had gone to bed.'

`Did he leave a message?'

He nodded stiffly. `He will be in Stockholm tomorrow night. He will telephone you when he reaches his hotel.'

She felt instant relief. `But Rena ...' her father

said reprovingly, causing her to halt on the stairs and look back at him.

`Tomorrow night is Friday night, Rena. He is not coming to Stockholm for business. Do not tell me that. He is coming only to see you. So you must bring him home for us to meet with him.'

Rena's heart sank at such a prospect. `Perhaps you would prefer me to tell him goodbye,' she said quietly.

`Perhaps that would be best,' he agreed gently. `There are many good men here in Sweden, Rena. You do not need to settle for a foreigner.'

The late-September weather was warm in England, but brisk in Stockholm. The wind from the sea had an icy bite to it. Phil was glad he had brought some reasonably warm clothes along.

`*Hej!*' The young bellhop at the Grand Hotel greeted him as if he was an old friend. Five minutes later he was in his regular room and as always it was stocked with fresh flowers in crystal vases.

Before he had a chance to telephone Rena, there was a knock on the door. He opened it and stared in surprise to see her standing there. She looked very serious and didn't smile.

`Hej, Phil.'

Instantly he knew something was wrong. She had never come near his hotel before. And the fact that she was here now, told him they had finally reached the end or the beginning. She had made a decision.

Judging by her clothes, it was the end. She had dressed as if for a funeral: black coat, black stockings and black high-heeled shoes. Even her blonde hair was tied back as if she didn't want it interfering with her thoughts.

`What's wrong?' he asked.

`Everything.'

She walked into the room and sat down on the side of the double bed, her hands clasped in her lap as if she was sitting in church.

`I want to speak with you,' she said quietly. `I want to tell you something else.'

`Would you like a drink?'

`No.'

`Do you want to take off your coat?'

`No.'

She looked up at him and he saw that she was very nervous. `I want to know if you are in love with me?'

He looked at her for a long time. `You know I am.'

`This is not just a Swedish affair?'

He half smiled. `This is not any kind of affair, Rena. Last I heard, it was a platonic friendship.'

She nodded, and looked down at her hands. `Yes, and I want to tell you why—' She did not speak again until he sat down beside her.

Even then she found it difficult, drawing a breath as if to speak, then letting it out unused, her hands clenching and unclenching on her lap.

`I had a bad experience ... ' she said awkwardly. `It was horrible, disgusting. Since then just the thought of sex with a man – ' She shook her head, then suddenly looked towards the door and stood up again, as if to leave. `No, no, I should not have come, you are a man so you will not understand, you will think it is nothing.'

He leapt up, put his hands on her shoulders, and pushed her back down. For the first time ever he lost patience with her.

`Rena, whatever is wrong with you, you'd better tell me. and tell me now. Maybe I'll understand, and maybe I won't. But since we're speaking the truth, I want to tell you truly that I am tired of playing your devoted eunuch. So unless you give me some kind of explanation now, you can stand up, say goodbye, walk out that door, and you'll never hear from me again, I promise you.'

She stared up at him, her ice-blue eyes flooding with tears. `I don't want to say goodbye.'

He sighed, and sat down beside her again, reached out and took her hand. `This man, the bad experience, the one who made you hate men, who was he?'

She bowed her head. `His mouth ... that's all I really remember. His lips ... cold and wet and disgusting.'

`You must remember more than that,' he said gently.

`Yes,' she agreed. `He was five years older than me...' And she could remember far more than his lips. But worst of all was her own shame, her own guilt. Even during the greedy assault of his mouth, even before the rough pain of the penetration into her body, she had an uneasy feeling that there was more in the room than met the eye, more than the rape. In cold terror she had struggled, and then she had seen them – his friends at the door, watching ... They had been watching from the beginning. And from the smirk on his face, she knew he had arranged it so.

Even when she had struggled free, mouse-like she had cringed, unable to speak, unable to do anything more than stare at their shameless faces, their insolent eyes, listen to their upper-class voices. Then she heard a sound, which made them all alert – a car outside. The front door closing, voices raised cheerfully – his parents had come back. They all quickly disappeared.

She was left alone, left to button up her dress with trembling hands and pull down the skirt – left to stand and stare at herself in the mirror and see another person there. Never had she felt such hatred. Never had she felt so ugly. Never again.

Don't you see?' she said, tears spilling from her eyes. `They just used me as a sex object. One to do it and the others to watch. They must have planned it. Because the house seemed empty when I arrived, but they must have been already there, hiding and waiting. And if his parents had not come back ... maybe I *would* have been raped by *all* of them.'

`How old were you?'

`It was my nineteenth birthday. I thought he was in love with me. But that day ... he turned into somebody else before my eyes ... they all did ... all men.'

For months afterwards she had gone through life on the verge of tears. `Everywhere I went I could feel eyes looking at mc. Men's eyes, everywhere, looking at me. I thought I was going to go mad.'

Then, she explained, something strange happened, a mental click in her head. She had actually felt it – a mental click – and she had frozen. Clinically clean, emotionally sterile, sexually frigid. A perfect nurse.

Phil felt sick with disgust and rage as he thought of the scumbag who had raped her – especially the scumbag watchers, abusing her with their eyes – a mental gang-bang by a bunch of filthy cowards.

He was looking intently at her face, the nurse's face that had first awakened him in the hospital.

He remembered the girl he had first seen. Poised, dignified, correct – going about her duties with a quiet manner and ice-calm control.

Not so now. She looked terribly young now, out of control, with tear-filled eyes. Desperately he wanted to take her in his arms, to comfort and reassure her and love her beyond words, but he held himself back.

He lifted the hotel's box of tissues from the side table and handed them to her. She began to dry her eyes.

`I told my father,' she whispered. `He was the only one I told. He wanted to go and kill them. He had his hunting rifle in his hand. But I stopped him, I begged him to keep safe my dignity. He agreed, but he drank and drank and stayed drunk for a week, which was shaming for him, because he is a strict Lutheran. Since then he has tried to keep me away from all men. Always he is afraid for me. And now he is very afraid of you.'

Phil was still holding her hand, holding it tightly.

He said, `Rena, are you afraid of me?'

`No ... I—' she shook her head and sighed helplessly. `Phil ... oh, I can't explain, the words won't come ... but I know how I feel about you ... and I want you to know how I feel about you...'

She looked down at her hands. `*Jag älskar dig*,' she whispered.

His eyes were puzzled. `I don't understand what you are saying.'

`I don't want to say it in English,' she said, unable to meet his eyes. `Only in Swedish.'

`Then say it again.'

`*Jag älskar dig.*'

He stood up and lifted the phone on the side table. When the telephonist answered, he asked

162

her, `*Jag älskar dig* – what does it mean in English?'

A chuckle, then her reply: `I love you.'

`Thank you.'

He put down the phone, but did not speak immediately, tilting his head sideways to look at her.

`It's true, I do,' she whispered.

He moved towards her and caught both her arms, pulling her up from the bed so quickly she was not even aware it had happened. He wrapped his arms around her and held her so tightly she could feel his heart beating. She lifted her mouth to his and kissed him with the tenderest hunger. A moment later he was kissing her with all the intensity and passion of a lover.

It was the beginning.

She took off her coat.

Phil drew down the blinds against the evening light and in the dimness they came together again. They kissed passionately, and kissed again, more desperately, his hands slid down the back of her thighs and slowly pulling her skirt up. He had to know if she wanted him in the way he wanted her, and he was asking her without words.

"Yes, yes, ...' she gasped in answer, 'I do ... I want to make love with you.'

In bed, her body was breathtaking, even more beautiful than he had imagined. She had no skill in lovemaking but she gave herself to him fully and trustingly, her lips opening under his lovingly. It took them hours to come to their senses. Long, wild, luscious hours of limitless love when he had lavished kisses of fire all over her body.

`I just knew you would be exquisite,' he

whispered, and she smiled dreamily and whispered back, 'You too.'

By the time the midnight sun had vanished into the darkness, he was more in love with her than ever.

He reached for the telephone and rang Room Service and ordered champagne on ice. Twenty minutes later she lay back on the pillows, her smile full of mischief and delight as he fed her small delicacies from a smorgasbord of light food.

He grinned. `Makes a change, the patient looking after the nurse.'

Ten minutes after that, she wanted to make love again. He sighed, `Rena, you're not frigid – you're the sexiest woman in the world.'

She smiled. `I've been saving myself for you.'

`I'm beginning to believe it.'

She stayed with him at the Grand for the entire weekend. They scarcely left the room and slept only fleetingly. The hotel provided 24-hour Room Service and they used it for breakfast and lunch. In the afternoon they lay in bed and sleepily watched a movie on TV. They had no desire to be in the company of others. The hotel was quiet, as most hotels are in the afternoon. No loud voices. No sounds of rushing feet as guests hurried back to dress for dinner.

In the evening they showered and then dined in the hotel's restaurant. Afterwards they took a stroll along the waterfront, walking as they had never walked before, as lovers, his arm around her shoulder, and her arm around his waist.

Under the evening shadows the water was dark and dancing. The lights all along the waterfront took on a more luminous brilliance. The air was as fresh as it must have been on the first day on earth. They felt as if they were the only lovers on earth. They stood in the breeze and kissed and forgot the world. Isolated in love and tenderness. Devastated by sexual passion. Every moment of the walk back to the hotel became more exciting. They glanced at each other and smiled in sweet expectation of another wonderful night together.

As they reached the main doors of the hotel, he paused to tell her something. `I love you, Rena,' he said. `You do know that?'

She nodded. `*Ja,* I do.'

He smiled. `You're my own beautiful *swede*-heart.'

She laughed and pulled him inside.

SEVENTEEN

Rome & Stockholm
October – November 1993

_____/

Sofia was ecstatic when Phil brought Rena for a long weekend in Rome.

`Capitale del Mondo!'` Sofia exclaimed proudly. `Roma is the head of the world! The city of *La Dolce Vita*.' She lifted Rena's hand and kissed it. `You agree, *cara?*'

Rena agreed with most things Sofia said – because she understood less than half of it. But she delighted in the lovely big Italian woman who had taken charge of her from the moment they had met, two days earlier.

`He has brought you to Roma to meet his darling Sofia and beloved Alberto,' Sofia whispered to her secretly. `So you are very special to him, very special.'

Rena already knew that, but it pleased her to hear someone like Sofia say it with such certainty.

`The Agony and the Ecstasy. Michaelangelo's Eternal City.' Phil smiled at Rena. They were sitting drinking cappuccino in the lovely square of *Campo de' Fiori* with Chef and Sofia.

The only sadness of this meeting was that Miss Courtney could not be there to meet Rena, because she was no longer alive.

`In her sleep,' Sofia whispered to Rena. `A year ago. Said her prayers, went to bed, and died peacefully. I blame her dog.'

`Her dog?'

166

Sofia nodded. `When Marian died – Phil has told you about Marian?'

Rena nodded. `Yes, he has told me.'

Rena knew she would always remember the night Phil had told her about Marian. He had known such sadness in his life. Both parents killed violently. Too much sadness for one person to suffer. They had talked for hours that night, all their private thoughts, sharing everything and sparing nothing.

`... and so the flat in Hampstead was sold,' Sofia was saying, `but the money from the sale could not be given to Phil until he was eighteen years old. So he came to live with his darling Sofia and his beloved Alberto. And when he was eighteen, they sent him the money, the lawyers who held the trust. He tried to give us some money but Alberto said no. He was our son now. We wanted no money. He must save it for his future. But Phil gave some money to poor Miss Courtney. And Phil bought her the dog.'

`The dog you blame?'

`*Si*.' Sofia sighed. `Poor Missy. When Marian died, poor Missy, her heart was too broke. So she stopped work, stopped everything, and never went outside the door. Phil was so worried about her. Then he bought her the dog, and Missy was happy again, looking after Barney like he was her child, out walking with him every day, walk, walk, walk, she and Barney.'

`How old was she?'

`Old when she died, but not so lonely as before. Her dog was old too. Twelve years old in dog life. And last year, when Barney got a tumour in his stomach and the vet said to Missy that he would have to give Barney an injection and send him to sleep, Miss Courtney said, "Very well," and was not upset on the telephone when she spoke to me about it. But two weeks later – Missy did the same as Barney – went to sleep and woke up in Heaven with Barney..'

Rena looked thoughtful. `Do dogs go to Heaven?'

`*Si!*' Sofia nodded her head emphatically. `Why should dogs not go to Heaven? Many are better behaved than humans!'

And Rena, who had often noticed this herself, found it impossible to disagree.

Chef and Sofia had moved to Rome at the end of 1987. In their youth they had met in the Eternal City and it had always been their dream to retire there. They loved the noise and the vital, throbbing life of Italy's capital. And during the long and tiring everyday existence of their life in the restaurant in London, they had often daydreamed about the long afternoon siestas in the heat of an Italian summer.

`Some dream,' Chef used to say, looking glumly at his till receipts. "Never enough to allow me to retire.'

But then Phil had inherited fifty-three million pounds, and a few months after his graduation he had bought Chef and Sofia a beautiful townhouse in the residential, but central, Prati district of Rome. He had also bought them a small villa in the cool greenery of Tuscany for when life in the busy capital got just *too* hot in July and August.

Chef had protested vehemently, but Phil would entertain no arguments. `It's little enough, Chef, because I'll never be able to repay all you did for Marian. And for me.'

And Chef had sighed, because he knew that Phil

was a man who believed in giving back as good or as bad as he got. An angel to his friends, but merciless to his enemies.

So the restaurant in London had been sold, and now Chef and Sofia were living without labour in Rome, enjoying, at last – *la dolce vita* – the good life.

Sadly childless, but always possessing a natural love for children, Sofia's greatest pleasure was that she now lived so close to her younger sisters and brothers and their children, a crowd of nieces and nephews of whom many now had their own children, and despite their general Catholicism, every one of Sofia's relatives loved Alberto, even though he was neither Catholic nor Italian.

`What I love about Italians,' Chef said to Phil, `is the way they excel in the art of *nonmifreghismo* – not giving a damn.'

In the crowded square of Campo de' Fiori, a young man strumming a merry guitar strolled past their table in a world of his own, singing about the *Girl from Ipanema.*

`And most Italians adore music and dancing!' Chef added, his shoes beginning to tap to the music.

Later that evening, in the courtyard garden of Chef and Sofia's house, Phil and Rena joined Sofia's crowd of relatives for a party. The night glowed with coloured lanterns and music and dancing and laughter.

`I didn't realise that Italians, on the whole, were such good-looking people,' Rena commented to Sofia, causing the older woman to clap her hands in delight. `Now look at me, I'm sixty-five,' said Sofia, subtracting five years from her age, `but I am still beautiful! And still in love with my Alberto!'

And five minutes later Chef and Sofia were dancing happily together to the lively music, both grey-haired and larger than life, both refusing to grow old, glorying in the ease of their retirement.

`Whoever has nothing else left in life should come and live in Rome.' Phil said to Rena and smiled. `Perhaps Chateaubriand was right.'

`Look, Alberto...' Sofia whispered to Chef. `Look – see how in love they are?'

Chef looked over his shoulder to where Phil and Rena had retired from the noisy family throng to a small wooden bench in a shadowy corner of the courtyard scented with overhanging baskets of trailing vine, red geraniums, bougainvillea and white jasmine. They were talking quietly together.

`See, Alberto, see how she looks at him, how she adores him, how she worships him – '

Chef turned back and continued to dance like Zorba the Greek. `You approve of her. Oh, that *is* a relief.'

Sofia suddenly flung her plump arms around Chef's broad shoulders, forcing him to slow down into a waltz, her chin tucked into his neck – not for any romantic reasons of her own, but because she wanted to pretend to be dancing while keeping her eyes on the young couple in the corner.

`See, Alberto, how beautiful she is ... so young and feminine ...'

Phil and Rena had their heads bowed, touching each other's fingers and speaking quietly. Phil was saying, ' ... I want you to know what you mean to me. I love you, and I love you in my heart. And from now on, wherever I go, whatever I do, none of it will mean anything without you.'

They were married in Stockholm a month later.

Phil experienced some difficulty during the ceremony, because everything was said first in Swedish, and then in English.

Apart from the language it was a simple wedding, no fuss, no flash. Rena wore a long-sleeved white satin dress, and Phil thought she had to be the most beautiful bride who ever stood before an altar. She looked like an angel, her blue eyes sparkling, her golden hair crowned by a circular headpiece and hanging down in loose curls. And whether it was the custom in Sweden or not, he was unable to resist leaning forward and kissing her on the lips.

It was the happiest day of Rena's life. And even her parents looked happy. They had liked Phil from the moment they had finally met him. And, they reasoned, Rena might be marrying an Englishman, but at least she was marrying him in Sweden. And *he* had even agreed to marry her in a Lutheran church.

And she would come back to them. Rena had promised. At least once a month she would come back from England to see them. And every night she would telephone and speak with them. She had promised. And Rena never broke a promise.

Rena slipped her arm through Phil's as they turned from the altar, smiling radiantly at Minna, and David Gallagher, and Miranda Alvin, and all the other intimate friends who had gathered in Stockholm for this special day.

Sofia was dabbing the tears from her eyes with a handkerchief, her extravagant hat taking up half the church.

But when Phil looked at Chef, and an unspoken message passed over Chef's face, Phil grinned at the older man and almost laughed.

Rena whispered to him. `Phil, what is so funny?'

`Oh, just one of Chef's old Jewish sayings – "A wife, a life."'

Part Three

James Duncan

1994

EIGHTEEN

London
May, 1994

_____/

James Duncan was studying himself in the bathroom mirror as he slicked the comb through his hair – completely grey now.

Pity about that. If he had taken Vitamin E in his prime it would have prevented his hair from turning grey – according to Joanne – who had just found it out from her nutritionist. But he hadn't taken any vitamins then. Not one from A to Z. So now he had to content himself having his hair rinsed a distinguished silver.

He gazed at his reflection with admiring satisfaction. He was fifty-five, as tall and straight as an officer, but elegant, very elegant, and still a very attractive man. The fact that he thought this himself made it no less valid, he decided. It was simply true.

He returned to the bedroom where Joanne was sitting in front of her dressing table putting the finishing touches to her make-up. At forty, she was fifteen years younger than him, but she never admitted to being over thirty-five. Always expensively dressed, she prided herself on being a `mirror of fashion'. Her bouffant of blonde hair was swept up into a chignon – à la Ivana Trump.

`Well,' said James determinedly, `no rich ruthless whiz-kid of a publisher is going to push me around.'

`Don't be silly, darling. All Phil Gaines has done

174

is to invite you to a party at his home this afternoon. Is that pushing you around?'

James sighed heavily. `I'm not going to get annoyed, Joannie, I'm not even going to bother to explain, because let's face it, you are fundamentally a very stupid woman.'

Joanne dabbed a tissue to her lipstick. `What's there to explain?'

`You think our invitation to this garden party today is something social?' James shook his head. `You've got no idea how business deals are made, have you?'

`Be a darling, James, and stop grumbling. You are *spoiling* my party mood.'

James eyed her coolly as she stood up and did a fluttery walk over to her wardrobe and began to slip into the skirt of a white suit.

At times like this, James felt deeply aggrieved.

He had not realised Joanne was so stupid when he married her, but at the time he had not been overly concerned with her cerebral fitness. She had been a great looker in those days, a great body, and all he had been able to think of then was how to secure her as his regular companion in bed. Marriage – that's what she had demanded. Claiming to be an old-fashioned girl of high morals, she would settle for nothing less.

After only one week of living with her in marital bliss, he had discovered Joanne's one tragic flaw – she was an airhead. Didn't have the brains of a gnat. Sometimes she was so stupid, so dumb, so deficient in ordinary common-sense intelligence, he often found himself wondering if she had truly been born on this planet? Her parents were dead, so he only had her word for it.

But despite all that – he stood for a moment

basking in self-congratulation – he was *still* married to her, after twenty years, which proved what a truly *decent* man he was. Reliable, dignified, a man who knew how to shoulder his responsibilities. Still, *someone* had to look after the stupid cow, and sadly it was him.

`Come on, Joannie ... It's a long drive from Berkshire to Hampstead. I don't want to be caught in the Saturday afternoon traffic.'

Joanne slipped her arms into the jacket of her suit and smiled at her reflection as she fastened the buttons. The white jacket had a deep `V' neck and all she wore underneath it was a half-cup bra and the tan from her sun-bed. But then, Joanne had always enjoyed giving men a good eyeful.

Finally, perusing herself in the wardrobe's full-length mirror, her eyes travelling down from the sexy jacket to the slim-line skirt cut just above the knee, Joanne murmured demurely, `How do I look, James?'

James was still watching his wife, the vainest woman in town, his eyes on the low `V' of her jacket which revealed the deep cleavage of her breasts. `That suit is new!' he challenged, his eyes like flints. `How much did that cost?'

`Oh*, pouf, pouf, pouf*!' Joanne waved a hand dismissively. `It's only money, James. And you don't want me to look *cheap* do you?'

James half opened his mouth to reply, changed his mind, turned and stormed out of the room.

He thumped heavily down the stairs, thinking to himself that if it weren't for the fact that she was always so commodious in bed and happy to indulge all his sexual idiosyncrasies, he would take her out to some lonely field and strangle her. Not only did she have the intellect of a paralysed flea, she was also a spend-happy catastrophe.

`If you're not down in one minute,' he shouted up to her, `I'm going without you.'

And he would, too. The old bastard! Joanne rushed over to her dressing table in a flurry and clipped her earrings on ... she would simply *die* if she missed seeing Phil Gaines again. That man was just so *appallingly* good-looking. She would wrangle a lunch-date out of him if it killed her.

She smiled sexily at herself in the mirror – yes, what man could resist such a seductive smile? She lifted her perfume bottle and shot another spray down her cleavage, then grabbed up her purse and did a fluttery run out of the room and down the stairs to hear James starting up the car's engine.

`I'll poison him one day,' she muttered angrily. `I'll put weed-killer in his coffee in small doses, and then I'll weep tears of joy at his funeral.'

In December of the previous year, after their honeymoon in Bali, Phil had bought Rena a beautiful Georgian house near Hampstead Heath.

Although the deeds of the house were in both their names, it was his special wedding gift to her, because down in the basement there was a thirty-foot indoor heated swimming pool, which the previous owner had installed.

The marble floor of the pool was deep blue and the overhead lights were as golden as the sun, and it was to be her own little Lake Mälaren whenever she yearned to leave the world and become a mermaid. A compensation for leaving her beloved Sweden and coming to live with him in England.

But now, on this warm Saturday afternoon in May, the basement was locked because the house was filled with people enjoying a party, and Rena did not want any strangers frolicking in nor invading the privacy of her swimming pool.

*

The party was turning out to be a spectacular success. The huge drawing-room was buzzing with conversation. Outside in the sun-streaked back garden more guests relaxed in clusters while waiters moved around dispensing champagne and hors d'oeuvres of beluga caviar.

There were more than a hundred guests gathered to celebrate the fourth anniversary of Gaines Publishing Limited, now one of the most successful independent houses in London. Since the publication of its first book by Marian Barnard four years earlier, Gaines Publishing had continued to publish a stream of exciting new writers, defying the recession and regularly reaching the bestseller list, regularly increasing their profits.

At thirty years of age, Phil Gaines still had the relentless energy he had when he first entered publishing, and everyone knew he was the driving force behind the firm's meteoric expansion and profitability. No one knew from where he had got his business acumen. Rumour still had it that he was already a millionaire before he entered publishing – and indeed he must have been – because no matter how successful, few independent publishers could afford to live in a house whispered to have cost three million pounds.

At first he had been branded as 'lucky' and a 'gambler' but now he was considered to be an innovator and regarded with respect. If he had simply been some rich dilettante dabbling in publishing he would have moved on by now, investing his money in films or television companies or some other equally exciting game.

But no, he had made the publishing world his world and was making it very clear that he intended to stay.

James Duncan wandered around the lower rooms of the house, sucking on his cigar and sighing at the monstrous injustice of it all.

Three years of the worst recession the publishing world had ever known, yet Phil Gaines was still rolling in it, and still making even more. According to the published figures, Gaines Publishing results for 1993 showed pretax profit up 46%. That hurt. That really hurt. Garland's figure for the same period showed a loss.

James reassured himself that one thing Garland's had *not* lost was its reputation. Quality literature. That's what Garland's published. Nothing but. And *nothing* in the world would ever persuade him to publish the type of mass-market crap that Gaines published. Yet everyone admired Phil Gaines, insisted the man had *style,* for God's sake! A man who blatantly *poached* another publisher's authors!

James was still furious over the loss of Howard and McAllister, but he wasn't going to let anyone see that he cared. At the time he had publicly laughed it off, wished the two ungrateful beggers to hell, but privately he had seethed at the way Phil Gaines had pulled two profitable rugs from under him.

It made you wonder just what the hell was happening to the publishing world! It was turning into a group of lunatic asylums for money-mad careerists. Slips of girls and arrogant young men all ruthlessly chasing the next bestseller. There was no *goodwill* left in publishing any more. No *gentlemen* left.

Well, there were still a *few* gentlemen left, including himself, but on the whole the entire publishing business was rapidly going downhill. And it was upstarts like Phil Gaines who were helping to accelerate the process.

Joanne Duncan usually adopted the air of being slightly superior to her surroundings, but this house in Hampstead truly met with her approval.

Fascinated, she even crept upstairs to take a peek, and there, down the long landing, she found bedrooms beautiful and silent, fresh and lemony – not smelling of lavender bags as most spare bedrooms do.

The most exquisite room of all was the matrimonial bedroom, radiant and romantic in the rays of the afternoon sun – a peaceful oasis of muted blues and cream; the bed a luxurious affair covered in blue silk.

Apart from personal oddments, the only colour that differed from the room's overall blue and cream colour scheme was the television – square and black and as big as a small cinema screen. Beside it stood a huge library of video films. Her eyes scanned the videos: every sort of film imaginable; she rummaged quickly through the shelves, but no – not one porno movie amongst them. She tutted her tongue in disappointment.

Two doors – one at each side of the bedroom – led to a His and Hers bathroom, with a dressing-room adjacent to each one. Now *this* house, she decided, was a house she would *kill* for!

Moving back into the bedroom, her eyes rested once more on the romantic-looking bed and wondered at the mystery of it, wondered just how much activity went on there. She stood, pondering on the unknown, her heart beginning to beat with the thrill of secret desires – and wondered whether his wife occasionally went away?

Surely the girl popped back to Sweden every so often? To see her family? Oh, surely she did!

Well, whether she did or not, it made no difference. It would take time of course, he was very aloof, but Joannie always got her man in the end.

On the floor below, James Duncan was still wandering around the house trying to estimate its cost, his ears sticking out like two question marks.

He went into the dining room. The French doors were opened onto the patio and garden. Guests were wandering in to refill their plates from a long table covered in dishes and attended by two waiters who seemed to be there solely for the purpose of ensuring that no dish descended below the half-full level. As soon as it did they rushed away to the kitchen and returned with a full one.

`Good evening, M'sieur,' said one of the waiters, offering James a large gleaming china plate and gesturing an elegant hand over the table of food.

James decided he might as well tuck in, and found himself listening to some of the conversations in the room as he moved down the table filling his plate.

As usual, the talk was all about the ups and downs of publishing.

`... believe me, it's quite true! Twenty-eight publishers turned down John Grisham's first book.'

`God, I hope I never make such a terrible mistake. If I did, David Gallagher would fire me on the spot. He's a lot tougher than he looks – '

James Duncan sucked his teeth in contempt. David Gallagher – another low-life whiz-kid posing as an intellectual.

By the time Duncan had reached the end of the table, a familiar voice caught his ear, the voice of a young woman. He glanced over his shoulder and saw that yes, it was her – Miranda Alvin. He had met her for the first time a few years ago and thought her very attractive and refreshingly intelligent.

Now he despised her.

She had turned down his offer of a job at Garland Press without even pausing to think about it.

She had also responded to his invitation to join him on a weekend trip to Paris with a condescending look that went from his face right down to his shoes and slowly came back up again.

`Certainly not,' she had said dismissively. `You are married, Mr Duncan, and I am a feminist who firmly believes in the sisterhood code of never betraying other women. So, why don't you take your wife to Paris instead.'

Bitch! As if any sane man would waste a weekend in Paris on his wife!

She had a rich, upper-crust voice, and a propensity for using the word 'bloody' whenever she wanted to emphasise a point, just as she was doing now.

`When we published Marian Barnard's book four years ago,' Miranda was saying, `we promoted it and backed it all the way because we knew we were giving the readers something they expect all publishers to give them – a bloody *good* story. Written by a bloody *good* writer. And at the end of it all – bloody *good* value in return for their money.'

James Duncan picked up a silver fork and napkin and carried his plate out of the dining-room into the garden, unwilling to listen to another word from Miranda Alvin. Such arrogance! Such smuggery! What that toffee-nosed bitch deserved was a good slap. And God knows – he'd like to be the man to give it to her. Right across the face. Miss Alvin – slap! take that with your afternoon tea. *Slap!* – and that – and that – and that!

Just thinking about it made him feel slightly aroused. Anger with a woman always had that effect on him.

Joanne stood in the doorway of the drawing-room, her eyes frantically searching out her host until she saw him. He was sitting sideways on an oyster-coloured long sofa, his shoulder turned away from the door, leaning his head back in very relaxed fashion as he listened engrossed to the conversation of an angelic-looking, auburn-haired girl.

Joanne smiled as she weaved her way towards them. The girl was no rival – she was no more than seven years old.

Joanne sat down on the sofa quietly, her presence unnoticed as the child continued chattering ... `It was at her wedding. My mummy and Charlotte are friends you see, and that's why we were invited to the wedding.'

`And that's where Richard Attenborough kissed

you on the cheek.' Phil looked hugely impressed. `At his daughter's wedding.'

`*And* he called me darling.'

`Did you like that?'

`Welllll – ' she put a finger to her lip as if deeply pondering the question. `Mummy *always* calls me darling,' she said `So I didn't *really* mind. I've met a lot of famous actors too. Do you want me to tell you their names?'

`Famous actors? Oh yes, tell me who?'

She suddenly giggled and pointed past him. `That lady is listening to us.'

Phil turned and looked.

Joanne's stomach did a delicious flip when their eyes met.

`Such a darling child,' she said sweetly, although she hated all children, `but isn't she rather young to be at a party for adults?'

`Her mother could not get a babysitter,' Phil replied, his face expressionless. He turned back to the child and smiled. `Mrs Duncan is without a drink, Agatha. Do you want to come with me while I get her one?'

Agatha scrambled off the sofa. `All right, if you want me to. ' She looked earnestly at Joanne. `Do you want lemonade or coke?'

`Neither, thank you,' Joanne replied, put out by this desertion. Still, early days. She turned her most seductive smile on Phil. `I'll have champagne or Pimms,' she said in a whispery warm voice. `Either, I really don't mind.'

Joanne sat back po-faced as they walked away. Oh well, she thought, cheering up, he'll be back in a few minutes with my drink, then, like the child, I'll get him into a nice little tête-a-tête.

`Why don't you like her?' Agatha asked Phil once they had left the room.

Startled, Phil laughed at the child's perception. `What makes you say that, Agatha?'

She shrugged. `I don't know. But I can always tell when someone doesn't like somebody else.' She looked up at him earnestly. `*Do* you like her?'

`I can't say, because I don't really know her,' Phil replied evasively. Which was a total untruth.

Although Joanne Duncan was unaware of it, he knew everything about her. Everything he needed to know. She was feckless and stupid and for years she had been cheating on her husband and having short-lived affairs with a succession of young men, mostly young waiters, foreign and penniless. For a woman like Joanne, they were as easy to pick up as a cup of coffee.

Agatha returned to the drawing-room alone, carrying a small tray in both hands on which stood two glasses. She smiled sweetly at Joanne. `We couldn't decide which – champagne or Pimms – so we got you both.'

Joanne glared at her. `Where's Mr Gaines?' she snapped.

The child's face paled nervously in response to Joanne's harsh voice. `He ... he had to take a phone call ... in his study ... from America.'

`That you, Marc?'

Phil smiled. `Hi, Jimmy.'

`Can you hear me?'

`Sure, Jimmy, I can hear you loud and clear.'

`Only I've got a real bad cold, a real stand-down. Hang on a minute while I get out my hanky, I need to blow my honker.'

A few seconds later Jimmy came back on the line. The nose-blow seemed to have cleared his mind.

`That you, Phil?'

`Yes, it's me, Jimmy. How did you get the cold?'

`Aw hell, it was just a bit of fun. Me and some of the guys decided to try a bit of fishing in the lake. Middle of the night. Damn well started to rain. Thunder and lightning. All I caught was a cold.'

`Any particular reason for phoning, Jimmy?'

`Yeah. Listen, son, I got something to tell you, something to show you, so jump in your car and rattle up here quick as you can. Can you drive up today?'

Phil rolled his eyes. `I'm in London, Jimmy. You're calling me in London.'

`Am I? Damn, I meant to ring your number at the Pierre. Thought you were still in New York? When did you go back to London?'

`A few days ago.'

`Ah, that's a pity.'

`Jimmy, what is it? This thing you want to tell me?'

`Last time you were up here – you remember that book you gave to me to read? *Some Kind of Wonderful*? The one written by Marian? The book about her and Marc ... 'cept for the names being changed?'

`Yes.'

`Started to read it last night, went to bed early with my cold, and you know what, it made me remember. Can't think how I forgot ... Lord Almighty, son, *where have all the years gone*?'

Washed away by the tide, like all sandcastles, Phil wanted to say, but he knew Jimmy was referring to the gaps in his own memory.

`What did you forget, Jimmy?'

`You see, son, I never meant to hold anything back from you. I guess I just locked them away with the rest of my souvenirs and tried to pretend they didn't exist. Only explanation I can think of. But last night, while I was reading Marian's book ... well, I began to wonder if maybe I was only dreaming ... So I got up, put my leg back on, searched through that big ol' brown suitcase of mine, and sure enough – there they were!'

Phil said patiently, `What was there, Jimmy?'

`Marc's diaries. Five of them. Five thick books. Covering the years from 1960 to 1965. All his thoughts written down in them. All about Kennedy and Khrushchev. All about Marian. All about you.'

`*What?*'

`Yeah, well, these diaries, I've had them since he died in Nam. Don't know why I took them. Guess I didn't want the army guys reading through Marc's personal stuff before sending it back home with his body. There's some photographs inside, a few of Marc with Marian, and a few of Marc carrying you ... looks like he's walking around some zoo. There's an unfinished letter too. A letter to Marian.'

Jimmy went on talking ... unaware of what Phil was going through, a possibility beyond all his imaginings, being able to read Marc's diaries – Marc's *own* private thoughts and words about that time out of time. Words that would reveal and give Phil a greater knowledge and deeper insight into the young man who had been his father.

After he had put down the phone, it was twenty minutes before Phil could leave his study and return to the party.

And a house like this was not the only thing that

stacks of money bought you, James Duncan was thinking. It also bought you something like *that*.

He stared at the Swedish girl standing in the garden, sipping wine as she spoke with David Gallagher.

God, she was sexy! She looked as cool as dew, but was probably panting hot underneath. An experienced man could always tell. And a wonderful figure! He had noticed that earlier when he had caressed her breasts with his eyeballs.

He sighed, sucked harder on his cigar, envying Phil Gaines for having a woman like that fall into his hand.

But of course, the reason why was obvious – money. Women like that, young and sexy and beautiful, women like that were only happy with men who kept them happy with lots of money. And looking around this place, every room a masterpiece by some interior designer, she was clearly getting as much money as she needed from Gaines.

A waiter paused before him, holding out a silver tray of glasses of champagne.

`M'sieur?'

James shrugged, dumped his empty glass on the tray and scooped up a fresh one. He might as well make the most of this shindig while he was here. But as soon as the chilled smoothness of the excellent champagne rolled over his tongue, it only gave him greater cause to feel umbrage.

The smile faded from Rena's face when she saw James Duncan standing by the French doors, watching her. Every now and again throughout the day she had noticed him watching her in a way that made her feel uneasy – the same way a hungry fox stares at a chicken.

`Who is that man?' she asked David Gallagher.

David glanced over his shoulder at the man standing alone sipping champagne, then turned back to Rena in surprise.

`You know who he is. You met him earlier. James Duncan.'

`Yes, I know his name, but who *is* he?' Rena asked. `Phil has never mentioned him before. Yet all day he has been walking around the house like an estate agent doing a valuation.'

`He's a publisher,' David said. `A business associate of Phil's. It's strange, though, now you mention it. Phil always gave me the impression that he thoroughly disliked James Duncan. But now it's all turned around and – '

At that moment James Duncan approached them and the conversation changed.

Simply because he was Phil's guest, Rena did her best to be pleasant and polite to the man who was so rudely ogling her breasts while he talked, but before long she was blushing and squirming in embarrassment.

She secretly squeezed David's arm in a silent plea to rescue her.

David immediately did so, with a quick and polite `Excuse us a moment,' to James Duncan.

Joanne had swiftly eaten a plate of delicious food, gulped down two glasses of champagne, and had returned to sit on the sofa where, she decided, Phil could easily find her when he returned from his telephone call.

A very *long* telephone call, as it was turning out.

But `America' the child had said. The phone call was from America, so what could one expect?

Those Americans never stopped talking. Once, in the late seventies, she had sat next to an American woman on a plane, and the woman had talked so much, never pausing for breath, she finally lapsed into a coughing fit in mid-sentence, then later blamed it on the Russians.

`The Russians?' Joanne had exclaimed, and immediately regretted asking the question because she would be forced to listen to the woman's answer.

`Interfering with the oxygen, honey, that's what they're doing. All this hullabaloo about their Space Programme. All a front, all a blind. The Ruskies don't give a damn about space. It's the world they want. America. Trying to make us weak by sending up their space probes and interfering with the oxygen. That's why my chest was affected. Not enough oxygen in this airplane. Never used to be like that. Always plenty of good oxygen in airplanes before the Russians started interfering.'

Joanne had avoided Americans ever since.

So, that had been the plan – to return to the sofa and sit waiting in a nice, attractive pose, long slim legs in good view ...

Moments later, Joanne jumped up with a burst of excitement. God, what a ninny she was! Why hadn't she thought of it before? If the man was alone in his study taking a telephone call, then that was the place to waylay him – in private!

Phil was coming out of his study, closing the door behind him when Joanne breathlessly rushed up to him. `Oh, Phil!' she gushed in a whispery voice. `May I *please* have a few words with you?'

He stood looking at her silently for a few moments, and her stomach did another flip ... *Oh,*

190

those eyes, those sexy dark eyes.

`Certainly,' he said, in a way that pleased her. `Go ahead.'

She glanced towards the closed study door, then looked at him appealingly. `May we go in there? It *is* rather private.'

`I can't imagine what it is,' he said, watching the way her bosom heaved seductively, `we hardly know each other. If it's something personal, something so private, then I'm hardly the person – '

`No!' she said quickly, having hastily sketched a plan. `It's about a book! I'm writing a book.'

`You – are writing a book?' Phil's eyes widened in what Joanne was certain was interest.

`Well, not exactly, I mean, I haven't actually written it yet, but I have this wonderful idea for an absolutely wonderful book. If we could just talk about it – ' Again she glanced at the closed study door.

Phil appeared perplexed. `But, Mrs Duncan, why talk about it to me, when your husband is a publisher?'

`Oh, *please*, call me Joanne.'

`Very well, Joanne, if you have an idea for a book, why don't you discuss it with your husband?'

`Because he simply *refuses* to take me seriously,' she whispered conspiratorially. `Simply *refuses* to believe that his own wife is capable of being a writer. But, believe me—' her voice pulsated with a subtle passion, `I am very capable. Some of my short stories have reduced my friends to tears.'

Joanne had never written a story in her life, but she roused her bosom into another seductive heave, and waited for his response.

`This book?' Phil said. `Your idea for it. Can you

give me the gist in a few sentences?'

`Yes, well, some years ago, I met this beautiful Italian girl, and became very friendly with her. And, eventually, she told me her life story, which I think would make a *wonderful* book.'

Phil thought she had paused for breath, but when the pause became prolonged, he looked at her questioningly. `An Italian girl – life story – what?'

`Well, her name was Isabella ... and she was distantly related to Mussolini ...'

Joanne couldn't think what to say next, but covered it up quickly. `But really, you're absolutely right – it's very unfair of me to ask you to discuss business during your party. So why don't you allow me to take you out to lunch one day, and we can discuss my book then? How about Monday? Lunch at Claridges?'

Phil looked at her thoughtfully – at the blonde who had been in court and laughed with delight when her husband got away with killing Marian Barnard. Another self-centred egotist who didn't have the decency to remember the dead woman's name – not even when it was on the front cover of the book which, she had gushingly told him at Martin Pellmann's party, she had read *three* times.

Intrigued, more than anything else, during the past few minutes he had allowed Joanne to play her hand, and now she had laid her cards on the table. Lunch on Monday at Claridges. Lunch with *her*.

He would rather eat dirt.

His inner feelings did not show on his face. He even allowed himself to smile apologetically. `I already have a lunch appointment on Monday.'

`Tuesday then? Well just about any day next

week would suit me.' She heaved another sigh, the
`V' of her jacket opening wider. `I have simply
nothing on ... 'she purred, looking at him with a
kitten-like innocence. `Not next week.'

`Joannie!'

James Duncan was walking down the hall.
`Wondered where you were!' he grunted. `It's time
we were going.'

`What – so soon!' *The old bastard! Trust him to
come along at the wrong moment.*

`It's a long drive to Berkshire.' Duncan looked at
Phil. `Thanks for the invitation to the party,
Gaines. Can't say I enjoyed it much. Too much self-
congratulation and backslapping going on for my
liking. Especially from some of your sales staff. But
still, it was interesting. However, we must be off.'

Now it was Phil's turn to ask for – ` ... a few
words? In private?'

James Duncan chuckled sarcastically. `Thought
you might ask that. I knew your reason for inviting
me here today wasn't solely social. Always time for
business, eh? Even during a party. Very well, let's
get it over.'

And seconds later Joanne saw her irascible
husband succeeding where she had failed –
disappearing into the study with Phil, the door
closing behind them.

What *is* it about men and business?' she
screamed inside herself, mincing away furiously in
search of a drink.

Damn James! If he hadn't come along when he
did, she would have had her lunch date with Phil
Gaines all arranged by now.

`Now that is a question to which I can give you an
answer here and now.' James Duncan sat back in

his chair and smiled at Phil with pleasant malice. `No. Not now. Not next month. Not ever.'

Phil stood in front of his desk, slightly leaning against the edge, his arms folded, his eyes considering his shoes. `Why don't you take some time to think about it,' he suggested quietly.

`I don't need to think about it. You see, Gaines, you're not as clever as you think. I've been one step ahead of you for months now. But the only way it's going to happen is over my dead body!'

Phil looked up from his shoes and fixed his dark eyes on Duncan's face until the silence became uncomfortable.

`Well?' said Duncan. `You've had my answer. Anything else?'

`But I think we *should* merge,' Phil said quietly. `It would serve both our interests in the long run.'

`Not mine! No sell-out will serve my interests. My father started that firm, built it up from scratch, turned it into one of the most *respectable* publishing houses in London. And I've kept it going. So why should I hand it over to you?'

`A merger is not a hand over.'

Phil turned and lifted a book from his desk. He held it square in front of Duncan. It was *Some Kind of Wonderful*, by *Marian Barnard*.

`This book, by Marian Barnard...' As Duncan looked blandly at the book, Phil saw not a glimmer of recognition. `This book, so far, in worldwide sales, has earned us millions. And that's just one book. Jimmy Overman's book is still back-listing at fifty thousand paperbacks a year. And that's just in the British territories. Others – all doing well. Our titles this year number over two hundred. So a merger with us could only prove profitable.'

James Duncan sat back in his chair, big and

194

solid in a silver-grey suit and silver-grey tie, both the same colour as his hair. Even his eyes were silver-grey, smiling now as he took a pack of cigars out of an inner pocket of his jacket.

`Mind if I smoke?'

Joanne was upset. But James seemed unconcerned as he turned the ignition key and started up the car's engine. `You've had enough champagne for one day. And I've got to be up early tomorrow morning to play a round of golf.'

`But, James, it's because of all the champagne that I desperately need to use the bathroom. And it's such a long drive to Berkshire. Please, darling, please let me go back inside?'

`Sometimes, Joannie,' he said with a sigh, `I think the only person you are capable of having any consideration for is yourself.'

`That is just not true, James. You know how much I worship you.'

`Oh, all right,' he relented, `go back inside, but be quick.'

`Bless you, darling, you really are the sweetest man in the world,' Joanne murmured as she opened the car door and swung her legs out.

Crabby old bastard! she fumed, doing a fluttery run on her stilettos back up the drive. *Weed-killer in his coffee is too kind. I think I'll just stab him in his sleep.*

As Joanne rushed inside the open door of the house, it was not the bathroom she was frantically seeking. And as she rushed along the hall – *Hallelujah* – she saw Phil standing at the foot of the staircase talking to the child Agatha and her very attractive mother – an actress in her thirties who was called Mary something.

`*Daaaahling!*' Joanne gushed apologetically to the child. `I almost forgot to say goodbye to you. And you were so kind, bringing me drinks. And you, Mary, it was *sssso* nice meeting you.'

Mary, who was usually nice to most people, found herself being kissed affectionately on the cheek, then Joanne bent and kissed Agatha affectionately on the cheek, `Such a *beautiful* child,' then she grabbed Phil's arm and drew him aside.

`Phil, about my book ...'

By midnight, only David Gallagher remained.

He was standing in the dining-room, by the French doors, staring out at the dark garden, turning around when Phil came into the room.

`Everyone gone?'

Phil nodded. `Everyone except you.'

`It was a good party.'

`Yes, I think so.' Phil poured himself a scotch and soda, an unusual drink for him.

`What was wrong with Rena?' David's eyes were studying Phil intently. `Why did she leave the party so early and not come back?

`She felt unwell. The noise and the crowd. I made her go to bed.'

`Oh, I see,' said David quietly. `Only we spent most of the afternoon together. Rena seemed to be enjoying herself ... apart from one disagreeable incident — ' David decided not to elaborate further. `Yes, she seemed to be really enjoying herself. But then suddenly, she was gone. She *is* all right, isn't she?'

Phil smiled at his friend. David and Rena were two people who just couldn't help liking each other.

`She was exhausted, David. She was called in to do an emergency shift at the hospital last night, then refused to go to bed when she came home this morning, insisting on overseeing all the arrangements for the party. So she's had no sleep since Thursday night.'

`Thursday night? My God, she *must* have been exhausted. But I never would have guessed. And she didn't mention it.'

Phil sighed. `Well, that's Rena, a true nurse. Keeps her own problems hidden while she attends to the job in hand.'

Phil slumped down in a chair by the table, sat back and loosened the knot of his tie, changing the subject. `Did you have any talk with James Duncan?'

`Yes, I did.' David nodded gloomily. `He seems to be the sort of man who would sell his grandmother if he thought she would fetch a good price.'

`His grandmother, yes. But not his firm.'

David looked sharply at him `He said no?'

`He said "Never".'

`Well thank God for that!' David exclaimed in relief, his face breaking into a sudden boyish grin.

`It's all for the best,' David said a moment later. `Phil – that Duncan! Him and us? It wouldn't work. He belongs in a world of antiquated typewriters. Even his literary gossip is from another time. He was telling me what Kingsley Amis said about Graham Greene, and what Graham Greene said about Evelyn Waugh. Not – you'll note – what James Patterson said about John Grisham, or what Dean Koontz said about Stephen King. No, no, I don't think Duncan's even *heard* of them!'

David shrugged. `To be honest, I can't understand why you even considered a merger with Garland's in the first place. It's not a house for young men or big profit, it's covered in dust.'

He poured himself a glass of red wine. `Even now, the whole thing is still a mystery to me. No matter which way I look at it, none of it makes sense. Point one: business goes from strength to strength, so who needs a sinking ship like Garland's?'

He looked questioningly at Phil but, getting no comment, he went on, `Point two: it can't be that you want to *rescue* the man. Help him out of his financial difficulties. It can't be that, because you truly *dislike* the pompous old sod. I know you do. So why?'

Phil was silently considering. `Well,' he said, `I tried to be merciful – tried to do it the civilised way, with a merger, to save his face – but now James Duncan has left me no choice but to return to my original plan.' He shrugged indifferently. `Either way, the end result will be the same.'

`Original plan?' David stared at him, confusion and exasperation returning. `*What* original plan?'

Phil took a drink of his scotch. `David,' he said, `what you don't know, won't hurt you.'

NINETEEN

**Berkshire
May 1994**

_____/

`A feather in his cap! That's what Phil Gaines is after, Joannie. Another feather in his cap!'*

Joanne ignored her husband's voice from their en-suite bathroom, adjusted the clock-radio, and slipped into bed with her *Hello!* magazine.

Wearing navy pyjamas, James returned to the bedroom, sat down heavily on the edge of the bed, flicked open a box on his side-table, removed a cigar, and began to light it.

`James, must you smoke those things in the bedroom!'

James always smoked a cigar in the bedroom, every night, and had done so for more than twenty years. It was his last ritual to unwind before sleep. Just as it was his ritual to ignore his wife when she complained.

He smoked contemplatively on his cigar; his eyes fixed upon the dressing-table where, tilted at a perfect angle, the mirror gave him a full reflection of his own image.

His eyes narrowed, he puffed a cloud of smoke in the air, and made a sharp tutting sound.

`A bastard, Joannie, that's what he is. An arrogant bastard.'

`True,' Joanne said amicably, thinking how much she simply *adored* arrogant bastards. Had she not married one?

She shot a sharp look at her husband's back –

although she didn't think much of *him* anymore – he was a brute! To the outside world James's face was usually arranged in an expression of gentlemanly humour, but he had a cruel streak in his nature and possessed a need to dominate everyone around him. And he sometimes took great pleasure in inflicting pain and humiliation on those who displeased him – even her.

Of course, there was a time, years ago, when she had seriously considered leaving James. But, well, she was not trained for any role but that of a wife, had no real skills, other than a passable hand at typing. And being forced – as she once had been – to sit in a stultifying office all day! Just the thought of having to *work* for a living left her feeling quite ill.

Marriage to James at least kept her free from all that. Free all day and every day to do what she wished. It also provided her with a pleasant home, a generous allowance on her credit cards, and – *best of all* – with James she had never needed to worry about being saddled with tiresome children.

Poor man – because of some boyhood illness, James had discovered very early on that he would be unable to father children. A fact which had dismayed him somewhat. But to her it was simply an *exquisite* relief, and one of the reasons why she had married him.'

`Gaines – who is he?' James said with narrowed eyes to his reflection. `Where did he come from in the first place?'

Phil Gaines ... Joanne's eyes illuminated with a lusty glow. She had rubbed one earlier and smudged her mascara. Her hair was unpinned from its chignon and hung around her face like a yellow halo of steel wool.

Phil Gaines ... Joanne wriggled her toes, a hot sexy demon licking up her legs to her thighs. She simply could not *think* of that gorgeous munchie man without wondering what he would be like in bed?

But then, these days she was unable to look at any attractive young man without wondering what he would be like in bed.

She had thought by the time she reached forty she would have eased up on sexual attraction, but no, life went on same as ever. The only difference was that now she was attracted to younger men, not older.

But Phil Gaines ... `Call me at the office,' he had said when she had gone back to ask him about her book. `At the office,' he had repeated, taking her arm and escorting her to the front door – and Joanne knew from experience what *that* meant. No married man liked 'the other woman' calling him at home.

`Don't worry, Phil,' she had whispered seductively in her husky warm voice. `I'm *very* discreet ... And the ideas I have for my book will *certainly* give you something to sleep on.'

Then James – the impatient bastard – had banged the horn of his car and she was forced to leave, glancing back over her shoulder with a seductive little murmur of `*Ciao*.'

Well, a little of the lingo gave her suggestion for a book about an Italian heroine a bit more authenticity.

So, she would do as he asked, and phone him at his office, on Monday afternoon, and arrange a lunch-date with him for later in the week – Claridges, of course. A nice hotel full of bedrooms above the restaurant. She hunched up her shoulders and smiled deliciously – she *always* got her man into bed in the end. Never yet failed. Not once!

`Gaines, you see, we know so little about him.' James chewed on his cigar. `We know all about his business life, his relentless success, his skill in making money, but when it comes to the man himself, knowing what makes him tick, what drives him, he's as deep as hell.'

Joanne sighed dreamily.

`Deep as hell!' Duncan glared at his reflection in the mirror. `I'd give anything to find out how he managed to get the *world* rights to Marian Barnard's book. A dead author. An unpublished manuscript. No hungry agent baying for a bigger advance. I mean, just how *lucky* can one man get?'

He glanced over his shoulder at Joanne. `Makes you sick, doesn't it?'

`What?' Joanne snapped out of her erotic fantasy and glared at him sourly. *What* makes you sick?'

`Gaines getting the *world rights* to Marian Barnard's book. Total control. No bloody agent. A book that made his firm a fortune.'

`It could have been David Gallagher,' Joanne suggested. `He's the Editorial Director there. And from what I heard that Miranda woman saying, David Gallagher has – what did she say? – "unerring talent for finding good scripts." She seems to respect him enormously, but I think she respects Phil Gaines even more.'

`It makes me puke! The way everyone treats Gaines like Mr Wonderful. But what does anyone really know about him?'

James drew on his cigar, sitting thoughtful while his lips manufactured a smoke ring. `I still say there's *something* strange about him. I've known it since that first day I met him. At Pellmann's party. I was introduced to Gaines and I'd been told beforehand that he was a very polite young man, very likable. So when we were introduced, I reached out to shake hands with him, very pleasantly, welcome to the club young man, all that kind of thing – but he just ignored my hand!'

Duncan looked over his shoulder at Joanne and nodded, as if he still could not believe it. `Would you believe it?'

Joanne merely shrugged, bored, utterly bored. She had listened to this tale at least a hundred times before. And even more galling was the fact that she had *been there* when it happened.

But could she stop James from telling the story over and over again? Could a fly hold back a steamroller?

`Just ignored my hand!' Duncan turned back to glare indignantly at his image in the mirror. He chewed furiously on his cigar, then spat. `Gaines stood there with one hand in his jacket pocket, and the other holding a glass of wine, and merely inclined his head in acknowledgement – leaving me standing there with my hand held out like a fool!'

`And you *looked* like one too,' Joanne thought happily.

James ruminated for a minute as he considered the ash on his cigar, then repeated the incident to her yet again.

`Now, it was Martin Pellmann who introduced us, and he looked as embarrassed as I felt, although he covered it up with conversation, and a short while later he took Gaines off to introduce him to someone else. But before that, never once while we stood talking did Phil Gaines acknowledge anything I said. His conversation was solely for Pellmann and one of Pellmann's authors. Disregarded me as if I wasn't there. Cut me dead.'

Joanne opened her *Hello!* magazine.

`I couldn't understand it. I'd never before met the man. He was a total stranger. But still, whenever I joined in the conversation, Gaines just stared past my shoulder at other people in the room as if he was bored to death. You get the picture?

Joanne's head was lowered over her magazine.

`So finally I thought, Oh, for God's sake, this upstart doesn't know who I am. And later Pellmann assured me that was the case, that Gaines had not realised I was the head of Garland Press.'

Duncan sat for a moment fuming. `But I've always hated Gaines since then, always despised him. Not that I've seen very much of him. And then the bastard goes and *poaches* two of my most reliable authors! No – not poached, he did more than that, Joannie – he deliberately *seduced* them away from Garland's with big money and promises of big promotions. Well, I tell you, Joannie, the sheer arrogance of that man takes some believing.'

Duncan sat frowning, still baffled.

`But now, these past few months, I've been wined and dined by his accountants and lawyers and every other puppet he's got dangling on his string. All sucking up to me for a merger. And then comes a call from Gaines himself, inviting us to a party at his home. Of course I knew straight away what he was after, but that's not what he got!'

Duncan tapped the ash off his cigar.

`You see, Joannie, when I make my strike

against a man, I strike hard. And the only reason I accepted the invitation in the first place, was because I wanted to put that arrogant bastard to the trouble of waiting on me hand and foot, pouring out my wine and so on. But he never did. I should have known there'd be people on hand to do all that for him ... Never even shook my hand. It was his wife and David Gallagher who greeted us. Did you notice that? Yet later on I saw it was Gaines himself who greeted and smiled and shook hands with others.'

Duncan mused. `Now what's his game? I thought. What's his bloody game? For months he's been leading me on some cat-and-mouse dance trying to get me up his own garden path – and when I get there, he's not even there to greet me! So what's his bloody game?'

He shrugged. `I mean, if you want to persuade a man to go into business with you, *that's* not how you do it. I thought I was going to be the guest of honour. I didn't expect the host to leave my welcome to his wife and one of his staff. Christ, *that's* not the way you do it.'

He sighed. `You know what it made me realise, Joannie? It made me realise that Gaines doesn't know as much about business dealing and wheeling as he *thinks* he does.'

Joanne suddenly looked up from her magazine, thoughtful. `Do you think they're having an affair?'
`Who?'
`David Gallagher and the Swede. I didn't like her one bit. Cold as ice. She hardly said two words to me all afternoon.'
`Yeah, just like that Miranda Alvin – a real stuck-up bitch. Did you hear the way Alvin was slapping herself and all the other members of

205

Gaines staff on the back? Made me sick. These upstarts – they publish crap and crow about it! They're destroying the publishing world, Joannie. These upstarts. Especially the women. If I had my way, I'd erase them all from the face of the earth with a blow-torch.'

`Yes...' Joanne was looking thoughtful. `I was watching them, James, and well ... they certainly seem very *fond* of each other. Do you think they are having an affair?'

`Who?'

`David Gallagher and the Swede.'

`How the heck should I know?'

He suddenly swerved his attention in her direction. `By the way, what were you and Gaines talking about?'

Joanne blinked, an alarmed crimson colouring her cheeks. `When? Where?'

`When and where I saw you. Outside his study.'

`Oh, *that?*' Joanne shrugged. `We were talking about books. All very boring, I assure you.' Joanne patted back a yawn. `He was interested in my choice of literature.'

`Literature – you?' James chuckled sarcastically. `The nearest you've ever got to a piece of real literature was a quick thumb-through *Lady Chatterley's Lover.'*

Joanne gave him a clowning smile, stuck out her tongue, then rested her head back against the headboard and closed her eyes as if sleepy. *What a stinker! What a pig! What was the best way to kill him without being found out?*

Duncan turned back to the mirror and continued the conversation with his reflection, rehearsing how he would tell it to his friends at the Golf Club tomorrow.

`But once Gaines and I were alone in his study, that's when I gave it to him. That's when I got my own back. "You know, Gaines," I said, smoking my cigar. "You *do* surprise me. You really do. Did you *honestly* think I would consider merging a respectable house like mine with one that published mass-market crap?"'

`James – you didn't!' Joanne sat up, eyes glaring.

`I did!' James heaved in silent laughter for a moment. `You should have seen his face, seen his eyes, mad as hell, mad as Caligula. Of course, he's a good actor. Managed to cover it up. Calm as calm can be.'

`But James – ' Joanne was in a state of panic. `What did he say? When you said what you said?'

`Well, as I said, he's a good actor, he covered it well, calm as calm, never even raised his voice, but I knew he was furious. I knew I had paid him back – '

`What did he *say?*'

`He said: "You've had your chance, Duncan. It won't come round again. And now the party's over. So I suggest you gather up your cigars and your wife and get the fuck out of my house."'

`Oh my God!' Joanne's hand was over her mouth.

`Oh, it's a true fact, Joannie, these upstarts are quite happy to sell crap, but they don't like it when you rub their faces in it.' Duncan chuckled. `Makes them curse!'

`But he has *money*, James,' Joanne argued, thinking desperately of her lunch-date and the Cartier watch she had set her heart on. `Absolutely *oooodles* of it! And you said yourself that you need all the money you can get just to keep Garland's afloat.'

James shot her an unfriendly look.

`I don't need it *that* badly. Not *Gaines's* money!' He stubbed out his cigar. `Do you think I'd seriously consider going into business with a man like Phil Gaines? Do you seriously believe after all my years as a Gentleman Publisher that I'd allow myself to end up in the sewer with the rats. With the very people who are destroying the respectable world of publishing!'

`But James, what about the bank?

`Come on, Joannie.' Duncan was tired of the subject. `Come on, Joannie, I've finished my cigar. And I'm in the mood ... a bad mood, so I need cheering up.' He turned and smiled at her, a long bilious leer, which turned her blood to ice.

`Come on, Joannie, let's play Master and Maid.'

An hour later, Joanne's backside was so sore from all the hard smacking the 'Master' had given her, she staggered into the bathroom and searched for her sleeping pills. She leaned against the sink and swallowed one with a sip of water.

Slowly she raised her head and looked at her reflection in the mirror above the sink. Her tears had streaked two sludges of mascara down her cheeks.

He'd better keep his promise and buy me the Cartier watch in return for this. He'd bloody well better!

TWENTY

London
May 1994

_____/

The morning looked anaemic, a hazy grey light filtering into the bedroom. Phil slowly opened his eyes and seconds later he realised that Rena was not in bed.

A flowery scent drifted out from her bathroom and the open doorway was steamy. No doubt, she had just taken a hot shower.

She came into the bedroom a few minutes later wrapped in a large white towel around her body and a smaller towel turbaned around her head. She caught his eye and smiled.

`You should be well rested,' said Phil. `You were asleep by nine o'clock last night.'

She removed the towel from her head and loosened her long pale hair. `I know, and I know it was rude of me to leave our guests so early, but I was so *tired* after my night shift at the hospital.'

`I don't know why you do it. You don't need to work.'

She sat on the bed and bent over to give him a toothpaste-flavoured kiss. `I *do* need to work.'

`Not night shifts. You never said anything to me about doing night shifts.'

`It was only a one-time.'

`A one-off.'

She looked puzzled. `Is that how you say it? One off? But it was the only once I have been on duty at night. So shouldn't it be a one-on?

He smiled and ran a finger down her cheek. `No more night shifts. Promise?'

`*Ja*, I promise.'

From the earliest days of their marriage, Rena had refused to be nothing more than be the idle wife of a rich man. She did not care, she had told Phil, how much money he had. She could not just sit around all day. What was she to do? Read magazines and arrange flowers?

Nursing – that's what she wanted to do. She was trained for nothing else, and it was what she loved best – nursing.

Nothing Phil could say would dissuade her.

Despite being married to a British citizen, she had endured weeks of red tape, but had finally been employed by a private hospital in central London. And from the first day she had loved it there. Her biggest surprise was the friendliness of the other nurses. None had the English stiff upper lip she had been warned about. All were welcoming and helpful, and within days she had felt accepted as one of the team.

So she was disinclined to refuse when the hospital had telephoned her on Friday evening to ask if she could cover for a nurse who was away sick.

She bent and gave Phil another toothpaste-flavoured kiss, holding the top of the towel over her breasts with one hand. `Do you want me to cook breakfast now?'

`No,' he sighed, `I don't want you to cook breakfast. I want to know what you've got on under that towel?'

She smiled. `What do you think?'

He breathed deeply but said nothing. They had not made love for two nights running and for them that was an age.

`I've missed you,' she said softly.

He tugged at the towel and it opened under his hands. He slowly skimmed her breasts with his palms. She leaned forward and kissed his lips, her tongue darting into his mouth in quick tantalising movements of erotic enticement. He groaned and grabbed her, and seconds later she was sliding into the warm bed beside him. From then on it was all sensation and ecstasy.

Later, she looked down at her naked body, shiny with sweat. `I need another shower.'

`So do I. Nice and cool.'

`Then breakfast,' she decided. She was an excellent cook and she asked him, `How would you like some crêpes with bacon and cheese, and some delicious Swedish roasted coffee?'

`Sounds perfect,' he said. `Just like you.'

`I am not perfect.'

`Maybe not in your eyes.' He sighed. `But to me, Rena, you're the eighth wonder of the world.'

TWENTY-ONE

London
May 1994

_____/

On Monday, Phil's lunch appointment was at the Grosvenor House Hotel on Park Lane.

As soon as he entered the Red Room bar, he saw Joseph Irving sitting alone at a table reading a newspaper. Whenever he and Irving met here at the Grosvenor, they usually had a drink in the bar before going in to lunch.

As he approached, Joseph Irving looked up from his newspaper and smiled.

`Ah, Phil, on time as usual. So, how are you, dear boy?'

`Fine, Joseph. And you?'

`Oh, tip-top as always. Now, I'm going to start with my usual straight malt,' Irving said, beckoning to a waiter. `What about you?'

`Club soda, nothing else.'

Irving gave the order to the waiter, then sat back and looked at Phil with a shrewd expression in his eyes.

`I think I know why you wanted this meeting today. You are becoming somewhat irritated by the tedious photographs we continue to send you.'

`That's right,' Phil agreed. `Every delivery is just more of the same. Waiters, gym instructors, more waiters. The photographs all say the one thing – the lady obviously likes her playmates young, the younger the better.'

`Indeed.' Irving's tone was as dismissive as

flicking dust off his sleeve. `She is clearly nothing but a cheap tart in expensive clothes.'

The waiter arrived with the drinks. Irving sipped his malt and regarded Phil intently. `I take it that the lady and her sordid little sexual dalliances are of no further interest to you?'

`No. Forget her. Now I want you to concentrate solely on the man himself, James Duncan.'

Irving sighed deeply. Phil's hatred of James Duncan had not abated over the years, but then Irving had not expected it to abate. And as the years had passed Irving knew that Phil had never once lost sight of his hated enemy, slowly and quietly pursuing him, nibbling and biting at the edges, irritating and annoying him, waiting for the day when he could finally make his real attack.

He asked curiously, `What exactly do you mean, Phil, when you say, "concentrate solely on the man himself"?'

`I want you to put someone back inside Garland Press,' Phil said. `I want Duncan put under twenty-four hour surveillance. Night as well as day. I want you to dig up everything you can on his two sisters, his present relationship with both of them. I want to know everything there is to know about James Duncan himself, every detail, no matter how small, how trivial, I want your people to find it out for me.'

Joseph Irving said thoughtfully, `The two sisters, yes, we know very little about them, so perhaps we can help you. But James Duncan...' Irving leaned closer, `Phil, there is very little that you *don't* know about him now. So what else are you looking for?'

Phil frowned. `I don't know, Joseph, I don't know ... I just feel there has got to be *something —*

'

He hesitated, not sure how to explain it. `It's his eyes, Joseph, there's something about Duncan's grey eyes ... up close, looking at his eyes, there's something not right, something about the man that's not, well – not *right*.'

Joseph Irving merely waited.

`I feel certain,' Phil continued, `that if we watch him close enough, and for long enough, we'll turn up something. Everyone's got something to hide, and a man like Duncan is so basically selfish, so innately *unpleasant*, the way he treats his staff, his authors, his wife ... I'm sure there must be something lurking in the shadows that I'll be able to use against him.'

Irving agreed simply. `We'll see what we can find.'

TWENTY-TWO

London
June 1994

_____/

Phil slowly manoeuvred his Mercedes through the evening traffic in St John's Wood, heading up towards Swiss Cottage, the music of Queen's *'Bohemian Rhapsody'* thumping through the back speakers.

Since his meeting at the Grosvenor with Joseph Irving three weeks ago, the reports on James Duncan had been sent to him at regular weekly intervals, always in a plain manila envelope, marked `Private and Confidential,' and always delivered by hand through his home letter box.

Much of what the reports told him, he already knew – Garland Press was doing so badly that if James Duncan did not find some good writers soon, he would have to find some very good accountants.

He smiled grimly as he cleared the lights at Swiss Cottage and accelerated up the long hill of Fitzjohn's Avenue towards Hampstead.

*

James Duncan seemed impatient and preoccupied as he ate his dinner that evening.

He placed a forkful of fish inside his mouth, muttered a few astonished words to himself, `... *adapt to circumstances ... Helen and Felicity ...!'*

213

and swallowed the fish with an expression of acute irritation.

Joanne laid down her fork. `James, are you listening to me? Have you heard even one word I have said?'

Duncan's eyes darted up from his food to Joanne's face. `What? *What?*'

`Oh, really, this is all becoming very tedious, James. What on earth is wrong with you tonight?'

He scowled at her. `Nothing that a bit of silence from you wouldn't cure!'

`Darling, that is *ssso* nasty! And doubly nasty because I have done and said absolutely *nothing* to upset you.'

`How dare you say that? When you do *nothing* but upset me! You and Helen and Felicity! A bunch of greedy cows bent on destroying me!'

Joanne's hand drooped towards her wine glass. There was really no point in arguing with James when he was like this. At times like this, she had long ago learned, it was simply best to butter him up until he was back in a good mood.

`Well, yes, Helen is very tiresome,' she agreed. `All those aggressive telephone calls – I do believe that if she telephoned the Speaking Clock she would disagree and argue with it. And as for Felicity, well, I can hardly believe that such a *timid* creature is truly your sister, James. All that cringing cowardice whenever Helen lays down the law. But now, I wouldn't say poor Felicity is a greedy cow ... no, she is more, let me see ... more *porcine* ... a bit like that sweet old sow we saw last year at the farm in – '

`Joannie – shut up!'

Joanne glanced beneath the table as she slipped a slender foot back inside its shoe. `James dear,' she said patiently, `we really can't go through the entire evening having you feeling so unhappy, now can we?'

She stood up in her high heels and minced over to the drinks cabinet. `What you need is a nice scotch. A nice smooth malt. We'll have one together, shall we?' She lifted down two glasses and poured two shots of Glenmorangie.

She minced back and handed one to James. `Go on,' she said. `Ease up. Knock it back. It will calm you better than any heart pill.' She raised her glass. `Cheers!'

James looked from her face to the scotch in his hand. `Cheers,' he said, and emptied his glass in one gulp.

`I've already had two nifedipine tablets today,' he said miserably. `My angina seems to be getting worse.

`And understandably so,' Joanne soothed. `Lunching with Helen and Felicity – both at the same time – is enough to distress anyone's poor heart.' She tapped his glass. `Another?'

`James nodded. `Why not.'

She took his glass and turned on a swivel back to the cabinet. `I tell you what, why don't we just take the bottle and go and relax in the sitting-room and have a nice long talk.' She scooped up the bottle and swivelled again. `Come along, James, come with Joannie...'

James fixed his eyes on the neat roundness of her rear as she minced away, and found himself following her. His mind was agitated, his stomach was nervous, and his angina was getting worse. But no matter which way you looked at it – Joannie still had the cutest backside in Berkshire.

`After all, James,' said Joanne, when he was

seated comfortably in his favourite chair in the sitting-room, `I really *dooo* need to talk to you about money.' She pressed a fresh glass of scotch into his hand, at least four shots full.

`My dear, your husband is not rolling in money like the rat pack,' he said impatiently, reaching for a cigar. `Your husband, Joannie, has problems. Serious money problems.'

`But, *Jaymesee*,' she said, unfolding herself languidly onto the settee. `A little gold Cartier watch won't make much difference, will it? It's one of the cheapest in their range. An absolute snip at twelve hundred pounds.' She pouted perfectly. `And you did promise — '

`No, Joannie. I can't do it. And if you think I can, then you're a stupid bitch barking up the wrong tree!'

He stared at her. `Don't you realise how bad things are for me? For Garland's! Don't you realise that for almost a year now I've been forced – on occasion – to fund the firm with my own money! Joannie, the situation is becoming desperate! The bank is on my neck every week. But there, that's banks for you!'

He sucked viciously on his cigar. `I hate banks. I despise them. When you're doing well and the money's rolling in, the bastards are grovelling at your feet like coolies. But come the problems, come the shortage of cash flow, and the bastards are snapping at your neck like vampires.'

Joanne sipped her scotch and looked back at him sympathetically while wishing she could strangle such a miserable, mean specimen of a provider. What was twelve hundred pounds? Compared to the villa in Portugal that Emma Friedman's husband had just bought for her. Well,

Gretta Curran Browne

bought for them both, but still...

Joanne sat in stark jealousy and suddenly felt like being very nasty.

`But, James,' she cooed, `why don't you get some new authors? Some *exciting* authors for a change! Half the stuff you publish goes straight to the libraries and nowhere else. And when was the last time you did any decent advertising or promotion? No wonder all the good authors take their second books elsewhere.'

`What?' James stared at her, furious. `What do you know about the business of publishing? What do you know about anything?' He sat forward and stabbed the cigar in her direction. `All you know about the publishing business is the amount of money you've been able to scrounge from it all these years.'

Joanne realised she had worked him out of his bad mood into a temper, but she didn't care. She unfolded her legs gracefully, and reached for the whisky bottle. `I know more than you think I do, James. A lot more.' She nodded her head, and poured a good measure of scotch into her glass.

`That afternoon I went to the Romantic Novelists Association with Sylvia, I was in the ladies, in a cubicle, and I heard some of the authors talking around the sinks. "Oh for God's sake," one said, "whatever you do, *don't* send your book to Garland's. They'll pay you peanuts and your book won't get any further than the libraries.'

James attempted to laugh it off. `Listen, Joannie, surely you know by now that authors are the biggest load of whingers ever born.'

He puffed a cloud of smoke in her direction. `But as for that bunch of bitchy cows you overheard, I can tell you this – not one of them

217

would be *good* enough to be published by Garland's. Romantic novelists! Romantic rubbish!'

He took a slug of scotch, his eyes suddenly jumping with fiery malignancy. `No, if it's crap they want published, then they will have to go to Gaines.'

`Well, ye-es, that's *exactly* what those authors said – if you want a decent deal, why not go to one of the big conglomerates, or even one of the smaller but more modern independent's like Gaines.'

Livid, he stared at her. `You stupid cow!' He slapped his knee furiously. `Don't you realise that it's those big conglomerate whales and *sharks* like Phil Gaines that have me in the mess I'm in. They just go around, those greedy fishes, swallowing up all the stalwarts. But here's one die-hard that will *never* merge, and *never* sell!'

`Then don't sell,' Joanne sulked. `Do what you like. I don't care. All I know is that Phil Gaines offered to merge with you, and I thought that was a very nice, and very *friendly* thing to do.'

`Well *you* would, wouldn't you? But I'm no fool. I know his game. The only reason he wants to merge and take away my independence, is because he wants the respectability of Garland's name to add weight to his own. But afterwards I would be left exposed and scarred with my own failure.'

James sighed and wondered again at the monstrous injustice of it all. What had he done to deserve such bad luck? He sat back, stretched his feet out, and stared up at the ceiling with a sad-dog gaze.

`Even if I had married someone with a little intelligence,' he said with a sigh, `I would now have someone to give me comfort and support in my hour of need. Instead of that I married you, Joannie. You, of all people. If I'd known how it was all going to turn out, I would have thrown myself in the Thames the day before I met you.'

`Ha-bloody-ha.'

`It's the truth, my dear. I should have married for money or brains. Only a fool would marry for shapely legs and a nicely rounded bottom.'

`Oh, stop pitying yourself. You were madly in love with me then, and you still are now.'

`I don't think I am, Joannie. I don't think I ever was. The fantasy is always much better than the reality. As most married men discover.'

`Most married women too.'

James's chin sank onto his chest. `Why do I have to get older year by year? Life was so much better in the old days. Even *you* were much better in the old days.'

`You sound like a dinosaur, James. Come to think of it, you probably *are* a Dinosaur. That's why you like eating fish so much.'

`You were my dream girl in those days, Joannie. The prop for all my sexual fantasies. I used to dream about you every night. In those days, Joannie, my life was one long lustful fantasy – but then you gave me plenty of provocation, didn't you?'

He sighed again. `Now you provoke me so much I often dream about throttling you dead and stuffing you under the floorboards.'

`Oh, enough of this marital bickering.' Joanne shrugged irritably. `And you're not so perfect either, James. There was a time when you used to be fun. But now all you do is moan, moan, moan. And *always* about money. And you hate everyone. You despise everyone. These days you're always so hot with rage against someone, I often wonder why you don't just blow up. Explode like a bomb. What do they call it – internal combustion? It happens quite frequently apparently. One minute the person is just sitting there having a cup of tea, and the next minute they explode into pieces. An arm here, a leg there, bits of body all over the place.'

`Joannie – shut up!'

It was too much for James. All he had to suffer. Not only from his wife, but also from his two sisters. He put his glass down with a thump, stood up in fury, and levelled a vicious scowl at his reflection in the mirror above the fireplace.

`Helen and Felicity want me to sell,' he said darkly. `The witches actually want me to sell! Told me out straight. They want me to take the money and run. Or as Helen put it, sell – but make them give you a seat on the board.'

As James launched into a word-by-word recitation of the lunch meeting with his two sisters, Joanne lifted her legs and reclined back languorously on the sofa, her head resting on the sofa-arm, a hand draped above her expensively bleached hair. All this talk of publishing had made her feel bored, utterly bored with the subject. Not that it was a very exciting subject at the best of times.

`Yes,' said James, `that was the biggest mistake my father made, giving those two witches equal shares in the firm. And Felicity parrots everything Helen says. If Helen says "Frog" Felicity jumps. If Helen has a cold, Felicity sneezes. And Helen wants me to sell.'

James took a slug of his scotch and grimaced. `But, just like you, Joannie, Helen doesn't seem to realise there is more to a man's life than money.

There is his life's achievement to consider. His self-respect. His standing in the community. His reputation amongst his peers ... Oh, I hate Helen, I despise her – '

Joanne stretched out fully on the sofa and gazed wistfully at the ceiling. It was *such* a long time since she had had any decent *amour*. Well, not since that young Spanish waiter more than a month ago – such an attractive young darling, so adorably *sweet*, but a mere boy ... Oh, how she longed for a *real* love-affair, full of warmth and passion, but most of all ... lots of *tenderness*.

James had turned and was staring at her. She smiled dreamily at him, not seeing him at all.

James stood looking at her with eyes that were narrowed. He knew that look – Joannie was in the mood. And, by God, so was he!

`Well, Joannie,' he said, consulting his watch. `It's nine o'clock. A bit early I know, but how about it?'

`What?' She snapped out of her dreams and frowned at him quizzically. `How about what?'

`Hitting the stairs and heading up for a roll on the old mattress.'

He shrugged. `You're right, enough of this marital bickering. And let's forget all about business. I'm sick to death of it. Come on, Joannie, let's forget about everything and play.'

`What?' Her eyes focused on him, and instantly she knew what he had in mind.

`Would you like to give me a nice hot bath with soapy hands?' he asked. `Or shall I tie you up? Yes, let's play the game where I tie you up and you plead for mercy?"

Oh no! She couldn't bear to even think of it – let alone endure it. Not tonight. She was not feeling at all robust or up to persevering with the old bully tonight.

`No, James,' she said, scrambling off the sofa and grabbing her handbag from the coffee table, snatching out a bottle of sleeping pills. `Not tonight.'

Then remembering that James was, after all, her bread and butter and credit cards and, hopefully, her new Cartier watch, she attempted to cajole him.

`*Jaymesee*, you know I think you're absolutely wonderful and I hardly know how I can resist you —' She tumbled a few pills onto her palm, `but I really feel so *queasy* after that fish, I think I'll just take one or two of my little sleeping pills and have a nice warm bath.' She popped a pill into her mouth and gulped at her scotch.

`Come on, Joannie, do your duty. Play your part. Be a good girl. Or I'll have to put you over my knee and smack your bottom.'

`No-no-no!' she almost screamed, frantically popping another pill into her mouth and gulping down more scotch.

`As much as I'd love to, James, it's really not possible.' She patted her stomach and looked at him apologetically. `I really do feel a bit sick.'

He looked at her suspiciously, sure she was lying, but what could he do?

`Well, this has been one hell of a hairy day!' he said furiously. `First those two witches of sisters. And now you.'

He lifted the bottle, poured himself another measure of scotch, and walked out of the room muttering to himself. `May as well go to bed anyway.'

As soon as he entered the bedroom, his eyes

went straight to his bedside cabinet and he let out a furious groan.

`I've no cigars!' he shouted as he came back down the stairs. `Not one upstairs and none left down here. Now how the hell am I going to unwind before sleep without a cigar!'

`Look in the study,' Joanne suggested.

`There's none in the study,' he announced two minutes later, standing in the doorway and staring at Joanne with such naked malevolence that she unconsciously took a step back from him.

She knew that look in his eyes, and feared it.

`Not one bloody cigar in the whole house!' he hissed. `Did you forget to buy some *again!* You lazy bitch! Just what the hell do you *do* all day?'

`D-darling,' she stuttered nervously, `let me see if there are any in the kitchen.' But his eyes blazed at her with such contempt, such malice, she took another step back, as if fearing a physical blow.

And she was right to fear him, because he wanted to grab her and slap her violently, leave her black and blue for a week. He had done it before, and she was asking for it again. He suddenly understood why husbands committed murder. Why the clever found life impossible with the stupid. His rage – how could he restrain it? Or release it?

`J-James,' she whispered meekly, shrinking under the gleam of violence in his eyes, `I really do feel unwell ...'

He stood for a moment glaring at her.

`Bitch!' he hissed, then abruptly turned and left the room.

Hundreds of rapid heartbeats later, Joanne heard the front door slam and the car engine starting up. She gave a huge sigh of relief, knowing where he had gone – driving off to the late-night supermarket or pub to get some cigars.

But now she must act fast if she wanted a peaceful night. So a quick bath, and with two sleeping pills inside her, she would be in bed and zonked unconscious by the time he got back.

Still incensed, still feeling like a bear in a trap, he came out of the supermarket having bought his cigars. He unwrapped one and lit up immediately, standing in the glow of the store window.

He sucked deeply on the smoke, and slowly exhaled. Dismally he looked at his watch: nine-thirty. He didn't feel like going back to bed and sleep. He felt like committing murder.

He gazed around him and mentally pleaded his case to an imaginary judge ... I was driven to it, Your Lordship. My patience and indulgence, which had lasted for twenty years, finally ran out. The woman conned me with endless glasses of scotch and flattery. She purred and pecked and kissed me and told me she wanted to be my slave. And I, Your Lordship, infantile in my love for her, believed her and married her. Then she turned into a mad vain bitch with a brain in her head that only a slug would envy.

But all that – all that I could have coped with, Your Lordship, if it wasn't for her constant craving for money. Every week something else, something new. I should have known the first time she invited me to lunch at Claridges – then left me to pay the bill. Oh no, Your Lordship, divorce was out of the question because I couldn't *afford* it! The money-mad bitch would have stripped me clean, tried to get everything her lawyers could grab for her! That's the only reason I stuck with her so long,

Your Lordship, because I couldn't afford to dump her.

He walked slowly back to his car, sat behind the wheel for some minutes, smoking his cigar, thoughtful. What was he to do now? He didn't want to go back, didn't want to go home, didn't want to be driven to murder. But there was still rage in his brain and he needed to release it.

An idea occurred him. He played it around his mind for a while. Then he smiled nastily and started up the engine.

As James Duncan drove away, another car which had been parked a few yards behind, driven by one of Joseph Irving's operatives, followed him.

TWENTY-THREE

New York & London
July 1994

_____/

Phil held one of Marc's diaries in his hands.

`Can't think how I forgot them for so long,' Jimmy said quietly. `I guess I must've just wanted to forget. Pretend they didn't exist. Moseying through life deluding myself that Marc didn't end up dead. That he was still alive somewhere.' Jimmy turned away, distressed. `Hell, son, I honestly didn't *mean* to keep these books from you!'

`I know you didn't, Jimmy, I know.'

And Phil did know. He had talked to enough Vietnam Veterans to know that many found release and peace in amnesia, convincing themselves that what happened to their friends was only nightmare, not memory ... GI Joe, that great guy, naw, he didn't fry in a VC firebomb ... No, he was back home somewhere in America...

A psychological symptom of combat trauma. So many wanted to forget the past, not remember it.

`I'm grateful to you, Jimmy,' Phil said, `for keeping them safe for so long. It's the best thing you could have done for me.'

Jimmy turned and looked at him. `Are you going to turn Marc's diaries into a book?'

Phil shook his head. `No. They're all I have left of him. And they're mine. Mine alone.'

Jimmy smiled, pleased. `You're just going to keep them safe. Same as I did.'

`I'm going to treasure them, Jimmy. A private

family legacy to pass on to my own children.
Someday.'

Three weeks after returning from America, Phil
was back at Heathrow Airport again. This time to
see Rena off on a flight to Sweden.

It was her paternal grandmother's seventieth
birthday, and the whole family were going down to
her home in Malmö to celebrate it with her.

`I wish you were coming with me,' Rena said.

`So do I,' Phil lied.

He had already met Rena's grandmother in
Malmö, and was convinced the woman was mad.
Like most Scandinavians she was bilingual and
spoke good English, but whenever she got Phil
alone, all she spoke to him about was Nordic myths
and legends and the powers of the supernatural,
always beginning with the words, `*Many full
moons ago...*'

It was for that same reason that Rena cherished
her paternal grandmother. As a child she had loved
spending summers with her in Malmö, loved
smelling the lilac hedge around her house, and the
Swedishly-clean rooms that always had the tangy
perfume of dried herbs.

And unlike her parents, who were not physically
demonstrative about their affections, Rena's
grandmother was very loving, allowing the child to
climb into her wooden bed at night, telling her
wonderful stories about the angels, and the
occasional flight of the soul during sleep, and the
power of dreams and wishes, always beginning
with the words, `*Many full moons ago...*'

Rena adored her, and was excitedly looking
forward to seeing her again.

`Do you think she will like my present?' Phil

asked.

Rena smiled. `She will love it.'

Phil had bought the present at Cartier. In miniature – an exquisitely-made gold angel with sapphires for eyes and outstretched wings poised for flight. On the same day he had bought Rena a similar miniature, but hers was of a mermaid.

They were calling her plane for the last time. At the departure gate Phil hugged her so hard it took her breath away. Then he gave her a last quick kiss and she went to catch her plane, waving to him over her shoulder, then turning again and calling back:

`*Jag älskar dig*!'

He nodded and smiled and watched her until she had disappeared from view.

The sun was dazzling as Phil drove out of the car park at Heathrow. He opened the glove compartment, took out a pair of sunglasses and slipped them on. Ten minutes later he received a call on his car phone. He put the phone on speaker and concentrated on the road. `Hello?'

`Phil, dear boy, I've been trying to reach you for hours.' The voice belonged to Joseph Irving.

Phil instantly became alert. He flicked a glance to the overhead mirror, then signalled a move from the fast to the middle lane.

`Yes, Joseph, what is it?'

`Something I thought you might like to know as soon as possible. About the subject under surveillance. We have at last come up with something.'

`Something good?'

`Something bad.'

Phil smiled grimly as he moved into the slow

lane. He had *known* there would be something.

`So tell me about it.'

`No, dear boy. Not on the telephone.'

`When?'

`It has to be tonight. My time is fully booked for a week otherwise. Are you free tonight?'

`Very free. My wife's just gone away for a week.'

`Then I'll see you tonight in the Grosvenor at seven.' Irving slammed down the phone with his usual abruptness.

Phil smiled. For an ex CID cop like Irving, some habits were hard to break.

TWENTY-FOUR

London
July 1994

_____/

Joseph Irving took his first sip of malt.

`So,' Phil asked, eager to get to the point, `what's this something you've turned up on Duncan?

`Sad, really sad. Incidentally, I was very surprised to learn that our man suffers from angina, and has a regular prescription of nifedipine as well as a nitrolingual spray.

`So? Why so surprised?'

`Because, dear boy, if he is suffering from angina, the silly man should not smoke cigars. What is the point of his doctor providing him with relief if he continues to agitate his condition by puffing Havanas?'

Joseph Irving sat back and frowned, as if such foolishness really annoyed him. `Angina is not a condition to treat lightly. And I should know. My wife suffered from angina for years before she died.'

`I'm sorry,' Phil said.

`No need to be.' Irving shrugged. `It was a long time ago. Her heart had never been good. But obviously our man's condition is nothing as serious. Still, he should be more careful and give up those damned cigars.'

`Okay, so the reports say Duncan has angina. But what's this "something" you've turned up?'

`He's a cruiser,' Irving said tersely.

`A what?'

`A kerb crawler.'

Phil was speechless. He had come up with at least five possible things that Irving's investigators could have turned up on Duncan. But *this* he had not expected.

`You mean — '

Irving nodded, a faint grimace of disgust on his face, as if all this was quite beneath him. He took a pair of spectacles from his breast pocket, put them on, and then removed a folded paper from an inner pocket, unfolded it, and sat for a moment surveying it sternly through his glasses.

`Three weeks ago, on the night of Tuesday the fourteenth of June, at exactly 9.20 p.m., the subject left his house and drove to a nearby supermarket where he bought a packet of cigars. He unwrapped and lit one immediately, and sat for approximately four minutes in his car smoking the cigar. After which, still smoking, he drove off.

`But instead of returning home, he headed towards the M4 motorway. Then drove non-stop to London at a recklessly dangerous speed of 96 miles an hour. When he reached London, he then drove to the red-light area of King's Cross. It was there he kerb-crawled and solicited a prostitute from the window of his car. A quick pick-up. A quick drive to a nearby railway goods yard. Then the subject drove back and dropped the prostitute off near to where he had found her. She appeared to have blood on her face, but my operative could not be certain. After which, the subject drove straight home.'

Irving looked up. `Kerb-crawling is against the law.'

Phil stared back at him, puzzled. `But what

made Duncan do it?'

`Oh, it's not the first time. After the incident we did a check through police records and discovered that, three years ago, in the area of Paddington, he was caught in the act of soliciting a female from a motor vehicle for the purposes of prostitution. He was taken to Paddington Green Police Station where he was cautioned, advised, and let off with a warning. Usual procedure for first offences of this nature. But his name still goes in the records. It may not have been his first offence, of course, but the first and only time he's been caught.'

Phil was still thinking, still slightly shocked.

`Being cautioned by the police usually frightens them off for life,' said Irving. `Our man, however, has obviously forgotten the fear as well as the warning. At any rate, he obviously decided it was worth the risk.'

`Do you think he will do it again?'

Irving looked down at his report.

`Six days later, on the night of Monday the twentieth of June, the subject made another trip to King's Cross. Then again on Wednesday the twenty-ninth. On this third occasion, my operative got a clear look at the prostitute when she was dropped off – a young girl of no more than sixteen. Her face was very badly bruised and she was holding a bloodstained handkerchief to her nose. The subject drove off at speed.'

`My God ... the bastard ... going out to beat up young girls.' Phil was feeling sick in his stomach.

`It's a risk all prostitutes take.'

`Yes – but a kid of no more than sixteen! I'm sure she didn't *agree* to get beaten up.'

`I suspect,' said Irving, `that our man is suffering severe stress in his business and personal life.'

`And that's not all he's going to suffer,' Phil said. `If he does it again I want photographs. Large twelve-by-tens of the prostitute bending down to his car. Then another shot of her getting into his car.'

He looked steadfastly at Irving. `That's what I want, Joseph. And I am prepared to pay whatever is necessary to get them. Photographs. And once I've got them, that will be the end of Duncan's whoring.'

`We already have photographs,' Irving replied, without a change of tone or expression. He looked down at the report in his hand.

`The young detective who supplied this report is an ex-police operative who never fails to do a perfect job. As soon as the subject first approached that particular area of King's Cross, he knew what was on. As it was dark he used high-speed film, 1600 ASA, and secured clear shots on each occasion of the subject soliciting the prostitute from the window of his car, the prostitute entering the car, and numerous other shots until the prostitute was finally dropped off. But, most importantly, in every shot, the car's registration number is clearly visible.'

`How soon can you get the photographs to me?'

`Within the next twenty-four hours. Delivered by hand, of course.'

Phil nodded. `This is it, Joseph. This is what I've been waiting years for. My time with James Duncan has finally come – time to make the payback.'

TWENTY-FIVE

London
July 1994

_____/

At two minutes before six, on the following Thursday evening, one of the telephones on James Duncan's desk began to ring.

Duncan ignored it at first, rubbing his temples with both hands and mumbling to himself as he studied the firm's accounts. Last year had been a disaster. This year looked as if it was going to be even worse.

He urgently reached for his nitrolingual spray and took the cap off and gave himself two shots under the tongue. Instant relief.

The telephone kept on ringing. Duncan glanced at it irritably, then saw it was his private line. It must be Joannie, wanting to know what time he was leaving – wanting to know if he intended to ruin her casserole *again.*

He grabbed the phone and opened his mouth to bark.

`Duncan?'

James Duncan sat speechless. He knew that voice. He had only spoken to Phil Gaines on the phone once before, but he knew that voice –

`What do you want, Gaines?'

`I think it's time we had a business consultation.'

`A *business* consultation?' Duncan sat forward on his seat. `Listen, Gaines, I've got no business with you, so there's nothing to consult about.' He slammed down the phone.

The silence seemed to blast the room.

Duncan sat staring at the phone, furious. Gaines! The sheer *nerve* of that man took some believing. A business consultation! So Gaines was still after a merger, was he? Well, he could wait till Hell froze.

His attention swerved back to the accounts on his desk, looking at them with glittering eyes. Gaines – the man with the money! As fast as he was losing it, Gaines was making it. How did the bastard do it? Of course, Gaines had stacks of money to begin with, and that was always a help.

The telephone rang, his private line again.

Duncan consulted his watch, and sprang forward. This time it was definitely Joannie ringing for a rant. Best to just mollify her.

`Hello?' he said smoothly.

`Duncan?'

`No! Listen, Gaines, I know what you're after, but you're not going to get it! Not now or ever! No merger!'

`I'm not after a merger, Duncan ... Not now or ever.'

Duncan blinked, then his lips curled suspiciously. `Then why ask for a *business* consultation? I've only got one business. *Respectable* publishing.'

`I've got some valuable information for you, Duncan. Something you should know as soon as possible. Someone's trying to cripple you. Someone's trying to close down that respectable little firm you're so proud of ... I just thought you should know.'

`Close me down?' Duncan searched for his nitrolingual spray. `Why should I believe you,

235

Gaines?'

`Because I'm telling you the truth. A lot of dirty business has been going on behind your back. And as one independent publisher to another, I think it's only fair that you should be told about it.'

`So tell me about it.'

`Not on the phone. Listen, Duncan, I'm being straight with you here. Personally I don't like you at all. I never have. You know that. But this business that's been going on – well, it's just too *dirty* to believe. And I think it should be stopped as soon as possible.'

`Gaines, listen, if what you say is true – if one of those conglomerate whales has been trying to nobble me – this is very serious.'

`It is, yes. The problem is ... you've made it very clear that you won't sell to anyone, haven't you? And the piranhas don't like that. They don't like the small fish clogging up their waters. If they can't buy you out, they'll chase you out. And when you've got nowhere else to go, they'll snap you up cheap.'

Duncan jerked upright in alarm. `Who?' he demanded. `Listen, Gaines, just tell me who?'

`Not on the phone.'

`Where then?'

`Well, let's see ... Can you come to Hampstead tonight?'

Duncan hesitated, the suspicious look back on his face. `But why you, Gaines? Why should you want to warn me – unless it *is* a merger you're after. Is that it? Is this some kind of scheming ploy to get what you want? You and me standing together against the congloms?'

`You can go to hell, Duncan. I don't really care what you do. I've done my best to warn you, but

I'm already tired of this conversation. My wife just happens to like your wife and that's the *only* reason I've agreed to warn you. But now my good deed is done for the year. My boy scout's badge is honoured. I'm hanging up now, Duncan.'

`No, wait, *wait!* Listen, Gaines, tell me – do you have an documental evidence to prove what you're saying?'

`Yes ... copies of letters ... with the name of the publisher who has already contacted your two sisters and secured their *willing* agreement to each sell their third share in the firm ... even if *you* cannot be persuaded to sell yours.'

`The dirty underhanded witches!'

`If you want to know more, Duncan. If you want to see the evidence, then be at my house at eight o'clock tonight. If you haven't shown by then, I'll be out.'

`Yes ... all right, eight o'clock, I'll be there.'

Five minutes later the telephone rang in David Gallagher's flat.

David could hear it ringing as he turned the key in the door. He rushed to answer it.

`Hello.'

`David?'

`No, this is Prince Charles.' David grinned. `Who else would it be, Phil? You know I live alone.'

`So what are you doing tonight?'

`Nothing.'

`Then will you do me a favour, David?'

`Depends on what it is.'

`I had a call from Rena, on my answering machine. She's not supposed to be coming back from Sweden until Saturday afternoon, but she's decided to surprise me and booked herself on a plane this evening. Could you go to Heathrow to meet her for me?'

`Okay.'

`I wouldn't ask you, David, you know I wouldn't. But Rena's call has put me in a tight corner and some business I planned to do tomorrow night has had to be brought forward to tonight.'

David shrugged. `That's all right, I'll go. What time is her plane due?'

`Nine o'clock. Scandinavian Airlines. Terminal 3.'

`I'll be there.'

`Thanks, David. You're a terrific friend ... and I mean that.'

TWENTY-SIX

London
July 1994

_____/

At ten minutes to eight, the doorbell rang.

`We'll have to make it brief,' Duncan said, his voice rough with agitation as Phil let him in. `I'm almost out of my mind wondering who they are. Which publisher? Names, that's what I want. *Names*. Christ, you can't trust anyone these days.'

`Come and sit down,' Phil said with solicitude, leading the way into the study. `Then I'll tell you all about it.'

As soon as he entered the study Duncan's eyes were immediately drawn to the drinks cabinet in the corner. `Can I have a drink? I need one.'

`A drink?' Phil's eyes were less friendly than his voice as he indicated a chair by the desk. `What drink would you like?'

`Scotch. I shouldn't really drink when I'm driving. But as it's just the one – make it a large one.'

Phil poured a scotch, not too large, and handed it to Duncan.

Duncan nodded gratefully, took a slug, smacked his lips. `I needed that! Listen, Gaines, I can't tell you what this means to me – and I've been thinking – and you're right! We independent publishers should watch out for each other. No mergers, mind, but no point falling out.' He reached into his inner pocket. `Can I smoke a cigar?'

`Certainly.' Phil found him an ashtray.

Duncan lit up and puffed a cloud of smoke. `Now, let's get down to business. Show me this evidence.'

`Very well.'

Phil remained standing as he opened a drawer in the desk and lifted out some large manila envelopes. From the first he removed a number of photographs of Joanne, in the company of various young men, and laid them one by one on the desk.

`Your wife, I believe.'

Duncan stared in puzzlement at the photographs, from one to the other. Then he slowly looked up at Phil in realisation.

`It was all a trick ... just to get me here. And the publisher – the one doing all the dirty business behind my back – it's you, Gaines, it's bloody *you!*'

Phil smiled. `As Muhammad Ali used to say – you ain't as dumb as you look.'

`You would go this far? For a merger?'

Duncan stared again at the pictures of Joanne. Then with a sudden lunge grabbed them into his hands and ripped them to pieces, flung the pieces across the desk, and jumped to his feet.

`There, Gaines. That's what I think of your dirty blackmail – *nothing!* Not shocked. And *not* impressed.'

He turned and stormed out of the room.

But out of the house he could not get. The front door was locked.

Puzzled, he turned the handle and pulled and pulled.

Then he realised it was Chub-locked. And Gaines had the key. He had been so distracted on arrival, he had not even noticed Gaines locking the door behind him. He felt even more distracted now.

He turned and stared towards the open door of the study as if suddenly sensing something direful. He was locked in.

He swallowed. Felt pain. He needed his nitrolingual spray. Needed a nifedipine tablet. But they were in the car. Outside. And he was locked in.

Slowly, he walked back into the study. Phil was still standing behind the desk, very calm, waiting.

James Duncan regarded him with a wary look of fear. `This is not just about business, is it Gaines? This is madness. What is it you want?'

`I want to show you these.' From a second envelope Phil removed another set of photographs and laid them one by one on the desk.

`Come and take a closer look, Duncan. They're good shots. Very clear. Especially of you.'

Duncan walked unsteadily towards the pictures. He stared, and stared, from one to the other.

`Oh my God! Oh my God—'

`Now this particular girl,' Phil tapped a photograph, `is what the police refer to as "a known common prostitute." Known, that is, to the police. In fact they all are. All of these girls have convictions for street soliciting.'

Phil looked at James Duncan. `Not very fair, is it? The man is allowed off with a warning while the girl is convicted. I mean, you *did* receive a warning, didn't you, Duncan? A few years ago? Before you went on this latest binge.'

Duncan was speechless, all his aggression gone. His face was like ceiling plaster. He reached for the glass of whisky on the desk, emptied the glass in a gulp, his voice coming out in a hiss.

`How did you get these? How did you get them?'

Phil shrugged, as if the answer was obvious.

`Money. Private Investigators. All ex-police. I bought the best.'

`You – ' Duncan shook his head in disbelief. `You vicious bastard.'

`Me? A vicious bastard?' Phil's tone was neutral. `I don't spend my nights beating up young prostitutes.'

`What is it you want, Gaines? A merger?'

`A merger?' Phil smiled contemptuously. `I had no intention of merging with you, Duncan. I intended to take you over, lock and stock, and then kick you out with the rest of the garbage. And I still intend to do that. But first, there's a lot of damage to be done with these photographs, isn't there?'

Duncan's eyes enlarged on the photographs. He flopped onto the chair he had vacated earlier, his face convulsed.

`You handed me the knife, Duncan.' Phil picked up a photograph. `This is *your* dirty work – not mine. If you hadn't gone whoring these pictures could not have been taken. If you had not set yourself up on a pedestal as Mr *Gentleman* Publisher, these pictures could not do the damage they inevitably will. You handed me a knife of your own making, Duncan. And now I'm going to use it to make you bleed.'

`What –' Duncan looked as if he was in some kind of unfathomable nightmare. `*What-is-it-you-want?* How can I even consider your blackmail, when you won't tell me what you want!'

`Blackmail?' Phil looked affronted. `This is not blackmail, Duncan. These photographs are not up for discussion or subject to negotiation. These photographs are going to be used. Have no illusions about that. Because first thing tomorrow morning, copies of these photographs – all

242

showing your car and registration number – are going to be delivered by courier to the Vice Squad at Paddington Green Police Station.'

Duncan was staring at Phil in a way he had never stared at anyone before, horrified and disbelieving.

`And also, first thing tomorrow morning,' Phil continued, `copies of these photographs are going to be delivered by courier to all your business associates. And to the wives of all your friends in Berkshire. Especially to the *wives* of all your fine old buddies at the Golf Club —' He smiled a little. `And so by tomorrow night, Duncan, you are going to be nothing more than a big buzz of bad news.'

James Duncan could not move, could not speak.

`You see, Duncan, what I actually *want*, is this. I want to see you ruined. Publicly humiliated. Drowned in your own degradation. I want people to see you for the bastard that you are. The fake that you are. The whore-fucker that you are. Oh, make no mistake, Duncan, this is *vengeance* I'm wreaking, and I've been a long time waiting.'

James Duncan looked as if he was impaled to the seat, his gaze fixed in rigid horror on his tormentor's dark eyes.

`Why?' he asked in terrified bewilderment. `What do you have against me? You hated me that first time I met you. You refused to shake my hand. I didn't even know you. You were a stranger! Why? For Christ's sake – *why?*'

`You brutally killed my mother.'

`Your mother?' Duncan looked even more bewildered. `I've never even met your mother! So how could I kill her?'

He stood up. `Listen, Gaines – all I know is that I'm locked in a house with a mad man. You've obviously mistaken me for somebody else. I've no idea what you're talking about. And I have a *heart* condition. I need one of my nifedipine tablets. I'm supposed to take two a day. But they're outside in my car.'

`I don't give a damn about your tablets! I don't care if you drop dead at my feet!' Phil's fist smashed down on the desk. `*Sit down!'*

Duncan was not even aware that he had stood up. He sat back down, faint with panic as his eyes fell once more on the photographs of the prostitutes. He reached out to touch one and saw that his hands were trembling violently. He had no doubt that Gaines intended to use the photographs, but if he did, it would be the end of him, the end of everything. Even the Golf Club would be barred to him.

`You still don't remember her, do you? Fourteen years is a long time, Duncan. But there are some things that some people *never* forget.'

`Fourteen years ... ' Duncan said slowly. `That was ... 1980...' And finally he realised what Gaines was talking about. `The woman ...'

`The woman,' Phil echoed. `In court, they described her as a waitress. But she was much more than that. Shall I tell you something more about her, Duncan?'

Duncan swallowed.

`She was lovely and caring and one of the hardest working women in the world. She looked in her mid-twenties but was actually thirty-five. It was late and it was dark and she was on her way home after completing a four-to-eleven shift at the restaurant. She was feeling happy, because the night before she had finished the final pages of her first book. She was delighted with herself. She had finally done it. And now, for the first time in her life, something might work out for her. Something to look forward to. Something good and something to come.

`But as eager as she must have been to get home, she waited at the crossing for the traffic lights to turn red. But her waiting didn't save her, did it? Not from the drunken maniac who came speeding through the red lights and broke nearly every bone in her body.'

The room was deathly quiet. Duncan tried to speak, tried to swallow again, but there was no spit in his mouth.

`You were stinking drunk, and you killed her. But due to the perversity of the law you could not be charged with murder or even manslaughter – you could only be charged under the Road Traffic Act with being above the alcohol limit while in control of a motor vehicle. Your sentence nothing more than a three-year driving ban and a fine of £150. Is that justice? And is that why you forgot it so easily? Because you got off so lightly?'

`It was an accident,' Duncan insisted feebly. `An unfortunate accident.'

`It was a bloody *crime!* You were stinking drunk and driving like a maniac at eighty-five miles an hour in a thirty-mile zone. Straight through a red light! Smashing into her as she walked on the crossing. She didn't even get a chance to turn her head and see you coming. And that's why you still don't know what she looks like, because the only time you ever saw her, her face was covered in blood!'

`Yes, yes, she died – but *my* only crime was having too much to drink. I never intended to kill her. If only you knew the grief it has caused me since. The years of silent suffering. The angina.

And no – I didn't forget! I could *never* forget. The death of that woman haunts me every day – '

`You dirty, snivelling, lying fake! Don't you *dare* insult me with your lies and false grief. You can't even remember her *name!'*

Phil was staring at Duncan with hatred and revulsion, asking him the same question he had asked himself a hundred times in the past three years.

`Christ! — how many people does a man kill in his lifetime? None, usually. So when a terrible event like that happens, surely the person responsible would at least remember his victim's *name*.'

`I do remember her name,' Duncan insisted. `Yes, yes, I do!'

`What is it?'

Duncan swallowed. `Gaines ... Mrs Gaines ... But I never knew she was connected to you ...'

Phil pointed to a framed poster on the study wall. Look behind you! Her name is *there* – big enough for a bat to see. And here —' He snatched up a copy of Marian Barnard's book from the desk and held it square in front of Duncan.

`Look at it, Duncan, the name of the woman you killed, *Marian Barnard*. The same name that fourteen years ago you heard read out in court at least *six* times – the name of your unfortunate victim. The same name that was printed in the newspaper report. Yet not *once* – not since that first night I met you when Martin Pellmann mentioned her book – have you shown even a hint of recognition or the slightest memory of her name. You killed her and then you promptly forgot her and her name ... my thirty-five-year old beloved mother ... Marian Barnard.'

Duncan was stunned. `Marian Barnard ... the dead author ... she was your *mother?'*

`Yes, and unlucky for you she had a son. But you didn't know that, did you? Because in court they kept referring to her as *Miss* Marian Barnard. But I've been on your tail ever since, Duncan, and now I've got you, I'm going to make you pay in full – not only for what you did to her – but for *laughing* about it afterwards.'

Oh God, Oh Christ – now Duncan knew there was no hope of a reprieve.

Suddenly Phil raised the hardback book in his hand and swung it across the desk — smashing it across Duncan's face. `You unfeeling pile of pigshit! You took away my mother's *life!* Smashed and battered her and took away her *life!* Then you didn't even have the decency to remember her name.'

Duncan was in shock, the smash from the book had brought blood pouring from his nose onto his shirt, his hand was over his chest, his voice shrill and shaking, `Gaines, Christ, Gaines, call an ambulance! I think I'm dying!'

`Then die,' Phil said coldly. `Do yourself and me one great big favour. Because whether you are well or ill, I'm determined to destroy you, finish you, take away your every hope, every ambition, every triumph. On her death I swore it.'

He threw down the book and began to gather up the photographs. `And I'm going to start with copies of these. Tomorrow morning. You can bet your house on it.'

`Gaines, please ... an ambulance.'

Phil glanced at him, implacable and unpitying, and continued filing the photographs back inside the envelope.

`Did you ring for an ambulance that night, Duncan? Or did you just stand there watching her bleed to death on the road. Yes, that's what the witness in court said you did. Just stood there, watching her bleed to death, while you smoked a cigar.'

He put the photographs back in the drawer and turned the key.

`But what I will do now, is open the front door for you. Now that you know what's going to happen, and why.' He raised an eyebrow. `Now you may leave.'

Duncan was slowly rising from the chair, clutching the arms as he pushed himself up, swaying dizzily. Through a haze of pain he saw Gaines come around the desk and walk past him indifferently.

`You bastard ... You vicious *bastard!'* A sudden upsurge of rage propelled him into a furious charge after Gaines, his huge fists raised to attack.

Phil turned swiftly as Duncan gasped and flopped against him; instinctively Phil caught him in his arms, staggered with him, regained his balance, then stood firmly holding the collapsed man against his chest.

After a silence ... after a very long silence ... when Phil could hear nothing but the sound of his own breathing, he slowly laid Duncan back down onto the floor.

James Duncan's silver-grey eyes stared up at him, enlarged and sightless. The eyes of a dead man.

Phil stood gazing down at him. `You swine,' he finally murmured. `You got off lightly again.'

TWENTY-SEVEN

London
July 1994

_____/

Rena almost screamed when she saw the white ambulance parked outside the house, its blue and red lights flashing in the dark.

`Phil!'

David rammed the brakes and brought the car to a stop a few yards behind the ambulance. Both jumped out and ran towards the house. The paramedics were wheeling a stretcher down the drive. The body and face were covered in a red blanket.

`Phil!' Rena gasped again, and clutched at David. They stood holding each other and staring as the body came closer.

`Who?' David asked the paramedics, then moved forward himself and lifted the blanket back from the face.

`Duncan!'

Rena stared, first in relief, then in bewilderment.

`How?' David asked one of the paramedics.

`Heart attack. Seems he just collapsed in the middle of a business meeting. The coroner's police found his nitrolingual spray and nifedipines in his car. Stupid fool had been suffering from angina for years, yet *still* smoked cigars heavily. He was smoking one not long before he collapsed.' The paramedic shook his head. `Why won't these people *listen?'*

David was feeling a strange sense of unease.

`Are you *sure* it was a heart attack?'

`Yeh, positive, all the signs.'

`Why has he got blood on his face?'

`Seems he was standing, then suddenly crashed down, hitting his face hard against the edge of the desk. The one I feel sorry for is the poor guy inside. Imagine having something like that happening to you? A business acquaintance dropping dead at your feet. The coroner's police are still in there talking to him.'

The two police officers were leaving the house as Rena and David approached the front door.

`Who are you?' the policewoman asked.

`I'm his wife – ' Rena pointed, `the man inside – I'm his wife.'

`Oh, I see. Well I'm glad you've come. Your husband seems perfectly all right at the moment, but later he may show symptoms of delayed shock. It's quite a natural reaction after something like this. At first it doesn't really sink in, all actions become instinctive, calling the police and so on. It's only on realising that someone is actually dead that shock takes over. I think you had better go inside.'

`Have you finished here?' David asked.

The policewoman nodded, calm and efficient. `Yes, we've finished here. The autopsy will probably be tomorrow.'

Her radio crackled into life, a voice spoke calmly with nightmarish automatism, informing her of another death somewhere else in London.

David and Rena went inside.

Phil was in the drawing-room. He turned as they entered, and calmly met the questioning look in Rena's eyes.

Rena still could not fully comprehend what had happened, but she also was feeling a strange sense of unease. `Phil ... James Duncan ... Who is he?'

`The man who killed my mother and laughed about it afterwards.'

`What?' And it was then Rena knew, with a sudden certainty, why James Duncan had been invited to the party. The merger had been a charade. A trap Phil had baited to draw James Duncan closer.

`Your mother?' Now it was David Gallagher who did not fully comprehend.

Phil looked at David. `My mother, Marian Barnard.'

`*Marian Barnard!*' David could only stare at Phil in disbelieving astonishment. `But you told me that Marian Barnard – '

`I know I did, David, but I lied.'

`Why?'

`Because the truth was nobody's business, but mine.'

Rena had to know the truth. `Phil ... James Duncan ... Did you kill him?'

`No.'

`The blood on his face?'

`I hit him with her book – the book of her *life* – I smashed it across his face.'

`But did you kill him?'

`No. He had angina. A rotten heart. A mean soul. And he drank heavily and continually smoked cigars, all culminating in a heart attack.'

`You did nothing else ... except hit him with a book?'

Phil hesitated. `Yes, I did do something else,' he admitted, `but don't worry, it was nothing that could be termed illegal.'

`What did you do?'

`I scared the life out of him.'

TWENTY-EIGHT

London
August 1994

_____/

Two weeks later, James Duncan's two sisters, Helen and Felicity, paid a visit to Gaines Publishing.

The two women sat on chairs opposite Phil's desk and he listened to what they had to say.

`You see, Mr Gaines,' Helen said primly, `although James's share in the firm now pass on in two equal parts to both myself and Felicity – Daddy did insist upon that in his own will, didn't he Felicity?'

`Daddy did, Helen.'

Helen nodded, and turned back. `But James also had a huge life insurance policy. And James always said that his will would provide a substantial bequest to each of us. But now we discover that Joanne is the *only* beneficiary of his will. James, in his meanness and duplicity, has left everything to the slut.'

`Everything to the slut,' Felicity echoed.

`And nothing to us.'

`Nothing to us.'

`So, what we wish to know, Mr Gaines, is whether you are still intent upon taking over Garland Press. At the figure formerly mentioned?'

Phil had no interest in Garland's, but he had used these two women when he thought he might need them, and now he would have to pay for it.

`Yes,' Phil said. `But there will be no seats on

the board. It will be a complete take-over.'

`Absolutely *no* seats on the board?' Helen asked. `Not even for James's widow?'

`No,' Phil said. `Not even for his widow.'

Helen smiled triumphantly. `Then we have no objections to the terms. Do we Felicity?'

`No objections, Helen.'

`No, by God!' Helen exclaimed. `She won't get a penny out of us! And that insurance money will only last her for a year at the most. The way *she* spends. And *then* what will she do?'

Phil had the absurd feeling that he was expected to give an opinion. He stood up quickly to signal the end of the meeting.

`I shall discuss it with my solicitor this afternoon.

Later that afternoon, Phil's solicitor was sitting on the opposite side of the desk, various deeds in his hands as he clarified the situation.

`Now, when you formed this company, you had no need of loans from banks. Every penny was supplied by you. At that time, David Gallagher, who was to be your Editorial Director, had no capital. But the board had to have two shareholding directors. So we agreed that you should own ninety-nine per cent of the shares, and David would own one per cent.'

Phil nodded, trying to conceal his impatience while the lawyer continued, `After that, a number of other department heads became co-opted directors, well remunerated with good salaries and bonuses, but no shares. That left – '

`All I want to know,' Phil interrupted, `is can I do this? Legally – can I do it?'

`Most certainly. This firm is yours, Mr Gaines.

You can do whatever you like. But remember, whatever you do, you still must have at least *two* shareholding directors.'

In his office, David Gallagher was staring at the brown parcel his secretary handed to him. It obviously contained a script, but it was what was written in huge black letters across the front of the parcel that made him stare – DAVID GALLAGHER – PERSONAL

`I don't believe it,' said David, glancing up at his secretary. `I know that handwriting. It's from John Houlihan! When did this come?'

`It was delivered to reception a few minutes ago, by John Houlihan himself. He told Carol that it must be delivered directly to *you* and nobody else.'

`Well, well,' David grinned. `The mountain finally came to Mohammed ... But is it a cut-down revamped version of his awful *magnum opus*, I wonder?'

An hour later, as everyone was leaving their offices and going home, Phil appeared at David's desk.

`Can I have a word with you, David?'

David didn't even glance up, too engrossed in his reading. `Not now, Phil. Later, later...'

Phil raised an eyebrow, and quietly left.

It was the office cleaner that made David eventually realise that everyone had gone home except himself.

`You not going 'ome, Mr Gallagher?' she asked him curiously as she lifted up his waste-paper bin. `You know what they say about all work and no play?'

`Yes, yes, I'm going now,' David said, as he

gathered up Houlihan's script to finish it at home.

As soon as he got home, David made a sandwich and a cup of coffee then sat down at his desk and returned with excitement to Houlihan's new thriller – typed at such a cracking pace that almost all the commas and stops were missing.

Nevertheless, it was brilliant, David finally concluded with a smile. The old pain-in-the-ass had done it again – written a uniquely original page-turning thriller that was almost impossible to put down.

Instinctively, David reached for his pencil and started editing.

At last he looked up, the final page completed. He glanced at his watch and saw it was nearly five o'clock in the morning.

He gathered up the pages, stacked them neatly, and was about to put them back in their folder when his eye was caught by Houlihan's accompanying letter – in particular, the P.S. scrawled at the end:

P.S. DG – *I'd be obliged if you would contact me immediately after you have read it – JH.*

David sat thoughtful for a moment, then a wicked grin moved on his face as he reached for the telephone.

Why not? Houlihan did request *immediately.* And Houlihan was a man who did not like to be kept waiting.

In blackness, the telephone on the bedside table rang.

A grunt, a groan, then a hand finally switched on the bedside light, illuminating the face of John Houlihan – looking like he'd just survived a bomb-blast.

He was still blinking as he picked up the phone. `Yeah ... yeah, this is me. Who are you? ... Listen, what time is it? Oh wait – the room is spinning ... Where am I? ... No, I've no idea.' Houlihan looked around him blearily. `I don't recognise this place at all.'

He looked over his other shoulder and saw Nancy fast asleep in the bed, oblivious to lights and the ringing of the telephone.

Houlihan turned back and nodded as he spoke into the phone.

`It's okay, I'm all right, I'm at home. Well I must be, because my wife's here in the bed and she's not a woman for sleeping with other men ... Look, will you wait a second while I go and get a mouthwash?'

He returned a minute later carrying a glass of Jamesons whiskey and sat on the side of the bed in his pyjamas. He gulped a slug of whiskey, and lifted the phone again.

`I'm back, but tell me, who did you say you were again? ... Oh, David Gallagher?' Houlihan's face lit up with delight. `You got the script?'

He took another slug of Jamesons. `Yeah, I'm back on the bottle and writing great. Total sobriety doesn't agree with me. Makes me too serious ... What? No, of course I'm not drinking too much. I promised Nancy I wouldn't. But she allowed me to have a few over the odds tonight because I'm celebrating the completion of my new script. I only finished it last night, you know? After *slaving* night and day for months on end ... What? You've read it already? So? Well? What do you think of it?'

Houlihan's face lit up in blissful radiance. `Brilliant? You're not jesting me now? You mean that?'

At the other end of the line, David smiled wryly. Houlihan was hoping for more compliments about his book, but 'Brilliant' was enough.

`I loved writing it,' Houlihan said excitedly. `Enjoyed every back-breaking and head-scratching minute of it!'

David grinned. `Yes, I knew you were back on form and writing up a storm. You left out most of the punctuation.'

`Ah, punctuation my arse! Who gives a damn about commas and semi-colons when the typewriter is pounding a rhapsody!"

He excitedly gulped another drink. "Listen – did I ever tell you what Christy Brown said about those writers who fiddle away with their and commas and colons? ... Christy Brown – you *must* have heard of him! They made a film about him with Daniel Day Lewis, *My Left Foot* ... Oh, you do? Well, some years ago Christy Brown once said to me in Dublin, he said – "You don't stop to depict each raindrop when you're painting a thunderstorm."'

David rotated his eyes upwards. Houlihan was simply incorrigible. No other editor would put up with him.

`So you'll put them in for me, will you? The commas and semi-colons and all that. Same as you always do.'

David smiled and rubbed his chin but did not reply.

`And you think the book is brilliant?'

`Even better than your first.'

`Honestly?'

`Honestly.'

Houlihan's shout of glee almost burst David's

eardrum.

`I knew I could do it!' Houlihan roared down the phone. `Those other cross-eyed bastards of publishers seemed to think I was finished, down and out. Rejected my last book flat, every one of them. Shows you how wrong they were! I'll *never* be finished. Not till I'm dead. Listen – just as long as I can hold a pen or bash a typewriter I'll always have a whip to crack. Betcher balls I will!'

`I'll let you go back to sleep now,' David said with a sly grin, knowing he had ruined Houlihan's sleep for the rest of the night. The man's excitement was almost palpable – even from the other end of a phone line.

Houlihan was speaking again but the words were obscured by a gurgling sound. `Sorry?' David said. `I didn't hear that.'

`Because...' Houlihan went on more clearly, `I was seriously considering – and I mean *very seriously* considering – giving the whole writing game up.'

`One more thing,' David said, his expression straightening. `Before I decide whether we should make you an offer for this script, and before I will agree to edit you, there is something I feel must be resolved between us, once and for all.'

In his bedroom John Houlihan frowned as he listened. He took a sip of his whiskey, and sighed sadly.

`Yeah, sorry ... sorry about that, David, I was just a bit, you know ... out of line.' He heaved another sigh, full of remorse, and answered the next question.

`Why? You want to know *why* I sent the script direct to you this time? Well now, I'll tell you just why. Because I was thinking – and I mean *very seriously* thinking – about everything. And what I came up with is this – you're a man that' has always treated me right, David Gallagher. Yes, you are. And I don't know why I never appreciated it before. But there you go. Success can blind a man.'

`Is that an apology, by any chance?' David asked.

Houlihan drained back his glass, then put it down with a thud of emphasis. `Even my sarcastic little digs – you always responded to my digs and jibes with the dignity of a gentlemen. Never lowered yourself to argue back. A gentleman now. That's what you are, David Gallagher. And my fist in the face of anyone who says anything different from now on. And Nancy agrees with me – all the way. You're a true *gentleman*, David Gallagher. And boyo, that's something rare!'

David was smiling.

At the other end of the line, Houlihan was frowning furiously. `Not like that Phil Gaines. That basket case! And a bloody *rude* basket case he is too!'

Phil laughed the following morning when David recounted the conversation.

`So it's me he hates now, not you?'

`Yes, I'm a gentleman and you're a basket case.'

`So? Is Houlihan back with us? Are we taking his new script?'

`If we don't, another publisher will snap it up in a week. It's a sure-fire winner. But apart from that, Houlihan says that from now on, he won't allow anyone to handle his scripts but David Gallagher – a *gentleman* of the first order!'

`So, how much?'

David shrugged. `Based on his last sales, I thought, perhaps, £250,000 for world rights. He's still got no agent, still distrusts them, so he'll give us the lot.'

Phil stood thoughtful. `This business of Duncan's,' he said, changing the subject. `The take-over. I think the name should be changed.'

`Yes, so you said the other day. Wipe out Garland's name altogether.'

`No, I don't mean that. I mean the name of our place. I think it should be changed to Gaines and Gallagher.'

David stared at him. `Bloody hell ... Phil, what are you talking about?'

`This publishing house. Gaines and Gallagher. My money and your management. A straight split.'

`You mean ... joint ownership?'

`Why not?'

`Why not?' David suddenly stood up, looking confused. `I'll tell you why not ... because although I may have made a lot of money in the past few years, I have nothing near the amount to buy a half share in the firm, not even a fifth. Do you *know* how much Gaines Publishing is worth?'

`David, all I want from you is your agreement, and your signature on the relevant deeds.' Phil shrugged tiredly. `You've run beside me all the way. Every step since Cambridge. So why not Gaines and Gallagher. Money doesn't come into it.'

David felt weak. He sat down. His brain was still in shock. It was like a dream. Long ago. His own publishing house. A foolish dream. A cruel joke. Phil may be a millionaire, but he was nobody's fool. He had more than doubled the personal fortune he had received from his grandmother. And although he was capable of being extremely generous, he was never *stupid* with money.

He looked at Phil. `This is a joke, isn't it?'

`No, David, no joke.'

`So, what you're saying – now correct me if I'm wrong, you want to just hand over half the firm to me – as a *gift*.'

`Why not?'

`More appropriately – *why?* There's no reason to it.'

`There's a lot of reason to it. Sound business reasons. What's the matter? Don't you want it?'

After a silence, David said dazedly, `Just like that? Straight down the middle?'

`Straight down the middle. Fifty-four per cent to me, forty-one to you.'

`Bloody hell!'

Now David knew Phil really was serious. Phil never made a deal which took away his control. And this was no exception. Nevertheless, forty-one per cent of a firm with a book value of millions – in return for the scratch of a pen.

`Hang on,' David said. `Fifty-four and forty-one is only ninety-five. Who gets the other five per cent?'

`Miranda Alvin. She too has run with us all the way, every step since Cambridge. I think she should be given a stake in the firm. Do you agree?'

`God, you really *are* serious.' David still couldn't believe it. And still couldn't *understand* it.

`I'm not going to pressure you, David, but why don't you and I go out to an early lunch and I'll explain to you some of those reasons of mine. Then we can discuss it with Miranda. Then you both can think about it, and let me know your decision in three weeks.'

`Why three weeks?'

`It will probably take almost that long to have the deeds drawn up. Apart from that, I won't be around for the next three weeks. I'm going away for a while.'

`Going where?'

Phil smiled. `Paradise.'

TWENTY-NINE

Bali
September 1994

_____/

The Balinese believed the sea was full of demons, but Phil couldn't see any. He swam deeper, coasting through the shifting patches of light and dark beneath the waters surface. He felt as light as a shadow gliding over the aquamarine depths dappled in sapphire and purple.

Surfacing, he pulled down his snorkel mask and looked up at the heat-hazed sky for a moment. He turned and floated on his back, savouring the sea's gentle caress. It was not a good day for surfers; the sea was very calm, almost as calm as he was. Over the past fourteen days the tight coil of tension inside him had slowly unwound. Now he felt regenerated, as ready to begin a new life as a newborn.

He had left Rena back in the hotel, fiddling with the humidity-control before indulging in a late afternoon sleep. She was tired, she said. Too tired to swim again. They had spent a week on the island of Moyo, enjoying a second honeymoon, but now they were on Bali itself, at Nusa Dua.

He looked towards the red haze of the sun, wondering how long he had been amusing himself in the sea. He turned and began to swim back to the beach.

On the beach, he dried his hair then threw down his towel and sat for a while, his arms resting on his knees as he watched the sea for a time.

Tonight. He would have to tell Rena tonight. He had thought of telling her a number of times over the past fourteen days, but somehow the right moment had not come.

So it had to be tonight.

Bali's Grand Hyatt was an exquisite hotel, built in the design of a Balinese water palace, surrounded by acres of tropical gardens, and linked by a series of lily ponds and blue lagoons, all leading down to a stretch of soft white beach. As dusk fell and the Chinese lanterns blazed into light, the view out to sea was stunning.

Hand in hand, Phil and Rena strolled under the silvery lights of the gardens, breathing in the balmy fragrance of the lush flowers. It was truly like Paradise – well, some place between heaven and earth, with one sunlit day following another.

They dined on Chinese cuisine in the hotel's air-conditioned restaurant. Phil waited until they had finished eating – deferring further until after the waiter had poured more wine. Then he took a deep breath and, hesitantly, began to tell Rena of his plans for the future.

She listened silently and without interruption, only the occasional expression flitting across her face gave him some hint of her reaction.

Finally, he looked at her questioningly. `Well, what do you think?'

`America? ... I know that's what you have always wanted, Phil. To live there. But—' she smiled excitedly, `I didn't think it would be so soon.'

He smiled with her, feeling relief. `You've always loved New York, haven't you?'

`*Ja,* since the first time you took me there.'

`And you always knew, didn't you, Rena, that we would be going to live there eventually?'

Rena nodded. She had known it from the day she married him. Phil was the son and grandson of an American and that was a part of his identity he did not want to lose. And as for her – the only place she wanted to live was the place where he was.

`But...' she repeated, `I didn't think it would be so soon.' The more they talked about it, the more excited she became.

He had worked it all out. Talked it all out with his friends in New York. Had been planning it for months. Working out all the legalities with Tom Kennett. He was going to start over – open another publishing house, in America. David Gallagher would manage the London house, and Phil the one in New York. It could be done, his friends had agreed. All he needed was the money and the guts. And he had plenty of both.

`Two of my publishing friends over there have already agreed to come in with me straight away, Phil said. `And Tom Kennett has already got a realtor in search for suitable premises. He'll be there to meet us when we arrive.'

`Tom Kennett?'

`Yes.'

`When we arrive?'

`Ah, didn't I tell you? We're not going back to England tomorrow. We're going from here to New York. Just for a few days.'

Rena was dumbstruck! `You have booked the tickets. Before we left London?'

`Well, yes, I did. Whatever your overall response, I knew you wouldn't object to a few days in NYC.'

She laughed. `Why did you not tell me?'

`Well, you were so excited about Bali, I thought, one excitement at a time.'

Rena's nerves were sizzling, she tried to calm down. `You are wise, Phil, I am so excited and I should not have too much excitement. I was going to wait until we went back to England, but as we are not going back to England, I may as well tell you now ... I am pregnant.'

Now it was Phil's turn to be stunned. `Pregnant? Are you sure? I thought you were on the pill? I thought you wanted to wait?'

She smiled at him. `You said it was up to me to choose when I would get pregnant, so I chose. I knew I didn't want to wait any longer. I stopped taking the pills.'

`Why did you not discuss it with me?'

`Why did you not discuss America with me?'

`Because I knew you wanted to live in America as much as I did. It was supposed to be a wonderful surprise for you.'

`And I knew you wanted me to make you a family and have a baby even more than I did,' Rena rejoined. `And is it not a wonderful surprise for you?'

Phil was silent, closed his eyes, and Rena felt moisture behind her own lids. They were going to become a family now ... it was what he had always wanted.

Phil lifted her hand to his lips and kissed her fingertips. `Are you sure?'

`About what?'

`Sure that you're pregnant?'

Rena nodded. `I had a test in Malmö. *Ja,* pregnant. Then I had another test before we left

England. Positive again. pregnant. Then this afternoon I went to the Hotel pharmacy and bought a tester and did another test. Yes, pregnant. That makes three positives. So, *ja*, I am sure.'

They left the restaurant and took the path along the beach, breathing in the warm air and ignoring the soft murmur of the sea as they discussed the future. With a baby on the way, Phil decided, the sooner they got settled in America the better. So, an apartment overlooking Central Park, and the occasional weekends at the country house in Massachusetts.

The beautiful big house on the outskirts of Harvard, Massachusetts was still there, still his, still owned by a Gaines.

Phil sighed. `Alexander, at least, would be happy about that.'

`And Jimmy will be able to visit us in New York.' Rena had loved Jimmy from the first day they had met.

`The thing about New York and New Yorkers,' Phil said suddenly, `is they all have a "Get it done yesterday," attitude to everything. Which, normally, I like. Even the way they speak is done with economy – the fewer the syllables, the faster they can say it.'

Rena giggled. `I love the way Americans talk, like Tom Kennett, all those wisecracks.'

`No, no, you're missing the point. What I'm saying is that it's okay for New Yorkers to rush, rush, rush – but you must not. You hear me, Rena? You must maintain that Swedish calm of yours, and take life very easy from now on.'

The sound of a plane roaring away from Denpasar Airport made Phil look up at the sky ...

he watched the plane climb higher and higher, its lights blinking, and then, as it disappeared into the distance, he noticed the silvery slice of a new moon high above them.

A new moon? New beginnings? It was a good omen.

He pointed to the new moon. `Make a wish, Rena.'

Rena closed her eyes and made a wish.

Phil looked up at the moon and made his own wish, with his eyes open.

EPILOGUE

New York
April 1995

_____/

The birth was much quicker and easier than Rena had expected. She gave one last push and there was a triumphant cry from the midwife. A few seconds later the midwife held up a baby girl and smiled. `Welcome to the world, honey!'

It had all happened so quickly, the baby was already born when Phil arrived at the hospital.

But as new as she was, the likeness was unmistakable. Phil's daughter was the image of Marian.

Her hair was black and her eyes were a dark sapphire blue – even the shape of the face – somehow all the cells and genes of his mother had passed down through him to his child. And as soon as he saw her, Phil knew. He knew that all the love and care and comfort that had been denied his mother would be given now to this child, his little girl, Marian and Marc's grandchild.

`She doesn't look anything like me,' Rena said, but didn't seem to mind, smiling adoringly at the baby in her arms.

`She's stunning ... gorgeous ... beautiful – ' Phil dragged his eyes away from his little girl and smiled at Rena. `Or maybe I should just borrow that old phrase from Jack Kerouac to describe her – "the only word is wow."'

Later that evening they named their daughter Marian Marcella Gaines.

Acknowledgements

To a terrific police officer in the Vice Squad in London, who shall, as promised, remain anonymous: my thanks for his unstinting help and technical guidance.

To Birgitta Sundström and Oscar Hellström at the SAS Strand Hotel for their delightful Swedish kindness and the help they gave to me during my research in Stockholm.

To the late and great Mr Truman Capote for posthumously providing me with the title for this book.

Thank You

Thank you for taking the time to read my book. If you enjoyed it, please consider telling your friends or posting a short **<u>REVIEW</u>.** Word of mouth is an author's best friend and is much appreciated.

Please follow me on ***BookBub*** by going to:-
www.bookbub.com/profile/gretta-curran-browne
and clicking the "*Follow*" button.

*

Building a relationship with my readers is the one of the great things about writing. I occasionally send newsletters with details of new releases, special deals or offers and other pieces of information or news I may have from time to time.

If you would like to receive my newsletters please sign up to my mailing list by clicking through my Website and clicking on the "Subscribe" Tab.

*

If you want to get in touch, please do, whether it is to ask a question, or make a comment. I'd be delighted to hear from you. You can contact me through my Website and clicking on the "Contact" Tab.

Many thanks – Gretta

www.grettacurranbrowne.com

Also by Gretta Curran Browne

www.grettacurranbrowne.com

Printed in Great Britain
by Amazon